STAMPEDE!

Thunder crashed, rolled, and rapid-fire flashes lighted the herd. Five men circled the startled stock. Lightning struck, sending balls of fire bouncing across the prairie. The cattle swayed like a mighty wave and bolted.

Rawls's roan reacted at the same time. Thrown back from the saddle, Rawls clawed desperately, stretched for the horn, and finally struggled back into leather. The quivering flesh of the horse beneath him told, plainer than words, that he rode in the lead of nearly 2,000 crazed and stampeding longhorns.

Darkness engulfed them, and the thunder's roll weakened and gave way to the roar of almost 8,000 hoofs almost on the roan's tail. The sound tore at Rawls's gut. He could feel the horse's heartbeat pounding through the saddle's fenders, and the animal stretched low.

"Dear, God," Rawls moaned, hardly hearing his own voice.

BLOOD FOR BROTHER

Mackey Murdock

LEISURE BOOKS NEW YORK CITY

For my wife Joanne
who has shared my life and love
for fifty fast years.

A LEISURE BOOK®

March 2006

Published by special arrangement with Golden West Literary Agency.

Dorchester Publishing Co., Inc.
200 Madison Avenue
New York, NY 10016

ISBN 0-8439-5657-7

The name "Leisure Books" and the stylized "L" with design are trademarks of Dorchester Publishing Co., Inc.

Printed in the United States of America.

Visit us on the web at www.dorchesterpub.com.

ACKNOWLEDGMENTS

Special thanks to Vicki Piekarski, who polished the rough edges while enhancing my literary efforts, to Jon Tuska, whose professional skills and guidance kept me proud and straight in the saddle, to Hazel Rumney of Thorndike Press, who read literary-road brands better than most, and finally to the DFW Writer's Workshop and friends at Western Writers of America.

BLOOD FOR BROTHER

Chapter One

Contractions, cramps, spasms, give it a name. Holy God! No word did justice to the demon struggling to steal her breath. She sensed her body spreading, tearing apart, and exploding into millions of fragments, brilliant stars of hurt in a black void of pain. Her breath roared. She panted, moaned: "Marcus, Marcus, you bastard! Why aren't you here?"

The bed once belonged to her grandmother. A tarpaulin rested beneath the lower sheet and blanket and over the feather mattress. Sheets and blankets could, perhaps, be saved from bloodstains. A soiled mattress was another matter.

Bess Slaton floated, wallowing barely conscious in troughs between crests of pain. For the last hour, the swells had increased in frequency and intensified. Above her, timbers swirled, spanned an opening below the roof and supported a loft. Corners of the upstairs room hid in darkness. A strong odor of onions drifted from the boards above and mixed with the scent of her body. Sweat dripped to the bedding, and wet strands of tangled hair crossed her view. She struggled to rise. Why hadn't she opened that window? Her head rolled.

Steam rose from the kettle hanging over the fireplace. Across the room, strips and squares of neatly folded cloth lay stacked on a table. At least she'd done some preparation, but she'd thought she had more time.

Liquid fire trickled between her buttocks, soaked and pooled in the blanket beneath her hips. Oh, God! Alone and birthing a baby—a baby without patience. The closed window buffeted her scream. The totality of the sound, its energy, clashed around her, gave relief to primal instincts too ancient to comprehend. She sensed a release of frustration. She screamed again, louder, then again.

Rawls Slaton shuffled, barefoot and haltingly, raising powdery dust from worn ruts. In the travel-stunted tufts of grass between the lines of bare earth, ants scurried along faint paths. He had come to know ants well over the past months, had developed a kinship to them. Hundreds of miles of walking, head down, would do that. Ragged clothing draped about him. His left side responded sluggishly, depended heavily on the walking stick in his hand.

Rawls stopped, raised his head and stared, blinked at the shaded area beneath a cottonwood near the stream: The tree dominated his senses. It sat to the side of the roadway. He cocked his head and wrinkled his nose, sniffed the sweetness of green growth and moist air. He'd have to think on it a while, but, yes, he knew this place.

His traveler's mind had no room for laziness. It labored constantly. Still, his thoughts arrived tardily, moved in and out slowly like water-logged beeves pulling river mud on a hot day. Bits of information floated aimlessly, disconnected, wandering through eddies of his mind to fall unused among the mental chaff that strained to command a body that reacted sometimes perfectly, at others half-heartedly. But, yes, this was a good place—this spot shaded by fat cottonwood leaves.

With a clumsy hand, he slowly stroked hair stubble and allowed his gaze to follow the winding ruts 100 yards up the roadway past the small barn to a smaller house. The mental chaff fluttered, stirred.

He was home. On ranchland his father had earned as a

land grant

He and Marcu

its wildness, hone

timately helped their

prairie had lived the pr

in-law.

She'd added her own beau

known her first as the tomboy k

Her family had had good horses and

but that was true of most in the Repu

while her father chased horses, every cow

chased her. She turned them all down, till his

won her heart and broke his.

The Slaton 5,000-acre grant lay west of San Antonio and north of the *rio*. His father had accepted it after shooting a Santa Anna soldier attempting to spear Houston with a bayonet. The general had fallen after taking a bullet to the ankle.

Rawls dropped the bedroll a few feet from the stream, then sank, belly down, to the sand at its edge. He lowered his face to within inches of the limpid water. From habit, he blew nonexistent trash from its surface before drinking. He sank his face deeply into the clear water, sat up, and cupped a double handful and poured it over his hair.

The narrow stream flowed from its source a half dozen feet to his left. Lowering to his elbows, Rawls responded to inner urgings and squirmed like a lizard to peer down into the depth of the spring. Along its bottom and inches below the water's surface, dozens of little sand bubbles mushroomed upward. At the top of their journey the bubbles rolled, then burst, and fine grains settled again, rolled to troughs and low spots, joined others for the next ride. Uncertainty surrounded the number of years since last he'd watched the underground pressure bring this spring's water to the surface.

...ents came slowly; ...ublesome. He pushed the ...e moment.

...reate a cloud of mud, Rawls sat and swung ...r the edge, then lowered them. He leaned back, ...ing a part of his weight on his hands and sighed. He had found his nest. The house belonged to Marcus.

The raucous *caw* of a crow broke the silence, then frantically the bird flew into view. A speck of feathered fury chased closely behind. The smaller scissortail broke off the pursuit. The crow hushed. Bees worked yellow blossoms along the stream. Only their *buzz* disturbed the shaded spot.

The peace and quiet rendered Rawls at ease, soothed frayed nerves. No gunfire, no explosions or hollering, no saber pointing death in his direction. How good it would be if the world could only hold this stillness. Still that scissortail had had to fight for it. He was a good bird.

A shriek from the house seared Rawls's nerves. He came to his feet, ankle deep in water. With the second scream he threw his arms over his head to stifle the sound. He bent, peeked beneath his arm at the shack down the road. He turned, as though to run in the opposite direction. A moan escaped his lips, then he turned again, bent, and picked up his walking stick, then his bedroll. With a half lope, half shuffle he lumbered toward the unpainted shack.

Nearing the house the unmistakable scent of burning mesquite welcomed him. He clambered up the porch steps and slammed his good shoulder into the door. Another scream from inside shook him.

The door latch offered little resistance, and two steps inside the cabin he fought for balance. He swayed, stood spread-eagle, his eyes adjusting to the interior dimness. The scent of onions overpowered those of cooking spices, soap,

10

and stale tobacco. Then he saw the blood-soaked bed and her large eyes staring from above her spread legs. Her right arm lay partially bent. It had been blown away. No—what was that?

He stepped toward the bed. The bloody mass, half on her belly and near the arm—it was a baby. For God's sake! Bess had birthed a baby. Rawls saw the pain, the fear on the blood-smeared face. She didn't recognize him.

"Be-ss, it's me . . . Rawls. I'm . . . I'm home. Lee, he give up." Recognition washed across her face. He warmed to the look, let the heat spread.

"Quick, Rawls, the knife and some of those strips of cloth. I need your help."

He moved to the table and picked up the butcher knife and cotton strips as requested. This was worse than bloody battle-fields. This blood came from Bess. He returned to the bed, looked down. The knife weighed heavily. He glanced up, met her eyes, quickly lowered his view, and continued studying the floor. She raised to her elbows, breathed a shallow sigh. He peeked at her face.

"You know what's to be done." Her voice trembled.

"Wh-what?" he asked.

"You've got to tie off, then cut this cord."

"I . . . I don't . . . know."

"You've been hurt." Her voice carried more statement than question.

"Some, but I . . . I may get . . . get over it."

"Stay with me, Rawls. We can do this." Her words were steady now.

Rawls's gaze searched the room, returned to Bess. "Where is . . . is Marcus?" Smoldering coals, deep in green-tinted gray eyes, startled him, let him know he'd picked a poor trail even before she shook her head.

"Use whiskey from the cupboard and sterilize the knife . . . there's water on the fire. Now, Rawls."

He found the whiskey, drenched the knife, then took a deep drink. Rawls stirred the blade in the bubbling pot of water. A few shuffling steps put him back at Bess's bedside.

"Here, sit here. You ready?"

Rawls nodded.

Chapter Two

The baby rested, warm against his chest. Rawls limped around the table. He made low, mocking sounds of the infant's crying. Now cleaned and with its cord covered, he held it wrapped in a blanket. It fit there against his body. He'd discover this infant that made him an uncle was a niece. Sadness came with the discovery. Guys could be pals.

After much effort, he'd succeeded in placing the gown Bess had pointed out on the baby. It was the diapering effort that had been his undoing. It proved too much for his clumsy hands. Bess had finished that job, propped on an elbow. Now she dozed. He listened to the rhythm of her breathing—it seemed regular—hoping she only slept. She looked so pale, solemn, her bright smile buried.

Yeah, everything had gone all right, but most of what he'd done had been at Bess's direction. Where was he going to place this kid while he tended to Bess? She, too, had to be cleaned. She belonged next to nice things, soft and fresh, not in that dirty bed.

Rawls's breathing came faster. Uncertainty grew, flirted with panic. Bess was unconscious, and he couldn't walk around like this forever. He couldn't put this little one down on the floor. What if a scorpion was down there? Hell, it'd be like him to step on her. No, he couldn't do that. But, where? He had to move Bess. Oh, God! If only he was whole again.

Rawls bumped the heavy oak table. Pain shot through his hip. He'd started to grab at his hip, but regained control just in time to prevent dropping the baby. He shook. He sat in a

13

straight-backed chair and rocked. Let's see, Marcus was oldest, then he came two years later. His mind slowed, allowed time for pleasant, childhood thoughts. *Then Momma died. Years later, Poppa remarried. The next year Sharon . . . yeah, that was it . . . his sister's name was Sharon.*

Rawls scanned the room, searching for a dresser. They used to put Sharon in a bureau drawer. He smiled. *Yeah, tuck her in there out of harm's way. But there is no bureau.* The effort of thinking became heavier. His view lowered, passed over the bottom of the cupboard. Flour dust clung to the cabinet's front.

Poppa had built that cabinet. There was a built-in bin from the floor to the top of the waist-high cabinet. It pivoted at the bottom to open or close. Just the right size, it held a whole sack of flour plus the sifter, and once ajar its own weight kept it open. He stood, leaned far back, proud of himself for remembering that limp neck. He bent his knees and picked up a small blanket from the table.

Rawls stepped to the cabinet, repeated his baby balancing effort, and opened the bin. Flour came to within several inches of the top. He removed the sifter and placed the blanket on the flour. He laid the baby on top and breathed deeply, cringed at the sound coming from her lusty lungs.

Rawls sat on the bed beside Bess, holding a pan of clean, warm water. It was more peaceful now. The baby had quieted. He placed the pan on the seat of a chair and squeezed water from the rag. If only she would smile. It didn't have to be directed at him, just a smile. He clumsily wiped at the mess on her face.

Her eyes opened. She looked wildly about. "The baby! Rawls, where is the baby?"

"The b-bureau, in the bureau drawer so nobody will step on her."

Bess lurched to a sitting position. She grimaced and grabbed her lower stomach. Pain colored her voice. "Rawls, you idiot, there is no bureau. Where's my baby?"

Rawls jerked upright and moved a half step backward. Was he an idiot? He bent and made fists at either side of his forehead. He closed his eyes, bit his lip. Reality drifted away. A hole opened beneath him, and he tumbled downward, lower and lower. *Sharon, bureau, bureau, no, not Sharon, the baby girl . . . the flour bin, she was in the flour bin.* Flood waters beat at the rising flame of panic in his innards, and he smiled and pointed. "The baby's in the flour bin."

Bess's gaze swung toward the cabinet and his own view followed. Above the front of the open bin a tiny fist clutched air, moved, and dipped from sight.

The stiffness melted from Bess's body. She brought her eyes back to his face, studied him. A perplexed look furrowed her brow, then she turned back toward the cabinet. The baby's feet and hands showed, wiggling over the top of the bin. She reached for the washrag. "Here, give me that."

Rawls handed it over, looked quickly in the other direction. "Maybe I'll go outside. Where's Marcus?"

"He and Ramón took some stock to San Antonio eight days ago. He said he'd only be gone three or four days. Said he'd be straight back. I don't know. Go, go on out. I've got to wash." He nodded. Her voice stopped him at the doorway. It came softer now, less frightened. "There's tobacco and a pipe on the mantel. Take some with you, if you like, and, Rawls, don't go far. I'll want you to hand me the baby soon as I'm cleaned up."

Rawls turned and took the pipe and a fill of tobacco, and shuffled out, closing the door. He stood on the porch, peered up the road after lighting the pipe. Marcus was obviously resting it. A couple of taps, packing the tobacco, and it drew sweet and easy. His view settled on the barn, warmed with a sensation of safety as he recognized a high-wheeled wagon. A bawling cow near the barn walked a lot fence that enclosed a calf. *Marcus should be here,* he thought. *It wasn't right. What did she say? He'd left with stock, how many days? Eight!*

Bess called. He reëntered the darkening room. She was barely visible, but he could tell she'd wrapped herself in a robe and sat beside the bed.

"Hand me the baby, then take that bedding outside, please. There are clean quilts in the trunk."

Rawls did as he was instructed. When he returned, the interior of the cabin had slipped into shadows. Bess sat with the baby. Rawls lit the lamp on the table, then found the quilts. It seemed he should say something, but what? He spread the first quilt on the mattress, billowed the second, and stiffened at the sound of smacking and gurgling coming from Bess's dark corner. His mind might be struggling with the aftermath of war, but he'd spent too much time around nursing calves and pups not to know that noise.

Bess crooned soft words to the baby, words he could not make out. Hair on the back of his neck tingled and he wanted badly to investigate the scene back there. For the first time in weeks, awareness of manhood pushed aside befuddled indecision. He sensed shame, and embarrassment stoked the fire burning his face. He smoothed the last quilt, turned to the fireplace, and punched buried coals with a poker.

He heard a slight rustle. "Help us to bed, please."

The lamp's light clearly illuminated mother and child. Bess had covered her breast. Rawls sighed, took the baby in both arms. Bess reached from the chair for assistance.

"I . . . I better put her down first." He bent and placed the baby in the center of the quilt. The holstered pistol, resting butt frontward on his left side, slipped slightly. He straightened, adjusted the holster, and offered his right hand to steady Bess for the step to the bed. "She is . . . is a girl."

Bess's expression softened, then a low moan escaped as she shifted her weight. She sat on the edge of the cover and took deep breaths, appeared to be studying her feet. She continued to hold his hand.

He shifted from one foot to the other. His mind whirled. This was both good and bad. She was his brother's wife. Marcus should be holding her hand. And he should see her as a sister, but she was a lot different from a sister. He didn't want to turn her loose, but he didn't know what to say. She must think him a fool. Maybe Marcus would never come home. If he had enough time, he'd show her he was no fool. "I . . . I don't mind that she's a girl."

Bess looked up at him. Her gaze rested on his face a long moment. It was the second time today she'd given him that hard look. The corner of one side of her mouth twitched slightly. "That's big of you." She released his hand.

Rawls felt a smile work at his lips, then realized she hadn't been sincere. He moved back toward the fireplace.

"Rawls, I want to thank you. I don't know what would have happened if you hadn't come along."

"I . . . I . . . I reckon, I wouldn't 'a' missed it." He pushed a forelock from his eyes.

"You must be hungry. There are beans and a hunk of ham in that pot with the lid on. Warm them up if you want. Cold cornbread is under the cloth on the cabinet." She pointed toward a cup towel.

Rawls looked up at the loft. "I . . . I know where the onions are. What about you?"

"Maybe I'll mix a piece of bread in milk later."

Rawls placed sticks on the coals in the fireplace and hooked the bean pot's bail so it would swing above them. He

17

lifted the lid, peeked inside the pot, and struggled not to show his hunger. The sight and scent of the lean meat bore no resemblance to his last meal. Yesterday he'd eaten rattlesnake. It hadn't tasted that bad; it was the sight and scent he had hated. "I'll go milk that old cow while that warms up."

Later, finishing his third helping, Rawls sensed Bess, watching him. He moved back from the table, propped his chair against the wall, and filled Marcus's pipe. With it in his mouth, unlit, he moved Bess's empty supper bowl from the bedside and placed it in a metal pan. He sat and took a deep breath, then sighed. He patted his stomach. "I'm obliged."

"Tell me, Rawls, what's wrong with you?" Bess spoke from her pillow. She'd rolled to her side, her eyes on him.

Rawls fired the pipe. "In a M-Memphis hospital . . . one sawbones thought apoplexy. Another said I'd just seen too much blood, heard too many screams or, maybe, been rolled on by too many damn' horses. He thought my brain had been squashed a little anyway, and had them get me out of there so he could fix somebody's hurt he could see." He stopped and took deep breaths, trying to steady himself. "In Fort Smith a doctor stuck a stick in my mouth and pushed down on my tongue, then said I was likely just tired. A-ain't too sure 'bout doctors. Think that last one may've been drunk."

"Where were you when it started?"

"H-hard to tell, not sure. It was a big fight. Learned later, Lee and Grant had already palavered at A-Appomattox." Rawls studied the pipe. It was a good pipe. "I was with Johnston . . . think somewhere in North Carolina."

"So, what happened?"

"Oh, uhn-huh, a lot of artillery fire, then a horse smashed down on me. Woke up a week later. At first I couldn't talk, couldn't move nothing on this side. All I could do was lie on my back, and, when someone w-would ask me things, I couldn't talk, just cuss."

"Cuss . . . you never cussed much."

"Must've learned. Once a lady came to shave me. She kept asking things and I'd try the hardest to answer, only nothing came out. S-suddenly I started mouthing bad words. Cussing, swatting flies, and shooting without thinking is all I'm at home with any more. I don't think about it. . . . The shooting's a little slower, but near the same. I popped that old rattler yesterday before I knew it. Funny thing, coming home, near the Sabine, I had a spell of walking for two days good as ever, no limp, nothing."

"All that and the war was over?"

"It . . . it gets cloudy. Think so."

"Well, it is now, Rawls. Welcome home. And there's more to do here than cussing and swatting . . . most times, anyway." Bess rolled, facing the baby. It made those noises again. She spoke with her back to him. "Will you get better?" Her arm stirred, moving as though struggling with her little one. She shifted her position.

"Maybe, maybe not." He silently thanked his mother for making him a boy. The less he had to do with babies the better. He'd hate to be wrestling with that little tyke, tired as he was. "The last doctor said, with time and exercise, I might completely get . . . get over it. I've done good so far, and I'd say, if walking counts, I've got the exercise."

Maybe his mother had had nothing to do with it—his being a boy. More likely it was God's doing. "It's just sometime I'm so slow. Others, my body does things, but my mind doesn't catch up till later . . . things like cussing or jumping out of the way of something. Sometimes I think it's getting better, but. . . ." On the other hand, it might have been his mother. He'd heard older cows had more bull calves.

Bess yawned, worked at her gown. "I'm going to sleep. No

need you going to the barn. Just unroll your blanket in front of the door."

He hung his pistol and belt on a nearby peg. Cupping his hand over the lamp's globe, his first puff put it out. Taking off his shirt, he lay on half the blanket, pulled the rest over his bare shoulder. He kept his pants on.

"Rawls, you really walked all the way from North Carolina?" Her voice was soft as though not to wake the baby.

Had a woman's voice sought him before from the dark? He didn't think so. "I . . . I . . . guess, mostly. The boys said after Johnston and Sherman talked, we started hoofing it. I don't remember, but I walked with some other hurt boys through Tennessee before landing in the hospital in Memphis. Shoes gave out in Arkansas."

No matter what had happened, Marcus was a fool. Seemed he should care for his older brother, but the man was a fool, and to be honest he sort of hoped he would stay gone. They could get together again when they were old men. That would be nice.

Chapter Three

Rawls promised himself as soon as things settled inside the cabin, he'd cook breakfast. Birthing children whetted a man's appetite. He felt sort of important today, important and hungry. Earlier, Bess had seemed desperate for him to leave the house. Likely she had her reasons. From the urgency in her voice when she suggested he milk the cow, Sherman's army could have been mustered above the spring.

Bess now walked beyond the porch and emptied a pan. He took a few steps, waited at the porch. When she walked back, he held out eggs in both hands. "F-found b-breakfast."

She nodded, placed her hand on his forearm, and with the other holding the porch post mounted the steps. Her eyes took in his shoddy garb, and she motioned her chin toward his waist. "The Yanks didn't leave you much, huh? After breakfast, you want to bathe and clean up some, I think you can find yourself a near-fit of Marcus's clothes in that chiffarobe. I know there's a pair of boots in the loft. They may need a patch, but they'll beat nothing."

Rawls cooked breakfast. After eating, Bess propped her chin in her hands with her elbows braced on the table and watched as he loaded the pipe. He got up, poured them both another cup of coffee, and lit his smoke from a fireplace ember before settling back at the table.

"Think the baby looks like me?" Bess asked.

He nodded, deliberately lying. A dried prune was what she looked like. A thin scar at the corner of Bess's eye caught his attention, teased for an explanation. Sight of it saddened him. She'd not had it before the war. His mind wandered past it, thought of how she had looked before. Strangely, in spite of his problem with memory, her image always answered muster. She'd been a bride of nineteen, fresh with dark-hair flying in the breeze, bright-eyed, always laughing. Those eyes had had only room for her husband—his older brother. At nineteen how do you capture a glance from a girl your own age? He'd joined Hood's Texas Volunteers shortly after the wedding. Still beautiful, he sensed she'd faced struggles of her own.

"Y-you want me to go look for Marcus?"

Her answer almost beat the question. "No, no! If he's coming, he'll come."

"I . . . I just thought. . . ."

"Let it go, Rawls." Her gaze wandered out the open door, settled on the cottonwood. "Rube is with him. I do miss Rube."

He stood, then gathered and put the dishes in the big blue pan. "W-who is Rube?"

"Our mutt. Just leave those on the cabinet and bring me a bucket of water. Here." She handed him a pair of scissors. "You want, I'll trim whatever is left after you hack it down some."

She had to be talking about his hair. He'd shaved, full, sometime last week. Rawls found Marcus's clothing and the boots where she'd said. Outside, he bathed behind an old canvas tarpaulin that hung beside a flat rock near the ditch from the spring. He managed to shave looking into a small piece of broken mirror Marcus had wedged in the fork of a mesquite. He needed a fuller view to trim his hair. A pool near the spring answered his need. Soon it reflected heavy strands of hair falling from above his ears. He tried unsuccessfully to shape the sides and back. Waves distorted his image, and his left hand grew tired of trying to gauge hair length by feel.

Later, sitting still for Bess's final trim presented a problem. He sat in a chair on the porch. She used a cup towel like a real barber to cover his shoulders and catch clippings. Still, the place where the towel wrapped around his neck itched. He'd not move, though, not if his head itched off. It felt too nice when she put her hand on his shoulder or blew hair from the towel. At least he'd finally seen her smile. One look at his botched haircut had succeeded where all his efforts had failed. Being a clown wasn't really what he had in mind, but she had smiled.

Questions concerning Marcus's whereabouts worried at his mind. He had the uneasy feeling he should be making an effort to fetch him home. But Bess was still unsteady on her feet. She didn't need to be left alone again. Besides, she seemed to miss the dog more than she longed for Marcus. Women were funny, though. Marcus said they didn't always say what they meant.

A soft breeze lifted the corner of the towel, then a stronger gust whipped it, and hair tickled Rawls's nose. He sneezed. Panic wormed upward, another disaster. A trickle of moisture wet his upper lip. He had no handkerchief. Women frowned on a man using the back of his hand. Everyone knew that.

Bess took the corner of the towel and wiped beneath his nose. The way she did it, she might have been just wiping loose hair, or maybe she had seen the moisture. At any rate, she said nothing, made no sign of awareness of his grubby habits.

Between the rolling hills beyond the cottonwood, a faint layer of dust rose then melted in the stronger breeze. The road wound behind that hill. Rawls squinted. After a moment his eyes watered and he looked away, rested them on the far hills. "H-how we doing?"

"About done. As I remember you used to do most things pretty good. Guess you never sheared sheep."

"OK, thanks. Bess, go inside with the baby. Somebody's coming." The force and steadiness of his own voice surprised him.

"Probably just cows coming to water." Her hurried movements disputed her words.

Rawls stood, brushed hair from his clothing, loosened the shirt's collar, and wiped at his neck. He leaned against the post's porch, fiddling one-handed with the button. A horse came into view. Its empty saddle's stirrups kept time with the mount's gait. The bridle's reins were broken. A flop-eared dog followed a few steps behind. Near the house, it broke into a trot.

"Bess!" he called.

Rawls heard the door open. From the corner of his eye he saw her standing just inside. She held the baby. His view swung back to the animals.

Sweat and road dust streaked the horse's shoulders and flanks, stood out on its darker legs. Behind the saddle's skirt a dorsal strip ran down the mount's hips, merged with the tail. He was a grulla.

"It's old Mouse and Rube," Bess said, and nodded when Rawls's gaze met hers. She lowered her eyes and reached to close the door. "See to the horse."

Rawls moved to the horse, took hold of the bridle, and led the pony to the fence. He opened a gate, pointed the horse inside, and, after removing the bridle, slapped the horse's rump. Maybe the fool thing wouldn't roll with the saddle still on. He moved to the harness stall and began a repair job on new reins.

24

He didn't want to leave. He might ride off, and the next minute Bess develop a fever. It happened often. The nurses had talked about the second and third day being dangerous for new mothers. Ladies in the ward next to his in Memphis often had had trouble with childbirth. But Marcus might be down, hurt. He owed Marcus, who had saved him more than once. In the presence of danger, pain or misfortune failed to distract Marcus.

Rawls shook his left hand. You'd think nothing could be as slow or clumsy as those fingers. Replacing reins shouldn't take so long. Somewhere on that prairie Marcus needed help, but where? Someone had to go—had to find him. Leaving the barn, his view caught Bess's figure. She slumped, looking frail, in her porch chair, the dog at her side.

Chapter Four

Bess's eyes ranged over Rawls's head, back to the hills, and up the road. "You're going?"

He nodded. "Where's the nearest womenfolk I can fetch to stay with you?"

"Four miles yonder, on the way to Plum Grove. Mouse's trail will likely take you by there, anyway. You'll see the house in a chinaberry thicket." Bess appeared tired. He shouldn't have allowed her to trim his hair. "Missus Meadows, she's a good woman. Just tell her no rush, everything is OK, and the baby's already here. If she can, just ask her to plan for a couple of days. Her man will likely bring her. He's dependable. And, Rawls, you don't have to come all the way back with them." There was pain in Bess's voice now. "If you lose them tracks, go on to Plum Grove. There's a place there, sort of a saloon. Chances are he's there." She stepped back.

She was out of sight, in the shadows. But if separated by the moon, he could list every feature of his brother's wife. She was tiny beyond belief, yet strong, bright-eyed, and smiling. Her dark hair soft as roasting corn-ear silk. She had a way about her of breaking into that half smile, just the beginning that teased with promise of more. The generous lips, the small creases about the mouth and eyes, all of it, high cheek bones framing her delicate nose and, somehow, God set all that in softness from another world—a softness that made him catch his breath.

Then there was that woman part of it. Curves, bulging

breasts and hips that made him turn in shame and head for the barn. Some secrets hid easier than others.

"Bess," he said, over his shoulder. "From the looks of you . . . every woman ought to have a baby."

The sun blazed over a big cushion of sky when he rode into Plum Grove. Earlier, the Meadowses had reacted immediately to his request. Mouse's trail led directly into town. The burg hadn't grown a plank since his departure. It had just aged with the rest of the South. Its wrinkles took the form of cracks and peeling paint. Hard times showed from the growing tumbleweeds at the edge of boardwalks to the fading signs on the buildings' façades.

He'd seen it throughout the South. Farms turned to weeds and underbrush, houses burned, and villages filled with hollowed-eyed hunger. Folks using scorched corn for coffee, barely staying alive. But, that was the old South.

This was newer country—frontier—not even organized into counties. This country was so raw, there had been no organized conscription. Marcus had stayed behind to manage the ranch. Secretly chafing at his brother's luck with Bess, Rawls had volunteered to go. Now, he'd come back to a land where the clock ran backward.

Seven structures faced the road from its north. Three were adobe, the others false-fronted frame. South of the dusty thoroughfare, sixty miles of greasewood, bunch grass, and cactus held the earth together. Somewhere out there the Río Bravo cut through. Mouse kicked sand puffs with more energy and seemed to sense the end of the journey.

Past the second building, noise and dust rose around a newly arrived stage. The dust swirled, engulfed Rawls, then moved on to the drying laundry. A handler worked at unhitching dripping spans of Mexican mules. Three other men struggled around the far corner of the building with six replacements.

Down the street, a sign hung over what used to be the Cattleman's Hotel. It swung level with the second story balcony and read: **The Gilded Posey.** Small pink flowers adorned each corner of the sign.

Rawls dismounted in front of the hitch rack beneath the sign. He entered the saloon. Inside, he paused, let his eyes adjust.

"Come in, pilgrim. A man without a hat is always thirsty." An older man fought flies behind the bar. The fly-swatter's handle seemed as large as the arm that swung it. His lusty voice belied his size, and his hatchet-edged face hid behind an oversize nose. "Must be coming a weather change. Flies gonna eat us up. What'll it be?"

"A-ain't got no money, so guess it'll be gossip." Rawls eased his elbows to the bar.

"Sign of the times. Country's got a hunert million cows and the whole caboodle worth about two bits Confederate. One customer and him broke. No money, no hat, looking for chit-chat, and me with, as the ladies call it, no tittle-tattle. Looks like we both drawed bad hands. You got any prospects? Maybe we can run you a bill. Name's Snort."

"Rawls Slaton. Y-you may know my brother . . . Marcus?"

"Know him, knew your daddy in Galveston before that Santa Anna thing. I traded cotton down there till the carpetbaggers ran all the honest folk out. Your daddy had a name people tipped their hat to."

"I . . . I been out to the ranch. Things sort of seedy out there. Here, too."

"Your brother's had more'n cows on his mind."

"H-he always had a weakness for cards and booze."

"Them, too."

28

Snort's last comment caused Rawls to scratch his head.

"Far as things going to seed, tending to business don't matter much. When they ain't no market for what you got, and the rains don't come, it's just as bad on the just as the unjust. I tell you . . . guess it's my age . . . but, at times, I wonder if all Texas is gonna starve."

"Still, looks like he could at least chop a stick of stove wood."

"True. But, Rawls, your brother's a complicated man. Complicated some ways, others good. Seems things is too easy for him, sometimes. Best with a pistol I ever saw. It showed in a scrap or two in here. When you ain't all frazzled out, you like that?"

"Guess so. We're a lot alike. Poppa rode with the guard, Rangers some called them. He come from a hard country . . . the Nueces Strip. He taught us guns before Mama broke us to the pot. We cut our teeth on pistols, one type or another. Don't 'member my first smoke, but we was packing iron at the time. It was nip and tuck who could beat who. That knack and a tobacco yearning is about all I kept through the war."

"Well, your daddy was a hoss, and any faults your brother's got, he's still proud of you. He told me so."

The older man rubbed thin chin-stubble and studied Rawls. His gaze moved slowly down from the botched hair to the ill-fitting and worn-out clothes. He couldn't have missed the hungry look. His face took on a pained look. "Boy, you are down on your luck, ain't yuh? But you're catching a break, though. Made Marcus pay his bill, 'fore he got wound up a few days ago. Said he'd sold some hides. Ain't that something, selling good beeves for their hide and that not worth enough to buy a drink."

The bartender poured a whiskey. "He's current with the house now. Here . . . you don't want this, I'll drink it." He pushed it toward Rawls.

"T-thanks, I'll make it good when I can. W-where is he?"

The barman hooked a thumb toward the upstairs. "Been up there most of the last three days. If he didn't go down them outside stairs, he's still there." The little man poured himself a drink. "If your brother ain't upstairs, he's over at the stage station. His old nag got tired of waiting and broke loose yesterday. Afoot, Marcus let 'em sweet talk him into heading for San Antonio. You cut it close. Stage is loading up now. Where's your hat?"

Rawls downed his drink, fought to keep down a gasp for air, and wiped the back of his hand across his watering eyes. "T-thanks. Your rotgut's smoother than I'm used to. Far as a hat's concerned, ain't had one in years. Lost my cap between Atlanta and Savanna running from the Yanks."

"You was with Lee and the rest of the boys?"

"No, Hood, then Mosby, then Johnston . . . saw Lee a few times."

"Wal, welcome home. Tell you what . . . something about the way that mane of yourn's been roached disturbs the orderliness of this place. The gals will be down directly. They're sort of genteel. Used to the finer things of life. We better get you a hat."

"T-told you, I'm broke."

"So yuh said. Tell you what . . . see that black, flat-brim dude's hat over yonder?" Snort pointed at the hat rack by the door.

Rawls used the bar's mirror to follow the direction. The black hat had only one companion, and sweat stains colored that one a dull pinto.

"The one with the table-top crown. A fellow passed through, wal, passed on fits better, and left it with us. He warn't as slick as he figured. Liked drawing to an inside

30

straights from up his sleeve. Hat's yourn, if you want. Folks here favor a little more crown, but it'll turn the sun, maybe not as quick, but it'll turn her."

Rawls faced the rack. "H-how much?"

"Said it's yourn. Little enough for the Cause."

Rawls shuffled toward the door. He'd go to the station first. It sounded like things had settled down over there. They might be about to get under way. He stopped at the hat rack, tried on the headgear. It fit fine, maybe a little loose, but thin rawhide inside the sweatband would fix that. He took it off, turned it in his hand. Dead center in front and a quarter-inch above the brim was a round hole. A ragged stain was smeared around the hole. Rawls poked his little finger through the opening and grinned at Snort. "S-somebody opened a window in her, huh?" He put the hat on and moved toward the street.

Snort called after him. "You find Marcus and you get thirsty, come on back! You don't want to drink on his cuff, I've been known to trade a shot for one of them Forty-Five shells."

Rawls raised his arm and kept walking. Outside, he turned toward the stage. Two handlers swung by their teeth from the ears of the swing span of the team of six half-broken Mexican mules. With a mouthful of mule's ear and a hand pulling down the other, the wranglers still managed to hang onto the animals' bridles. With the team in check, a helper hooked the harness. Another struggled with one of the leaders.

It lifted Rawls's spirit to see such ability. Someone had taught them well. Those boys knew their stuff. A mule had only two spots tender enough to give a mere human control. One was his nose when properly twitched, the other, those long, ugly, and sensitive ears. Prone to balk into rock-like immobility or lock the bit in their teeth to run out of control, a handler's only hope for survival was to get pressure on those tender areas. He and Marcus had learned the tricks at an early age.

The driver had one foot on the brake and another braced, against the front of the box. He leaned back with his weight on the lines. The rear of his pants seldom dusted the coach's seat. A heavy man faced the rear and, holding the jostling stage's top rail with one hand, worked to secure a saddle to the topside rack. He wobbled back and forth on his knees.

"Board up, god-damn it! Climb on, we're leaving. Last call! Board! Sons-a-bitching mules!"

One of the passengers was still at the door of the station when Rawls's shuffling trot put him at the stage's door. Inside the stage, Marcus slumped against the opposite rear corner, his dull eyes staring straight ahead.

Rawls opened the door, leaned in. "M-Marcus?"

"Rawls, little brover is that you? Get in. We're going to San Tone." Marcus raised an arm, let it fall. His words were slow, rasping. They started barely above a whisper, crunched clumsily over gravel, then grew louder till the shortened San Antonio competed with the hollered Spanish oaths of the mule handlers.

"C-come on Marcus. We going home. You're a daddy."

Marcus stared, squinted. His chin dropped. "Shit. What you talkin' 'bout?"

A worn lady passenger aimed an angry look at Marcus and crawled in over his outstretched legs.

"Y-you and Bess . . . your baby is here."

"Get in, Brover. I'm glad you back. The war's over. Babies can wait. We'll go play some poker. Maybe get you a dance. . . ." Marcus attempted to straighten, but slid farther down in the seat. His features twisted into a knowing grin. "A dance with a painted lady."

The stage lurched forward, then came to a stop. "Hold that damn' team!" Rawls shouted up at the driver.

The man in the box continued sawing on the lines, attempting to hold the mules. "Get yore ass away from that door and shut it!" he called back. "We're leaving now. Soon as he shuts the door, turn 'em loose boys."

The handler on the off leader apparently misunderstood. He released his animal. It jumped forward. The other men struggled in a losing battle to hold the remaining hitch.

Rawls took one step back, drew his pistol, and thumbed the hammer. The barrel lowered. The front sight settled into the notch even with the off-front mule's huge ear. Rawls squeezed off the shot. The roar of the six-gun pounded like drums in his head. Through the smoke he saw a small hole of daylight through the mouse-colored ear.

The injured leader skidded to a spread-eagle stop and dropped his head between his front legs. He brayed loudly, lowered his good ear, and flapped the injured one. Neither thunder nor man would move him now. The other five animals shied from the noise and their frozen mate. They dragged the balking brute sideways, then sprang forward. The stage bounced and stopped momentarily against the station's porch.

"S-said . . . hold that team," Rawls said.

The animals lunged again. The driver, fighting the team, looked over his shoulder. "You crazy son-of-a-bitch! Shoot him, Zeb."

The guard, Zeb, had his hands full fighting to stay on the stage's roof. He turned loose with one hand, leaned forward, and grabbed for a booted scatter-gun. He got the gun, but lost it, falling sideways over the railing. He landed with a dusty *plop* in front of the stage's wheel. The shotgun fell beside him. He snatched it up, rolled, and swung the gun

33

toward the coach door.

Rawls held the .45 pointed at the man's nose. The hammer rested back on the fork of his gun hand.

Zeb froze. He lowered the shotgun, blinked rapidly.

"T-that's good. L-living beats a draw. Just a minute, I'll have my baggage." Rawls motioned with his gun barrel for Zeb to remount the stage, but shook his head when the man looked at his weapon. His head motion set off those drums again. He reached in and Marcus, wide-eyed, raised an unsteady arm. They gripped hands, and Rawls locked his forearm inside Marcus's, and pulled. Marcus slid face down into the dust of the street.

From above came the driver's voice. "Leave him be, Zeb. Hang on. The son-of-a-bitch's crazy. Man shoots a stage company mule, no telling what next. Just look at that damn' hat. Sure is an ugly one. We'll turn him over to Rake. That's what he's paid for. Cowboy," the driver said, addressing Rawls, "Rake Darrow's in El Paso, but you'll be hearing from him." He turned to the hostler, saying: "Willey, bring in a replacement for that sulking, notch-eared son-of-a-bitch."

Rawls backed a few steps, dragging his brother. He stopped, and Marcus struggled to his feet. Rawls put his hand on Marcus's waist and clasped the belt. One of the handlers unhitched the balking mule, and the team moved forward, past the animal. In moments the hostler appeared with a replacement.

Behind them the boardwalk rattled. The *click* of a lady's heels signaled a fast gait. The woman didn't stop till her arms were around Marcus's neck. He staggered a few steps, holding the woman, then turned, grinning sickly past the woman's ear at Rawls.

"What happened? You boys celebrating with pistols again? Honey, you weren't going to leave without li'l ole me?"

Marcus's companion displayed a bounty of paint and bosom. Underneath the makeup were lips too full, and around the eyes a hard look belied her girlish tone.

"W-who are you?" Rawls asked.

"I'm Rose, honey, but I'm sorry, I only bloom for Marcus. You going to San Antonio with us?"

The stage groaned and squeaked over the sand-muffled sound of hoofs. It moved away, its noise growing fainter. The shot mule remained, immobile. It occasionally shook its offending ear. The ear showed no blood.

God! That was what Snort had been talking about. Marcus had jumped the fence, been tempted to stray from grazing in heaven with his wife by a harlot's debauchery. No wonder Bess was so torn up. After all Snort said, he'd taken this long to put it together. Bess said he was an idiot. She was right. "E . . . excuse us, ma'am, we headed home."

Marcus shook his head. "Ain't, by God, going home. You ain't my poppa."

That's what he thought! The drum in his left ear grew louder, moved toward his temple. Damn a brother that had the gall to treat Bess like dirt. He tilted the gun barrel to point at Marcus's crotch. "S-stay, if you like, but you'll do it shy of that. You're lucky I don't geld you right here."

Marcus blanched. He staggered, then, with feet spread wide, he caught his balance and swayed. "You wouldn't. We're brothers." Marcus squinted. "You ain't drunk, are you, kid? You walking crooked, shooting straight?"

Rawls clumsily tapped his forehead with a finger of his slow hand. "M-maybe I'm a little touched . . . could be that driver is right." He cocked and fired his weapon. The Colt roared. Dirt exploded between and slightly behind Marcus's legs.

Wide-eyed, Marcus jumped, fell, and sprang quickly to his

35

feet. "Let's go." He moved drunkenly behind Rawls.

Rose looked toward the disappearing stage. "Shit." She picked up her hatbox and bag and headed, alone, for the saloon's outside stairs.

Chapter Five

Fading light bathed the baby. Bess snuggled, warm, enjoying a sense of safety and well-being for the first time since her pregnancy began. The child slept in a cradle brought by the Meadowses. Her feedings were sort of a whirlwind of emotions for Mama, but it appeared the milk satisfied.

The older couple had arrived shortly after noon and created a cyclone of activity. Mrs. Meadows proved herself one of those efficient people whose every move counted double. She'd been here four hours, and the place was dusted, swept, and scrubbed. Laundry hung on the line.

Now, Mrs. Meadows bent forward over a bucket of hot water, plucking wet feathers from a fryer. She scolded her husband. "Just go on home, Sam. Us ladies will be all right."

"Hush about it, Mother. Things there are OK. These boys get home, we'll hit the road tomorrow."

In spite of Bess's admiration and respect for Mr. Meadows, she resented his reluctance to be near her or the baby. He treated the inside of the house like a den of snakes. It was as though he viewed childbirth as something to be kept in the dark. She had enough trouble feeling clean without that. The front door marked the man's self-imposed boundary.

Poor old Rawls, he'd had that stupid male modesty knocked out of him in a hurry. Bess sensed a momentary softening of her facial muscles at thought of the fumbling younger brother, then the brittleness returned. She was such a fool, such a complicated fool, resenting the very reserve in other men that she longed for in her husband. She blamed his crudeness and lack of modesty for her own coldness. Yet, when exposed to a different behavior, she still withdrew.

The serenity melted away. Familiar uneasiness replaced it. Questions floated in her mind. If only she could change, soften this barrier she'd placed around herself, and share her life with others. She thought of Marcus, of what he'd probably been doing. A knot tightened in her belly. She tossed her head, forced him from her mind, but the unanswerable question remained, cried for an answer. Could she ever again freely embrace love?

"Someone's coming," Mr. Meadows said.

The dog barked twice, sniffed the wind, and loped toward the spring.

"It must be them." Bess ached for excitement, sensed sadness.

A team pulling a buckboard bounced into view. The driver wore a flat-crowned black hat. He raised a hand in greeting. "O-old Mouse was about petered, s-so Snort loaned me his team and rig." Rawls pointed at the bed of the buckboard behind the seat. "M-Marcus is OK. He's just played out."

Marcus raised to a sitting position. His legs draped over the tail end of the buckboard. As they neared the ditch leading to the barn, he stepped to the ground, stumbled, and righted himself, then made his way to the water. He dropped to his knees and dipped water to his face.

"H-he took sick, coming home." Rawls pulled the team to a halt at the barn.

Bess moved toward Marcus. A few feet from him the stench of vomit fouled her senses. She stopped, whirled, and walked slowly toward the cabin. Tears wet her cheeks and she put her hands to her face.

"Get your things, Mother, I'll harness Zeke. We best go." Mr. Meadows walked toward the barn. He looked toward

Marcus, said nothing, then addressed Rawls. "You need us, we can come back."

"T-thanks," Rawls said.

"What about this chicken?" Mrs. Meadows held the plucked bird waist high.

"I'll bet Rawls can dress and fry a chicken," Sam Meadows said, disappearing into the barn.

The sob started low, moved upward. Bess fought it, surrendered, walked faster.

Mrs. Meadows reached her free arm and embraced Bess as she drew near. "Honey, honey, honey."

"Thank you so much." Bess steadied her voice. "You've done so much, been so kind. Won't you stay the night?"

"There'll be a moon. Old Zeke knows the way. You take care, honey."

Bess freed herself and moved to the porch. She stopped, determined to show Mrs. Meadows a brave smile. The woman took long strides toward Marcus.

Marcus stood, shaking water from his hands. He looked blankly at the lady bearing down on him. He made a motion toward a nonexistent hat.

Mrs. Meadows stopped. The two figures were only a couple of feet apart. Her firm voice dripped ice—ice that burned. "You ought to be ashamed of yourself." She still held the nude chicken, and now she swung it with all of her adequate weight behind it.

Marcus reacted too slowly. The bird slammed against his face, resounded with a soft, plopping noise.

"Here, make yourself useful. You don't deserve what you got up there." Mrs. Meadows turned, her back stiff, and moved toward the barn.

Marcus looked down at the bird now in his hands. "Yes, ma'am."

The next morning, Rawls joined the family at the baby's crib. Marcus moved his finger to the child's hand, lifted one of the tiny fingers. "She's pretty like you, Bess."

Here it comes, she thought. *Now he wants to make up. It's always like this. Have his fun or his blow-ups, then try to weasel or cry his way back into favor.*

"Where'd the cradle come from?" he asked.

"The Meadowses."

"Bess, I'm sorry. I never dreamed you were this near. We couldn't sell the beeves, had to sell to hide buyers. I was just so damn' down."

"Not now, Marcus." Bess noticed Rawls looking from one to the other of them. He seemed hurt, ill at ease.

"S-she ain't got a name."

The diversion brought a sigh from Marcus. "Yeah, what we gonna call her?"

"S-she shines like new money." Rawls bent closer to the cradle. "I-Indians would call her Little Shiny."

She did look polished, Bess thought. *Bless his poor heart, he's right.* "You just named her Rawls. Her name is Patina . . . Patina Louise Slaton."

Rawls appeared puzzled. "I . . . I said Shiny."

Marcus moved to the coffee pot. "It means the same."

After the brothers finished their coffee and smokes, they headed for the barn. Later, the wind shifted, bringing a hint of fall and thoughts of long sleeves. October neared its end. From the doorway, Bess noticed the half dozen chickens peck their way to the corner of the barn. The new breeze fluffed their feathers, hurried their steps as they turned south. Marcus was working on the corral behind the barn. Bess could not see Rawls. She wondered if she should check the barn. *Just raw nerves,* she told herself. *The man walked from*

Tennessee, even farther. He'll be OK.

She'd barely shelved the thought when he walked from the barn. He held a small wooden box and walked, head down. She started to the baby, stopped, and turned back. Something wasn't right. He was limping much worse.

Rawls bent, shakily reached to the ground, picked something up, and slowly put it in the box. He continued his search. Hypnotized, Bess watched. Step by agonizingly slow step, he proceeded around the yard. Her concern grew. His effort to reach the ground without toppling over increased, and time after time he got down on his knees. He came closer, and she realized it was rocks that he gathered. He was going around the yard in ever decreasing circles, picking up small pebbles.

Bess hurried toward the corral. She passed Rawls, and spoke. He made no response. A few steps more and she stood by Marcus, pointing. "I'm worried!"

Marcus stopped what he was doing, and walked with her to the fence. They each leaned, resting on rails of different heights. She gazed through an opening. He looked over the top.

"I'll be damned. You suppose he's been walking so long, he just can't stop?" Marcus fished for his pipe. "He put a hole in a Butterfield mule's ear at Plum Grove. Shot him standing in his traces. Thought he was gonna do the same to me, but he backed off at the last minute."

Bess couldn't resist. "Never questioned the Slaton aim . . . it's his follow-through that casts doubt. I'm frightened, Marcus. What should we do?"

"Just leave him be. If he goes down, we'll find him a bed, but he's been on his own a long time. Gives you the creeps, though, don't it?"

On the way back to the cabin, Bess stopped in front of

Rawls. He stepped around her, making no acknowledgement of her presence. She noticed his shirt was wet with sweat. The few steps to the cabin seemed uphill. She had her baby, but was losing her one remaining champion. That was it; he'd always championed her needs.

Chapter Six

Rawls awoke in darkness, alone, wet clothes clinging to his body, his face dry. His rope-tight stomach scolded. The past few hours were a mystery. He walked through the barn and on toward the house. Midway across the yard he saw the glow of Marcus's pipe. He felt in his pocket to reassure himself he carried his brother's spare.

"Come up and light. Feeling better? I told Bess, rest is what you needed." Marcus's voice was sincere.

"Better, thanks. Sort of played out on you today, huh?"

"Don't worry about it. Get you a bite, then join us. Ain't too bad out here since the wind died."

"There's a bowl on the table," Bess told him, "venison stew. Cornbread in the bread box." Bess sat in the shadows across the porch from Marcus.

Rawls lit the lamp and ate, wondering what to say when he joined them on the porch. He seated himself near the porch step. "D-dry, ain't it?"

"Seen worse. Had a shower about six months ago." Marcus's face showed in the glow of a match.

"H-hold that," Rawls said. He took the light after Marcus had used it. "How do folks hang on?"

"They ain't holding on. Most are losing what little grip they had. North of San Antonio, they're still scratching, but it's all over here. We got nothing but cattle. And they ain't worth a damn."

"Where's the market?"

"There ain't none. Skinned, the hides will bring maybe

43

two or three dollars. Some tried driving to Missouri, but that's like feeding chickens to coyotes with a thief behind every oak. Welcome to your half of nothing." The fire in Marcus's pipe made an arc as he waved his hand.

"Poppa had this dream of owning all these acres full of cows. Just drive a few off to Galveston or San Antonio and bring a wagon load of gold home," Rawls reminded.

"Well, he always talked big. Sure, the cows are here, but Yankees and carpetbaggers got the gold. Fact is, they claim they're gonna take this land back if we don't come up with two hundred dollars in taxes."

"When?"

"I don't know. It's the talk. Politicos are fighting it now in Austin. Think I'll see if that jug's sweetened any. You want a little toddy against this breeze."

"Marcus!" Bess's tone was full of hurt, anger.

"It's a homecoming. My little brother's home." Marcus stood.

"No, not me, my head is just now acting like it belongs."

"What happened today, Rawls?" Bess asked. "You were wringing wet."

"I-it comes and goes. Don't know. Really, don't remember much about the day. S-seems I remember when I was a kid better than this morning. 'Member that pink dress you wore, first time Marcus and I saw you."

"Why, Rawls Slaton, how nice! Marcus!" Bess called. "Come out here . . . I want to ask you something."

Marcus brought out the jug and sat. "What?"

"Do you remember what color dress I wore the first time we met?"

"Your dress? How do you expect a man to remember something like that? I remember the time, though. Rawls and I rode by your daddy's place, down on the Croton Brakes. We saw your garments on them bushes a half mile away."

"Rawls remembers."

"I . . . I do. Marcus pointed at them garments and said . . . 'They's gals down there, and were a man hurt, I bet they would rub his forehead.' I . . . I said . . . 'Yeah, but we ain't hurt.' " Rawls chuckled. "He said . . . 'They don't know it.' "

Marcus laughed. "I jabbed that old bay, and he lit out, a-pitching, straight for that cabin."

"I know all about it," Bess said. "As I remember, it wasn't so funny when we picked you up, walking, three miles from the cabin."

"How'd we know everybody had gone to town? The washing hung out there on them bushes." Marcus stroked the jug, then took a drink.

"Point is, you remember you were riding a bay horse, but you don't remember my dress."

"I remember your daddy's buggy horse was a black."

"I . . . I don't think that's what she means, Marcus."

"Maybe not, but I was glad to see that black pacer pulling your family in that buggy." Marcus set the jug on the porch and walked toward the barn. "Be back directly."

Rawls sighed, turned, and straightened his legs along the porch. "I-it's good here, quiet."

"You don't ask for a lot, do you?" Bess's voice held sadness. He'd heard it a million times before. Homesick kids, battle-weary veterans, they'd all spoke with the same futile agony in their voices.

"A . . . a fellow first has to figure out what a lot is. Compared to some things, this is a lot. How about you, you ever want something real, real bad?"

Bess chuckled nervously. "Oh, yes."

"What?"

"Oh, I don't know, Rawls. How about dinner tomorrow, what sounds good?"

"That ain't right, Bess. You're always testing. Somebody asks you something, you run away."

"I what?"

"R-run away."

"Well, I have my wants. I wanted to be a good wife. I want this baby to grow healthy and happy."

"Y-you wanted! That sounds like yesterday."

"Rawls, maybe we better not snub that bronc' too close."

"O-OK, that ain't what I meant, anyway. I know you're a good woman and want all the right things, like we all wanted the war to end. B-but what about for yourself, like this place is for me, did you ever see something you wanted real bad?" Light flickered beyond the corral as Marcus burned a match.

"Someday, Rawls, you'll have a woman of your own, and you'll find us a vain bunch. We're constantly concerned with our appearance, coveting pretty things. But, yes, I've always remembered a bonnet I saw in San Antonio." There was a long spell of silence. A coyote yapped somewhere beyond the low line of hills. In the dark sky the evening star gained shy, barely visible companions. "It was the most beautiful bonnet. Daddy was bringing us from Galveston. We were in the lobby of the Menger Hotel. I was wide-eyed, taking it all in, a child, barely in my teens. There are moments when time stops. That was such a moment."

"Pretty, huh?"

"The night, the chandeliers, the heavy curtains, then there she stood on the wide winding stairs. The lady wore face paint, carried a parasol, and had an escort of several men dressed in uniforms with shiny buttons. They surrounded the lady. All eyes turned toward her. She had on a

46

bonnet . . . a dainty thing that barely covered her beautiful, dark hair. The crown and brim were of navy blue velvet with a yellow, ruffled silk band around the brim and a yellow sash folded to form flower petals near her ears. The sash tied in a huge bow beneath her chin. The woman wore a powder-blue dress of heavy material that covered all but the tip of her shoes." Bess paused. "Silly, huh? Aren't you sorry you asked?"

"N-no, bad times, you got to hang onto thoughts of that sort. Makes things worthwhile." Rawls stood. "Think I'll turn in. This air's got a chill in it."

If he and Marcus ever got their hands on some money, he'd see Marcus got that girl a bonnet. Lying in the dark of the harness room, his mind played with visions of a smiling Bess tying a bonnet's sash. He tried to think of another face, slip in a ringer, but his sister-in-law kept pushing back into the picture.

A scream jarred him from his slumber. He had no idea how long he'd slept. He fumbled, searching for his pistol. Thoughts of Yankees flashed through his mind, then he remembered. *Home. The war is over.* He reached the barn door and heard the struggle.

"Don't you do it. You've treated me like an animal for the last time." Bess's voice shouted from inside the house.

Rawls moved toward the cabin and heard a barrage of breaking dishes and tumbling chairs. Heavier sounds of bodies slamming against the wall caused him to look up just as the wooden bucket fell from its peg to the porch floor. He reached the step, and the door burst open.

Bess crossed the porch in one stride, plastered herself face to face against him. Her arms and legs tangled with his. Her force carried him backward. They went down.

47

Marcus appeared above them. He stood, straddle-legged, swaying side to side. Blood ran down his front and he held a dripping butcher knife in his right hand. "You cut me."

Bess reached her feet first, moved behind Rawls. He climbed to his knees. Her voice, wild and crazy with fear, screamed only inches from his ear. "You better stick me with that thing! I begged you, told you, I'd take no more. I'm not going to be hit again."

Rawls gained his feet and took a step toward his brother. "P-put the knife down . . . you crazy?"

Marcus swung his left arm and staggered forward. "Out of my way. This is my woman. I'll take care of her."

The arm caught him in the face, and Rawls stumbled backward and to the side. He sensed Bess retreating with him. He regained his feet near the corner of the porch and tried to gather himself to deliver a blow. Marcus continued toward him. Rawls swung, then saw his brother duck. His fist sailed harmlessly over Marcus's shoulder. Hard knuckles smashed Rawls's face, spawned blinding pain. He backpedaled. His feet found only air. A new hurt from the rear of his head hurtled him into darkness. Rawls tumbled, drifted like a feather through murky shadows broken by streaks of light. He reached, contacted only air. He failed to touch the sides of the tunnel through which he fell. Time became meaningless, an eternal moment.

Someone spoke, quietly, almost in whispers. Voices from great distances should shout. These words came from far away, but they whispered.

He awoke, realizing his hips still slept. The ants had to be imaginary. They stung both sides. He opened his eyes. Bess and Marcus stared back at him. They stood leaning their backs against the cabinet, looking across the foot of the bed.

Somewhere to his right the baby fussed.

Bess smiled. Really, she half smiled through a cut lip. One eye peeked through swollen lids surrounded by black and blue tissue.

Covers trapped him. He struggled, tried to sit. "What'd you do to her?"

Bess was instantly at his side, pushing him down. "It's OK. That was three days ago. It was a fight, but we're over it. It's OK."

"Rawls, I'm sorry," Marcus said. "I never meant to hurt nobody. It was the liquor. I quit the stuff. No more."

Bess sat on the side of the bed. She nodded. "We were afraid we'd lose you. When Marcus saw that, saw what he'd done to his little brother and me, Rawls, I truly think it changed him. I think we all got a chance now. You wouldn't believe how we've been praying."

"Little Brother, I'm sorry . . . sorry about all of it."

Their faces were fuzzy, but their voices louder. He wished they would be quiet. It was too much at one time. Seemed like words were running out of each of them. "It's fine. I'm glad y'all didn't kill each other. My fault anyway for being so clumsy. I'm hungry." If Bess would turn to that cabinet, maybe he could scratch.

Marcus grabbed a bowl and moved hurriedly to the fire-place. "We got stew."

Bess smiled, more confidently this time. "I never saw fever so high. We squeezed water from a rag into your mouth. You got a right to be hungry." She put her hand on his forehead. "I believe it's gone." She stroked his forehead.

Her hand felt cool and soothing. "Don't stoke that fire, Marcus," Rawls said. "It's hot in here."

"That's good. You been shivering for three days and so hot we couldn't touch you. We thought you were dying. One

49

night old Rube howled that ole mournful cry all night. I told Bess you were gone for sure." Marcus handed the bowl to his wife, then passed her a spoon from the cabinet.

Chapter Seven

Rawls's health improved each day. Bess saw a change in his moves, his walk, and his facial muscles. Best of all, his spirits seemed to soar. It had been a week since he had regained consciousness. She forced her thoughts away from her brother-in-law and turned them inward. She lamented the fact that she'd been the youngest of four children. Her exposure to babies had been limited. She doubted her ability as a mother, and every nerve seemed attuned to Patina's needs. She had only to hold the child to sense overpowering emotion—emotion that ran the gamut from fulfillment to fear. She laughed, cooed mother/child, nonsensical sounds and stroked this new light of her life.

She dodged all doubts of Marcus's ability to curb his temper and stifle his taste for alcohol. He just had to be a good father. This child needed a father. When his actions—a short word or scowl of disapproval—stirred uneasiness, she stuffed them away like scraps of material for next year's quilt. But the questions returned, stole upon her, thieves that left her worn and sapped of energy. She could postpone or argue with her thoughts, but her instincts rebelled, brought periods of melancholy.

Her time and energy barely met the day's demands. Patina added to her load. Rawls pretty much looked after his own needs. At least he helped, heating the laundry water, keeping the woodbox filled. His military training might account for it, but he attended to his own needs better than most men she'd known. Perhaps it was just the distraction of his presence that wasted her time. More and more she gazed into space, scolded herself back to reality.

Now she watched as Rawls and Marcus crossed the clearing, moving toward the barn, both shirtless. Perspiration glistened on their shoulders as rays from the sun cast highlighting shadows on their every move. The Slaton brothers were indeed a closely matched pair, yet so different.

Rawls stood half an inch taller, his face more angular. High family foreheads were common to each and ended in shocks of wavy brown hair. Under those hats, she knew Rawls's locks to be much shorter. She felt amusement lift the corners of her lips at the memory of how poorly he had trimmed his own hair.

Perhaps the feature that set them most apart was their eyes. Both had varying shades of gray. But it wasn't so much the color as the expression projected. Marcus's were bolder, often staring from beneath a single raised brow, exposing a sense of boredom or easy-going carelessness. Rawls, on the other hand, had a power to create a sense of restlessness within her. One glimpse from beneath those heavy eyebrows, so readable and so much more intensely interested, never failed to turn her knees to jelly.

She continued to catalog the two, measuring her reaction. Marcus's face was broader, his nose slightly shorter. The strong jaw line of each balanced a firm chin marked with a short crease beneath straight mouths. Marcus's muscles bulged more obviously, his gait nimble as a frolicking colt. Rawls had no gait. He glided like a swooping hawk now that he was getting better, his thin body supple, but equally powerful. Hard, tough men. But only one offered total love and security.

She tried to convince herself that Rawls's health accounted for the watchfulness she afforded her brother-in-law. She could tell herself that daily, but it failed to account for her embarrassment at the closeness of her scrutiny and the guilt she sensed when her eyes lingered each time he filled her view. She was like a schoolgirl, reluctant to avert her eyes.

Today, the guilt deepened. Yesterday, Rawls had taken the borrowed team back to Plum Grove. He'd been gone all day. She had wondered if Rawls shared his brother's taste for the girls at the Posey. She knew he had no money for such adventures, but she could envision his gaining credit or other special favors. Bess slammed a diaper into the laundry water and, when the suds wet her cheek, wiped them away with the back of her hand.

A little past mid-afternoon a horseman rode up to the barn. His sorrel was road weary. The rider watered, then released his mount in the lot shortly after greeting the men. Not much later, Marcus advised her that the visitor would take supper.

The men sat in the shade and talked, drank spring water, and smoked. The stranger later joined in their work of unloading a wagonload of fencing rock. Near dark, they washed and filed in, each carrying his hat.

Rawls brought the fourth chair in from the porch. "Mister Slaughter, this here is Marcus's wife Bess. This here is Ned Slaughter."

"Mister Slaughter, welcome. We're having chicken, butter beans, and gravy."

Ned bent at the waist. "It's my pleasure, ma'am. I must confess it's been some time since I've enjoyed hospitality such as this." His eyes rested on Patina. "Wal, I swear! Look at that."

"That's Patina," Rawls said, seeming to straighten with pride.

Marcus waved them to the table. When each stood behind

their chairs, Marcus bowed his head. "Lord, thanks for your help in getting these victuals. Amen." The men sat down and turned their plates upright. Bess forked each a piece of chicken, then joined them.

Marcus's eyes fixed on the pulley bone resting on Rawls's plate. "You back on your feet and so frisky an' all, I'll match grab with you for that white meat."

The contest had been an ongoing match of quickness before the war. A pebble, or in this case a match, would be held by one or the other in an open hand. The challenger would attempt to grab it with his hand poised, palm down, and inches above the object. The one challenged got to hold the object, and the other gave the go signal. Marcus usually won, yet the challenge often came from Rawls.

They both stood. Rawls reached into his pocket, then held a match over the table. Marcus took his position, snapped— "Go."—and with the speed of a striking snake held the match aloft. Blood appeared on the back of his hand from Rawls's fingernail. The brothers swapped plates without a word. Marcus smiled. Mr. Slaughter chuckled. Bess turned away to hide her frown.

"Next week," Rawls promised.

The men ate in silence except for Slaughter's response when additional food was offered. "Thank you, ma'am. Don't mind if I do."

"You're a traveling man, Mister Slaughter?" Bess asked.

"Not usually. We ranch up along the Palo Pinto. Fellar in Fort Worth gave me thirty dollars to peddle some posters through this country. It's lonely work, but times you meet nice folks."

Marcus handed Bess a piece of paper. One side was printed. She read: **Joseph H. McCoy—Buyer of cattle for northern market at rail's end—Abilene, Kansas. Top**

dollar. Follow the Chisholm Trail: It's got more prairie, less timber, more small streams, fewer large ones, and better grass; no civilized Indian tax and no wild Indian disturbance. Lots, chutes, and rails at Abilene, Kansas.

She looked at Marcus. "Where's Abilene?"

"Due north, past the Indian Territory," he said.

"What does it mean?" They seemed awfully excited about something that was happening that far away.

"It means things may be looking up," Rawls explained. "We got cattle . . . till now, nobody wanted them." Rawls's eyes were bright, reflecting the lamplight. "There's fortunes out there."

"But they're here, that's there," Bess reminded. Rawls was sounding more like her husband. Marcus was the excitable one.

"Cows will drive," Marcus said.

Did Marcus's tone reveal impatience at her meddling in men's talk? Did she imagine it? Damn him! And it had pleased her so when he showed her the paper. "Drive to Kansas?" It seemed incredible.

"Yes, ma'am! I got thirty more of these handbills to pass out. Come spring, they's no telling how many will be headed north. This is the kind of news will turn this old state around."

Slaughter helped Rawls with the dishes while Bess, holding the baby, and Marcus sat on the porch. She'd just finished feeding Patina when Rawls and Slaughter came out on the porch.

"Think I'll turn in," Ned said.

"I'll show you where us help sleep," Rawls said, smiling.

The shadows of the two men drifted toward the barn. The

55

glow of Rawls's pipe appeared at intervals. Bess stood with Patina in her arms. "What is a steer worth in Abilene?" she asked Marcus.

"He said two- to four-year-olds might go as high as sixteen dollars," he answered.

"And here . . . how much here?"

"Around two to four dollars for a hide. Sometimes five or six a head, if you can find a meat buyer."

"And how many can you drive?"

"Depends on the men and the cattle. Rawls thinks big."

"What's big?"

"Five hundred to a thousand head."

"And they can walk all the way to Kansas?"

"Some've already walked to California and Oregon."

"You mean oxen."

"Never was an oxen could outwalk a longhorn. Most often they're one and the same. How come you gave Rawls the pulley bone?"

"What?"

"The pulley bone, you gave it to Rawls. You know we're both partial to it. How come?"

"If that isn't the most childish question I ever heard. I guess you'll just have to shoot me." She waved a hand in the air, grateful for the darkness. She knew of the brothers' life-long rivalry over the wishbone's choice white meat.

"That man will talk your arm off," Marcus said as Ned Slaughter disappeared around the rise. He leaned near Rawls. "What do you think?"

"I think, come spring, we best have us an outfit ready to roll."

"I don't know . . . it's aright ways to Abilene."

"Not for a couple of steppers like us," Rawls contradicted.

56

"Let's get another cup and see what Bess thinks."

"Why?"

"Because she's smart 'n' I'm thirsty."

"You git your own woman, you'll find smart is making up your own mind, then telling them." Marcus moved in the direction of the house.

Rawls followed, thinking that sometimes Marcus just liked to grumble. They reached the door, and Marcus entered. A moment later he returned to the porch with the coffee pot and three cups. Then Bess appeared, carrying the baby.

"I'm thinking," Rawls said, "if I got any say-so about things here, Marcus and me need to start road branding some stock to hit the trail with come spring."

"What?" Marcus asked. "Hell, you got as much say as anybody. This place is half yours, Rawls. I've told you that before you put on the uniform. If you hadn't gone, I'd likely have had to. I got the best of the deal."

Bess pulled the blanket tighter about Patina. "I can see you getting the cattle together, some anyway, but what about grub, men, and enough horses?" She pulled her shawl over the baby's head. "You gonna do this, you got to think it out. You can't just jump up some morning and start heading north. Won't you need a stake?" She watched Marcus. "Right now, we're so short of cash, all I hear from you is about losing this place. How many head you thinking of branding?"

"Ramón will likely throw in with us. Three of us working through next February should be able to put a herd of four hundred together. Old man Johnson might add another hundred for us to take north on shares. What do you think, Rawls?"

"Think we ought to shoot for a total of seven hundred and fifty. Maybe we can buy some on credit or get more on shares, but once they are trail savvy, with a couple of hands, seven

fifty should move about as easy as five hundred. Mounts . . .
no problem. The prairie is full of horses."

"Maybe that's your stake," Beth suggested. "They got a
market?"

Marcus showed his surprise at Bess's words. "Matter-of-
fact they're moving pretty good at San Antonio. Buyers are
shipping them to Galveston and then on to New Orleans."

"What's pretty good?"

The girl was smart, Rawls thought. *Why couldn't Marcus see
that? She asked the right questions.*

"Twenty-five dollars for rank stuff, unless you take them
on to Galveston, then thirty to forty." Rawls could sense
Marcus's doubts grow fainter.

Bess went inside and returned with a stubby pencil and a
piece of wrapping paper. She handed the baby to Marcus and
licked the pencil. She figured on the paper, using her thigh for
a desktop. She looked up, her color paled. She examined both
their faces. "Do you realize, if you brought home ten dollars a
head on seven hundred that amounts to seven thousand dollars?" She giggled. "I never heard of such."

"Seven thousand dollars, it's got a good ring, don't it?"
Rawls said.

"There would be expenses, of course," Marcus said, "but
seven thousand will buy a lot of coffee and flour. But it would
mean you and Patina staying here alone all summer."

"What about that Indian Corners country? Mustangs still
ranging around them mesas and box cañons over there?" The
country Rawls spoke of began fifteen miles to the west and
tended to deep soil and strong grass. A land with few trees
and well watered. Horses favored it.

"More'n ever," Marcus said.

"How many hosses we got around this place?" Rawls
asked. "Ones we can catch, that is."

"Ten, all together. There's six over in Hank's Hollow. They're boxed in. Then there's four down on the crick. The old bell mare they're with is hobbled."

Bess reëxamined the brown paper she'd marked on, then said: "You gonna try this, I think you need to get your hands on fifteen hundred head of beeves. By the time you get to Abilene, you may be looking at five dollars each. Who knows how many you'll lose on the way?"

Marcus tilted his hat back. "What happened to that gentle little woman that always said . . . 'Money don't buy happiness?' You getting greedy?"

"She had a baby," Bess responded. "If I'm going to stay here and lonely to death, I want it to mean something when y'all get back."

Rawls's excitement grew. "Y'all get the stuff together. To-morrow we're heading for Indian Corners, Marcus, to see Ramón about him becoming a cattle baron."

Chapter Eight

The high sky above Buckthorn Mesa framed Ramón Lopez's silhouette. Rawls and Marcus rode beside their father's old friend. Behind Ramón, as with the brothers, two remounts followed at the end of lead ropes. One carried a light pack.

The bald-faced animal Rawls rode nibbled at the old Mexican's gray mare. He'd nickered and rattled through his nostrils since nearing the animal.

The old Mexican fire-eater slouched, rolling a cigarette. "Rawls, I see Marcus, he mounted you on a beeg red stud?"

"No, the dern' thing's just proud-cut and won't admit the fun's over. Ramón, you're looking fit. Them ponies got any bottom?"

"*Sí,* never tire. Tomorrow we mount the Mesa Grande. We find mustangs, then you see."

For a moment, near sundown, they thought they'd beat Ramón's prediction. They sighted a lone horse, but soon its lack of alertness at their approach turned idle curiosity into caution. The animal raised its head, briefly studied them, then continued grazing till they approached within a few yards.

Ramón angled closer to the horse and spoke in low tones. "Thees one ees no mustang. It ees saddled."

The horse's saddle had slipped and now rode upside down under its belly. Rawls stood in his stirrups and looked from south to north. Only the grass stirred. Not even a buzzard floated in the sky. The animal walked toward the gray, its head turned to one side, dragging the reins. The riderless mount stopped in front of Ramón's mare, snorted, then touched noses with the gray.

"Thees saddle, all over she ees bloody. Eet was made by my people south of the *río*."

Marcus dismounted, straightened, and retightened the wandering horse's saddle. He fashioned a halter from a lead rope and added the stray to his string of mounts. "You'd think buzzards would give away this old boy's rider if he was down somewhere."

"You would," Rawls agreed, scanning the sky. Next he circled the area where the horse had grazed and finally picked up its trail. "He came from thisaway." He pointed northwest, deeper into the Indian Corners country.

The trio rode another hour, backtracking the horse, before the quiet pushed Marcus to speech. He leaned toward Ramón. "I've been to your place. You're fixed up pretty well down there. After all these years, I still don't know how exactly you come by all that?"

"I did not know your *papá* at San Jacinto, but fortune, she smiled on him at that place, and on me from the Alamo. Later your *papá* and me, we rode with the Rangers. Did he not tell you? Or that my *mamá* was from the family Seguin? Her brother, he die with thees important man, Travis, at the Alamo? In hees pocket they find a grant signed by thees same Travis. General Houston, he honor eet. Your *papá*, he rode here from San Jacinto, my sister and I from the Alamo. Today thees grant still ess my family's home."

"Why'd they call this Indian Corners?" Rawls knew the story, but found the rhythm of Ramón's English pleasant to listen to.

"When we get here, thees Corners country marked the southeast corner of Comanche land and the southwest of the Wichita. To the south and west lived the Lipan Apache. The

61

Tonkawa to the east. Later all ees changed. The Kiowa, he come in, and Comanche, he raid what he want. Then come thees Comancheros . . . they trade guns, whiskey, and slaves. They are the worst."

Concern showed on the old man's weathered face. It added to the dour expression of his neatly trimmed, but drooping mustache. Still, his eyes were bright and the set of his chin confident. His sombrero sat jauntily. Ramón rubbed the metal buttons adorning his tight-fitting, embroidered jacket. He nodded to the north. "*Padre* Alegre, he rested at my *casa* a short time ago. He spoke of performing last rites for a *vaquero*. As we, thees man hunted horses north of here. The *padre*, he tell me that Comanchero Grande's riders had left a bullet in thees man. Thees devil still raids thees badland as before the war."

The three men had been in the saddle only an hour the following morning when Rawls topped a rise and jumped a coyote. The animal gnawed at something it held with its paw. It dropped the object, darted sideways, then ran.

Rawls loped to the spot and pulled the horse to a rump-sliding halt. He dismounted and led the mount the last few steps back to the bloody remnant. He gagged, and raised the back of his forearm to his mouth. At one end of the coyote's prize, meat was torn, exposing an elbow joint. At the other end, the stumps of gnawed fingers identified a man's right arm.

"Found that pony's rider, leastwise part of 'im," Rawls said as Marcus and Ramón rode up.

Thirty minutes later, having spotted a number of circling buzzards, they found the remaining scraps of bones and clothing of the doomed rider. The rib cage was well stripped of flesh, but it showed the hole a slug had torn through bone.

By noon, they had discovered dozens of mustang tracks leading from a huge mesa into a well-concealed horse trap. They entered the enclosure. Prints from a few shod hoofs mingled with the others. Apparently they weren't the only mustangers about. At either end, a gate and a fence had been fashioned. Vultures picked at the remains of a single corpse at each opening.

They studied the abundant sign. Except for the buzzards their approach frightened away, the place was desolate. Tracks, scattered gear, and a few shell casings, plus the two bodies were all that remained of the men and animals that had been here a short time earlier.

The enclosure used a cañon that funneled mustangs between steep banks when traveling from the three-mile mesa to water. One end of the cañon had been blocked with cottonwood logs, the other with mesquite. The band of horses had milled and grazed inside the trap for some time.

After carefully scouting the large trap, Ramón and Rawls worked at two shallow graves. "Thees men are from below the *rio*."

"I'd say so," Rawls agreed.

Standing guard, Marcus sat his horse at the top of the mesa near the entrance gate. He had a good view and held his rifle. He hollered down to the others: "Boys, what do you make of all this?"

"From the looks of those blankets, five men bedded down here night before last," Rawls answered. "They'd been holding captured horses for about a week maybe, trying to get some of 'em hobbled and all of 'em used enough to man smell to drive."

"What makes you think a week?" Marcus asked.

"Other end down there"—Rawls pointed—"where they were drove out, showed tracks of maybe sixty head. Way this grass has been grazed off, I'd say sixty head for about a week."

Ramón watched Rawls's face as he explained, nodding in agreement.

"I'd say yesterday morning, about daylight, they were hit by maybe ten men. Some Indians, 'cause a few of those riders rode unshod horses," Rawls said, adding: "May all have been Indians on stolen stock."

"Could be Comancheros," Ramón offered. "Do not forget that dead *vaquero*."

Marcus studied a moment. "So you think these Mexican mustangers were robbed by Comanches or Comancheros?"

"My guess," Rawls said. "Looks to me like everybody was firing guns. I dunno, Ramón, what do you think? We've only found three bodies, but there were those five bedrolls."

"*Sí,* five men. I theenk there ees two *hombres* get away on one horse. Maybe one ees afoot. There are two saddles in camp. One, he could belong to the dead man at thees gate. One could belong to the one who hitched a ride. The man killed at the far end, maybe he had a horse saddled. We did not see thees bronco. Most likely it ees with the thieves. The herd, she went out that end. *Sí,* I theenk maybe two of these men ride away, two to one horse. Marcus, keep the sharp eye. Thees men, they waste no lead, three shots . . . three dead! Indians don't shoot rifles thees good. I think Comancheros, maybe even Comanchero Grande, ees about."

Rawls looked at Ramón. The neighbor's mouth was a tight, straight line, serious.

The two bodies were put in the shallow graves and covered by Ramón and Rawls. Ramón knelt, crossed himself, and prayed aloud in Spanish. Rawls added his own "Amen", then they gathered the horses.

Marcus solemnly watched them. "Little Brother, hope

that old soft army life didn't dim your shooting eye. 'Pears we may be going ag'in' some of them Comancheros . . . and, as Ramón says, could even be that Grande's bunch."

Ramón studied the distant horizon. He smiled at Rawls. "You shoot like your *papá* and thees brother, I hope."

Marcus chuckled. "He left here near as good as me."

"Is thees true?" Ramón asked, turning to Rawls.

"Shooting's kept me alive, Ramón," Rawls said. "Poppa taught us pistols, then, later, I rode with Stuart. Some think him to be the best with a sidearm. He ain't. Colonel John Mosby's Raiders were the best. They were partial to Colts. I rode next to him in 'Sixty-Four. Nobody . . . not the Texas Rangers, not the Comancheros, nor George A. Custer . . . could hold a candle to our worst shooter. Pistols is what we lived by, and Colts a-horseback is what we used. Old Dominion's fields are red today, with men's blood. They'd testify, if they could, to what I just told you. But as the old Indian said, that's yesterday's medicine." He looked about, sort of abashed at his loose tongue.

"You find shells for Poppa's old Sharps you're toting?" Marcus asked.

"Twelve for the rifle, seventeen for the six-gun," Rawls replied. "Y'all fixed?"

Both men nodded in response.

Rawls looked at Ramón. "Comanchero Grande, huh?"

Chapter Nine

The three men sat their horses. Ramón and Marcus discussed the Comanchero leader's latest acts of lawlessness. Rawls recalled that before the war blood marked the trail of the big renegade known by Mexicans on both sides of the river as Comanchero Grande. During the war the blood trail had deepened. On the ride to Ramón's, Marcus had mentioned that Grande still traveled the Indian war trails country, plying his brutal trade. He, his men, and his customers rode the country's shadowy paths, happy to be west of and beyond the reach of the law.

"Understand Indians started calling the man White Buffalo," Rawls said. "I've heard they treat him fancy, sort of with awe . . . you know, with respect . . . like for a medicine man or a crazy."

Ramón spoke tersely. "Whatever he ees called, he rides with death in hees gun and whiskey in hees belly. I hope he and hees stolen horses are out of the country. But I don't know."

As Ramón talked, Rawls's attention was directed at a black spot, only a speck, that dipped in and out of the distant mirage dancing on their back trail. "We got company." He pointed.

"You got good eyes, Brother. How you know that ain't a buffalo or a horse just a-grazing along?" Marcus asked.

"Traveling too straight . . . somebody's pushing 'im," Rawls responded. "Let's hole up, see if they don't come to us."

After the trio took cover, the speck took shape, revealing two men riding double. At the trap's gate they veered toward the freshly dug graves. They exchanged words, and Rawls, who had dismounted and taken cover a distance from Marcus and Ramón, caught the word *"bueno"* as well as the tension that rang in their voices. They turned and entered the open gate. The front rider kicked the mount into a lope, and they headed toward the trio's position of concealment.

A second later Ramón shouted: *"¡Alto, amigos!"*

The horse slid to a stop. The two Mexicans raised their arms.

"Keep your hands up and get down easy!" Marcus hollered, still not showing himself.

Ramón repeated the command in Spanish.

The two men obeyed. Rawls walked from his stand, holding his rifle ready, chin high. He approached the men from behind. They twisted and turned in his direction. Their wide eyes projected fear, and color had drained from their swarthy faces. Rawls took a sidearm from each man. Rifles draped from either side of the saddle.

"English, speak English!" Ramón commanded. "What ees your business? It ees OK, you are among Tejanos."

The men nodded, gestured with their hands. Rawls noticed a little color returning to their faces. "We are from south of the Río Bravo . . . mustangers," the older of the two said. "The men in the graves, one ees my brother, hees father." He pointed at the younger man who'd crawled from behind the saddle. "Comancheros, they stole our mustangs. Thees morning we find your tracks. You buried our people?"

"We did," Rawls answered, then asked: "How many thieves?

"I say seven, he thinks eight." Again the older man spoke. "He ees Miguel. I am Juan . . . Juan Santos."

"How do we know you ain't part of that pack of thieves?" Marcus asked.

Rawls thought it a good question. The story of these men fit with Ramón's reading of the sign, but, still, caution always beat a maybe. Especially when life was the ante.

"I saw the tracks where you find Tito's horse," Juan said. "The left shank of the bit in hees horse's bridle, she has the letters JS. I also make thees." He pointed at the initials on his bridle bit. "A Comanchero would not know. He might know thees one, he would not know that one."

"Let's check," said Rawls. "C'mon, follow us to the horses."

"It's there," Marcus said, hurrying his step to catch up. "Noticed it this morning." He put a hard eye on Juan. "Them Comancheros . . . they old Grande's bunch?"

"*Si, señor*. He ees the leader. He killed my *padre*." They were Miguel's first words. The young man blinked rapidly, yet his eyes filled and small knots of muscle danced along his jaw. "Ride with us, *señores*. We will keel thees man. We will geeve you many mustangs."

"Just how many horses they got?" Marcus asked.

"Fifty-four of ours, plus the ones they ride," Juan answered.

Marcus's eyes opened a lash wider. They locked on Rawls. "Let's do it, Little Brother. We'd have to work our butts off for two months for a chance at that many horses."

"Marcus, it'd be five of us against maybe ten," Rawls pointed out.

"Sounds about even to me," Marcus declared. "B'sides, we'll have half of 'em cut down before they even know they're in trouble." Marcus's steady eyes reflected the intensity of his argument.

"What do you think, Ramón?" Rawls asked.

Ramón nodded. "We're here. Grande, he ees close. We should go, I theenk. We don't, someday he come back. Maybe next time, he attack my family . . . your family. *Sí*, we should go."

Marcus handed the bridle with the initialed bit to Rawls. He shrugged and said: "It's like he says."

When Miguel had mounted the stray horse, he said: "*Muchas gracias, señores*. I follow the fat *gringo*'s trail. Anyone who rides with me, he ees welcome. Eef you change your mind, eet ees OK. Just tell the people you knew Miguel. Tell them, Miguel, he was a good *hombre*, one who rode to avenge hees father."

Rawls exhaled a deep sigh as he trailed the others through the trap's opening and onto the trail of the stolen horses. After the war, he had envisioned getting back to Texas and settling into a peaceful life. Marcus might be argued out of following, but the others were dead set on a fracas. Juan or Miguel, he could understand, but Marcus, he just saw a quick way to get mounts. As for Ramón, who knew about that old war horse?

Two days later, using the first light of morning, Juan picketed the last of the horses the group rode. The outlaw's camp lay a few feet in front and below in a horseshoe cañon Rawls and Miguel had scouted the evening before. Ramón had buried eight inches of Mexican blade in a look-out stationed across the narrow defile.

Now Rawls led the group the few feet to the bluff overlooking the renegades. Rawls knelt on one knee, the other providing a rest for aiming the rifle. His companions settled into positions next to him.

Six blanketed figures slept around the coals from last night's fire. The long tousled and matted hair of one indicated a girl. She slept uncovered, sprawled awkwardly, a short rope knotted around her neck, but untied at the other end.

It would not be the first time Rawls had fired at an unsuspecting enemy, not even a sleeping one. He'd seen war start with great rules. But, after burying a few dozen friends, honor, nobility, and codes of conduct played second fiddle to remaining alive. Once a man saw what killing was about, life and death were the only boundaries. Honor was for the elite and the hypocrites that hired others to fight their wars. It made little sense to risk death to capture a man whose fate was to be immediate hanging—less to die with him.

Young Miguel knelt beside Rawls. "The beeg one, I don't see the beeg one. There were seven, maybe eight men."

"Over yonder, in the ravine, there's another. I can see the top of his belly," Rawls whispered. "We'll have to get him with the second volley, when he stands. Just another minute now, wait for a little more light." Raising his voice, Rawls addressed the others. "OK, everybody pick a target. Left to right, aim at the man in the same position as yours. Juan, you take the one on the far left, and then . . . Marcus, Ramón . . . so on down the line. No need of maybe being killed by one, while killing another twice. But, watch out for the girl. Miguel, Juan, do you know anything about her?"

"No, *señor*, I did not see her when they took the mustangs," Miguel replied.

Minutes later, it was Rawls who squeezed off the first shot. His companions' four guns lengthened the roar of his weapon.

The blankets covering the enemy churned into action. An arm flopped from one, a leg from another, then both covers quivered and were still. A third man rolled to rest against a rock, gut-shot. He turned to face them, his eyes pleading.

It continued on and on, a scene all too familiar to Rawls. Figures ran, fired, then Comanchero Grande blotted all else from view. From the ravine, he moved forward, his rifle raised.

Rawls's Sharps was empty, so he reached for his pistol, knowing he was too late. From the corner of his eye, he glimpsed Juan taking aim. Then the *vaquero* jerked upward. The Comanchero leader's bullet erased the young man's face.

With the first shots, the girl had come to her feet, screaming. She circled the camp before figuring out where the attack on the camp was coming from and that freedom lay toward the ridge top. Then the girl bounded to the base of the bluff's incline. She fell to her knees, clawing desperately at the steep wall.

Grande's aim shifted to fire at the girl. Miguel's gun barked. The chief Comanchero's saddle gun fell. His right arm dangled, then turned red, bleeding from the elbow.

Relief flooded Rawls as he holstered his gun and moved forward to help the desperate girl. He leaned over the ledge, looking for her, then glanced up just in time to see the outlaw claw for a pistol with his other hand. The six-gun swung up, again aimed at the girl. Action bogged in quicksand, slowed. Time and eternity merged.

But the girl was making progress. Her face filled his view, a swollen, distorted face, a one-time pretty face. A smile of relief crossed her features. Rawls dove, throwing his body, hoping to knock her down, protect her. He reached into air, but, from below, the report of Comanchero Grande's weapon sounded. Rawls heard a *thud* as the bullet made impact with the girl's slight body, and he saw hope disappear from her face as she fell back, rolling and sliding to the bottom of the bluff. Then he heard the sound of Ramón's shot from behind.

Comanchero Grande's scream reverberated from the vertical cliffs. He dropped his pistol, his useless hands now hanging at his sides. The sounds of battle died, as the *caws* of startled crows grew more distant. A stillness settled over the campsite, crept along the crevices and outcroppings of the bluff's walls.

Rawls rose to hands and knees and shook his head. So near, but he had lost her. No victory here.

The distant sound of rapid hoof beats broke the quiet. Rawls leaped to his feet and clawed back up the few feet he had fallen. "Miguel, see to the girl," Rawls snapped. "Ramón, watch Grande. C'mon, Marcus, let's check the mustangs. There may be more of these Comancheros."

"I'll get the horses," Marcus informed him as he took off at a run.

Once on the black, Rawls spurred over the edge of the cliff, fighting to remain mounted. The horse slid, leaped, and partially fell down the embankment. They flashed past Ramón, who stood over Grande with one foot planted squarely on the big man's back, the end of his rifle barrel poked in the outlaw's right ear. Curses streamed from the Comanchero's mouth. Beyond, and to one side, Miguel bent over the girl's still form. Other bodies littered the campsite as they rode through.

Less than a minute later, Rawls found himself looking into the face of a dead man sprawled on the ground.

Marcus pulled his horse to a stop beside him. He studied the downed outlaw. "Must've tried to run out. He's done for. Stole his last hoss . . . neck's broke."

Rawls looked about. They were not far from the outlaw camp. To his left was a box cañon, and deep in its recesses was a herd of horses. Rawls nodded at a large cottonwood growing at the foot of a bluff. A strong, horizontal branch grew from the stout trunk. "We got need of that."

Marcus nodded. "Grande's still breathing. I'll go get him."

Rawls loosened the reins, allowing his mount to graze. He watched Marcus ride back alone, then he shifted and lifted his leg, cocking it around the saddle horn. The rope work he had in mind took two hands. He formed a bight in the end of his lariat, then lapped thirteen coils.

It didn't take long for Miguel and Ramón to gather their horses and return with Marcus. Miguel's rope was around the Comanchero leader's neck as he was led, half running, half walking, behind the horse. Both of his arms hung loosely, flapping like the tongues of panting dogs. The captive staggered, cursed, and fell. He righted himself, clamped his mouth, and strode forcefully forward when Miguel stopped at the foot of the tree.

Rawls rode to the renegade's side. He bent and placed the noose over his huge matted, buffalo-like head. After pulling the knot tight behind the man's left ear, he flipped the end of the hangman's rope to Miguel.

Ramón brought up the horse of the dead thief, stopping the horse directly under the cottonwood limb. He and Marcus helped Grande aboard. Miguel tossed the end of the rope over the heavy branch, pulled it tight, and secured it to the tree's trunk.

Rawls rode in front of the man's horse and stopped. He placed a hand on the horse's forelock and looked the killer in the eye.

The big man glared. "Git on with it. These busted wings is killing me."

"Got anything to say?" Rawls said, and held out his tobacco. "Want me to roll you one?"

Grande shook his head. He looked out at the horse herd,

raised his eyes to the new sun, then stared his hatred from bloodshot eyes. He spat at the black's hoofs. "Told yah these wings is killing me."

"I can't figure it. Why'd you kill the girl?" Rawls needed an answer.

"I know yah . . . yore a bunch of lily livers. She meant more to yah than all them ponies . . . all the ponies in Texas. B'sides, she was handy."

Rawls tossed his quirt to Miguel and turned the black away. His stomach rolled.

The Comanchero's bull-like voice bellowed from behind: "Ain't got the guts for it, have yah? Go ahead! Ride off. I called it . . . called it right. Lily livers!"

Rawls nudged the black forward into a slow walk as Miguel brought the quirt down with a smack on the horse's rump. Behind Rawls, the sound of stretched rope hummed, hoofs shuffled, and three loud gasps followed a gurgle from the big Comanchero. Rawls turned. Sour stomach or not, this was one dance he'd as soon remember. Comanchero Grande did not disappoint him. With his last reflex, his feet shot up above his head, then his body spun, relaxed, and slumped, swinging ever more slowly, back and forth.

Marcus sat his horse, unmoving. He swallowed and spit a blank. "Miguel, ride over and hold the herd on that ground. Rest of us are going to bury that girl and Juan."

"If eet ees all the same," Miguel said, "I weel help. A relative ees a good theeng at a burial."

Rawls reined the black toward the horse herd. "C'mon, Soot, let's you and me keep an eye on your cousins over yonder."

Chapter Ten

Rawls sat his saddle and hunched forward, riding stone-faced into a north wind. Marcus's gelding moved a step in front. The ears of both mounts pricked toward Plum Grove, sprawling a half mile ahead. The Grove had been Marcus's idea. Rawls had voted for the more direct trail to the ranch. He'd feel better when he saw Bess and Patina. It had been weeks since they'd ridden by the ranch on the return from Indian Corners to drop off some of the horses. They had hit the trail for Galveston the next day.

In spite of the cold, $15 in coin warmed his pockets and another $300 rode tied in a sock and buried in his saddlebag. Marcus carried a like amount. The Galveston horse market had treated them well. Ramón had waved *adiós* and angled toward home with his share earlier in the day.

Miguel, too, no doubt had his pockets full of *pesos* by now. The week after the shoot-out, he'd taken his leave, but not before Marcus had offered him a job on the drive, come spring. He rode to a friend's *jacal* and obtained the help of three Mexican boys. After returning, he and the boys had pointed his share of the herd toward Plum Grove and ultimately Mexico.

Marcus had argued the need for supplies at the ranch necessitated the detour through town. They were low on tobacco, and coffee was always short. After all, they'd been gone nearly a month. Besides, Bess deserved something. With the baby and all the diapers, he knew she needed a new tub to set on a bench beside the wash pot. Maybe she'd like some sticks of hard-rock candy. Still, Rawls wondered about his brother's motives. It seemed to him, it would be better to head straight for the ranch, especially with the three mules that made up the remnant of the wild bunch they'd collected at the Corners. Besides, Bess may have ridden in for supplies with the Meadowses.

The thought of his sister-in-law sharpened his impatience. This trip had driven reality home. Bess's absence proved only physical. Mentally she rode with his conscience, sometime scolding, at other times smiling. Images and thoughts she'd put into words infected his senses, spread a strange mixture of pleasure and sadness. His memory of her grew sharper each day.

His mind formed new visions—visions he longed to touch, to find real. Sometimes, alone at night, half awake in the privacy of darkness, he'd actually reached for her to find only cold emptiness where he envisioned warmth, a saddle's hard pommel where he'd sought soft flesh. He laughed at his stupidity. He'd fought and bled in war only to find real agony in an emotional entanglement with the impossible. He shook himself.

"When we get to town," Rawls announced, "I'm buying a Mackinaw coat, one thicker'n a side of beef. Been cold so much, I'll have to rub with rock salt to thaw by a fire."

"What you gonna do when winter sets in? It ain't but November." The scorn in Marcus's voice carried an edge of excitement. He'd pushed his mount since the tops of the Grove's buildings had come in sight. His features lightened when he said: "Maybe we'll get you warmed up at the Posey."

In town, Rawls munched crackers and cheese while dragging his spurs alongside Marcus's through the saloon's door to the bar. Both men carried saddlebags draped over their shoulders.

" 'Pears the Slaton brothers are back in town," the bartender said. "Edge on up here, boys. Tell ole Snort what's yore pleasure."

Rawls's foot found the brass rail. He admired his new coat in the mirror.

Marcus spoke: "Whiskey. Got a place under that bar for these?" He handed his pouches to Snort. Rawls hoisted his own to the bar.

Snort took the saddlebags and stuck them out of sight behind the bar. He poured a whiskey.

Marcus held out his hand, palm up to Rawls. It held a coin. "Grab."

Rawls smiled, removed his foot from the rail. He'd been waiting for this. He placed one hand over his brother's and eased the other under and toward Marcus's belt. "Go," he said, slapping upward with his left hand from beneath the open palm.

The coin flipped up, and Rawls's flashing right hand snatched it from the air.

"Make it two," he said to Snort, and handed him the coin he had won. "Thanks for the drink." His speed was back.

Across the room, sitting with his back to the wall, a tall, broad-shouldered man played solitaire. Caution took over, forcing Rawls to observe the man in the mirror while sniffing Snort's wares. The card player seemed oblivious to the others in the room. His attention followed the frayed cards he fingered and the suits arranged on the table before him. He was too neat for a cowman, too sunburned for a gambler. The table hid his belt and hardware. Perhaps he was unarmed. Perhaps panthers didn't sleep on ledges. He seemed a good man to watch—a better one to avoid.

"Been hearing some of yore goings-on," Snort offered.

"How's that?" Marcus asked.

"That young Mexican was through here with some broomtails a few weeks back. Bought a little grub and a bottle. Told about you boys clearing out old Grande's bunch."

"It was overdue," Rawls said.

The *click* of high heels sounded on the stairs, then a shrill voice drowned the sound. "Marcus, darling, where you been?" Rose glided across the room, spreading sawdust with her swishing skirts and the sweet scent of dance hall with her perfume. She pinned Marcus to the bar. He didn't seem to mind. "Buy me a drink, honey."

A subdued version of the bolder strumpet, a more reserved follower, shadowed her across the room. Like Rose, this girl showed a lot of shoulder. Rawls found the struggle between restraint and escape taking place between her flimsy blouse and her narrowed cleavage even more remarkable than the ocean swells of Rose's huge bosom. The girl's paint job, less garish than her friend's, dulled faint freckles that sprinkled a shapely nose. She was a few years beyond childhood and tender-looking to tired eyes. His new Mackinaw seemed a little heavy. Snort had too much mesquite on that fire.

"Lilly, this is Marcus's little brother, Rawls," Rose said. "Ain't he a cutie?" Rose had a lot of energy, managing to kiss Marcus, breathe, and make the introduction all at the same time.

Snort set two more glasses on the bar. He filled them from a different bottle.

"Howdy." Rawls realized he'd failed to leave his hat on the rack. He removed it and placed it on the bar.

The girl put one hand on his shoulder, pressed her breast

against his arm, and took her drink from the bar. "I'm enchanted, I'm sure," she said.

Marcus squirmed free of Rose and reached for his glass. "Ole Rawls is suffering bad from the cold, Lil, maybe you can help."

"You cold, honey?" Small furrows wrinkled Lilly's eyes, and light danced from her pupils. A smile tilted the corners of her mouth.

How could all that innocence survive in a place like this? "No, no," Rawls contradicted, "fact is I'm warming up good." *What a fool. Bess was right. Bess, great Lord! Damn it was hot.* "We been to Galveston," he declared.

"Galveston, I love Galveston," Lilly purred. "I like water, like to lie in it, take off my clothes, and feel it swirl around my body. You like water, Rawls?"

Did he like water? He took the bottle from Snort and poured himself another drink. "Ain't afraid of it," he responded. "We got a spring at home. You can see the water bubble up through the sand." *Dumb! Dumb!* Rawls tilted the glass, sensed the fiery liquid scald his taste buds, and balance the warmth of his throat to the heat of his face. He looked for Marcus and found only his back. Big Brother was heading with Rose for the stairs.

"Hey, damn you! What about Bess, Patina?" Rawls called out.

"Mind your own damn' business, Little Brother," Marcus said, turning. He held a quart in his left hand. His right arm surrounded Rose's waist. His face flushed. He turned back, and proceeded toward the stairs.

Rawls started to follow, took one step, and halted. He wanted to stop Marcus, but knew its futility. An image of Bess crossed before him, pain etched on her face. He retreated to the bar, slammed his fist against its surface.

Lilly's arm settled around him, one hand resting on his shoulder. He looked into her eyes. There was no laughter there now, no innocence, just that special wisdom, the knowledge men seldom glimpsed. The ways of the universe reserved for the softer gender lay open, exposed there for him to ponder.

"You lonely?" she asked.

"Yeah, but not now," he said. The heat of anger owned him. How could any son-of-a-bitch be so dumb, especially his brother?

"I understand," Lilly said. Her fingers squeezed his shoulder. "See you another time." She moved to a gaming table, and leaned carelessly against the wall, watching the cards fall in front of the four cowboys.

Snort poured another drink. Rawls rolled a swallow of the liquid fire around in his mouth before tilting his head back and downing it. Thoughts of Bess and Patina, alone at the ranch, worsened his uneasiness, prodded the anger.

"You make this stuff?" He nodded at the glass, made a face at Snort.

"Have you know that's Tennessee brewed," Snort said. "I ain't your brother. Don't come down on me, young man."

"Last I saw you, I was broke. You treated me square. I got a dollar or two now. Owe you anything for them other times?"

"No, as I remember, we let Marcus's bill tote you a little and squared the rest up with six-gun shells or sumpin'. Anyways, it's good to see you again. Grown attached to that hat, have yuh?"

"Beginning to like it. Catches people's eye." In the mirror, he noticed a figure cross the room. At first he paid little attention, but then he saw a square-built man pull back a chair and join the solitaire player. It was Zeb, the gunny who rode shotgun for the stage.

The tall man raised his drink at Snort, signaling him to bring his companion a glass. A bottle already stood near the man's cards. Snort made his way to and back from the table.

The mirror reflected recognition in Zeb's eyes when they settled on Rawls. He spoke to the other man and hooked a thumb toward the bar.

Hair at the back of Rawls's neck challenged his collar. He switched his drink to his left hand, letting the glass hide his lips. He asked Snort in a low whisper: "Who's the loner?"

"Rake Darrow, division agent for the stage line. He transferred down from Fort Smith a few weeks back. Think he and the judge up there ran out of trees to hang folks on."

Zeb poured a drink while talking rapidly. Darrow stared in Rawls's direction.

"Guess it figures . . . that's the stage's gun with him," Rawls commented.

"Yeah, but watch out for Rake. He's a cold-blooded killer. Got every crooked law from here to Missouri in his pocket. They say he hung a nester for stealing a pair of worn-out horse collars, and that was after the farmer's woman talked the man into returning the durn' things."

Rawls heard a chair scrape behind him. He glanced up at the mirror. Darrow was up, leaning over the table. He wore one gun belt. It holstered two pistols, tied snugly.

Snort's voice wafted across the bar, colder than the outside wind. "Watch yourself, son. They ain't forgot that mule you ventilated."

Darrow carried his bottle to the bar, stopping six feet down from Rawls, and deposited the liquor on the bar top. He let his arms swing free while his eyes locked on Rawls. "Name's Rake Darrow. You owe me fifty dollars for a mule."

"Don't remember buying no mule," Rawls responded.

"You didn't. But you did plug a hole in one's ear from a

span of Butterfield leaders. See, I'm partial to that outfit. You hurt them . . . you hurt me."

"Understand, Mister Darrow. I admit I acted some hasty that day. I'll pay what's reasonable, but fifty sounds a mite steep for a teeny hole in a half-broke Mexican mule's ear. We've both seen more than that lopped off just to mark 'em."

"Maybe, but you might as well have drilled that animal through the head. He ain't no good to himself or nobody. Snap a whip over his head and he thinks he's shot . . . throws on the brakes and he's there till it rains. I ain't here to argue." The agent leaned forward and raised his hands within inches of his holsters.

"In that case, have a drink," Rawls said. "We'll wrangle on it. Tell you what . . . I got three good mules over at that stomp lot. They are bigger, younger, and better than that runt I culled for you boys. You examine them, take your pick, then make me out a bill of sale, and we'll mark this matter settled."

Zeb had moved to within a few feet of the agent. "He's right, Rake. Their animals looked fit. I saw the gentlemen bring them in."

"Gentleman?" Darrow scoffed. "All I see is a son-of-a-bitch posing as Reb riff-raff. Fork over the fifty."

"Put some writing gear on the bar, Snort," Rawls said. "This Yankee carpetbagger just gave me the itch. He's gonna scribble out a bill of sale and sign it if he has to make his X with his own gut juice." Rawls's fingers spread. If he could beat Marcus, he could take this gunny.

The stage guard touched the agent's shoulder. "Rake, let's check Mister Slaton's stock. It seems reasonable."

"No Reb son-. . . ."

Snort leaned with his elbows on the bar, his features blank. "Rake Darrow, meet Rawls Slaton."

"Slaton?" Darrow seemed startled. "Slaton. That's the

name that Mexican kid mentioned. The one that hanged that Comanchero Grande . . . killed his men." Rake appeared less certain as his arms went limp. His breathing became audible. The agent thought for a long moment, then picked up the pencil. "Let's go look at that mule."

Chapter Eleven

Bess opened one eye and clumsily rubbed quilt-covered fingers at a loose strand of hair. Patina made happy grunts and gurgling sounds, just enough noise to indicate wakefulness. The crib's shuck-mattress pad rustled, confirming the child's contentment. Bess knew the noise would shift into demanding wails of hunger. Light filtered through crevices around the door and offered a pale glow of illumination through the kitchen window. Odors from seasonings, home-cured ham, and coffee beans blended with the faint scent of wet diaper.

Outside, Jefferson Davis crowed defiantly, challenging first light. Bess yawned, stretched. She tightened her leg muscles, then relaxed and trembled. She'd enjoy the quilt's warmth one more minute. The men were still away.

Later, with Patina changed, nursed, and her own morning needs met, she sat at the table with coffee, eggs, and ham. A cold biscuit from yesterday's pan served for a pusher, and the honey jar promised indulgence for the meal's last bite.

Bess removed a folded brown paper and a short pencil from her apron pocket, then smoothed the paper against the table with the edge of her hand. She studied its markings. She mentally counted five, ten, fifteen, then seventeen. She added a third vertical line to the other two. This was the eighteenth day of their absence. They'd be back anytime now.

The loneliness had not been too bad. Actually the first few days of not having to pretend had proven a relief. Perhaps the stooped stature and sour faces of those women who were always advising her were due less to toting babies and wash water than she'd thought. Lies were a heavy load, also.

From deep within, the words shallow and selfish continued to echo in her consciousness. Was she bad for wanting something—something better than dutiful love, obedient conception, and lonely childbirth? Thank goodness Patina did not fit in her unhappiness. She'd brought freshness back into the world, but even that was not enough. The pattern was real, and most of the women she knew reluctantly admitted to being trapped in it. She wanted to feel alive again, tingle from frost-laden breezes, the sight of wildflowers, singing birds. Enjoy the birth of new skies and the grace of a setting sun.

Yes, there had been a time—a time when Marcus stirred her, when his mere glance made her stomach flip, and she'd dreamed of the excitement life with him would hold. She couldn't put a date on it, but a vague yearning had appeared in his eye and it sort of grew, silently, barely visible like a weed in a garden, till it shaded their lives, tainted the union of their souls. The twinkle disappeared; the challenge faded. He stared into the distance, and spice and seasoning abandoned their bedroom. Life had become stale.

It wasn't the work, not the poverty, the uncertainty of what tomorrow held that turned the faces of this country's women toward bedroom walls. Oh, the good Lord knew they worked hard enough, but she didn't mind work. Neither did Marcus. She could be happy here. She wanted to be. Perhaps that explained it—a simple answer for a not so simple problem. She needed to be needed. If only she could fulfill him, but she couldn't. She'd tried. It was there on his face, discontent, stamped in stone. She saw it every time she looked at him.

And now, Rawls was here, eager, alive, and more important hungry—hungry for her. Yes, she was bad. She feasted on her husband's younger brother's hunger.

When they returned, she'd put it right. She'd make it work, but Rawls would have to go. Ramón could help Marcus with the cattle gathering. Rawls could work the outer ranges. That would give her family the house to themselves. They needed that.

Rube barked, then came down the road to meet them. He stopped fifty yards away and sat with his tongue lolling, dancing, and dripping on the dry-crusted earth.

Marcus threw his lead rope to Rawls and spurred his mount toward the cabin. Other than loud groans, curses, and the vigorous scratching he'd given his head, it was the first energy he'd displayed since Rawls had pulled him from Rose's bed at daylight. He passed the spring, stood in the stirrups, and whirled his hat overhead. "Bess, honey, we're home. Hello, the house! We got money to burn."

Bess opened the cabin door. She held Patina and waved. She hollered something Rawls could not make out. The mutt stretched low in a galloping run, striving to stay up with Marcus's mount. Taking his cue from his master, he added to the racket.

Marcus dismounted from a sliding stop. He took swift steps to the porch and hugged Bess. He stepped back and touched Patina's face.

Rawls turned from the scene, moved on to the barn, and swung to the ground.

Bess called: "Rawls, welcome home!"

He waved but got right to caring for the stock. He could hear Marcus's voice.

"Got you a new tub, Bess, and they's hard candy in that sack. Wait till you see what's in them saddlebags."

"I'll put the baby inside," Rawls heard Bess tell Marcus.

When Rawls was through with his chores and out of excuses, he could avoid Bess no longer. He went toward the house. Bess's face beamed as she counted gold coins, running her hand around the inside corners of the saddlebags. Marcus worked at his cinch strap.

"For heaven's sake!" Bess cried. "There's two hundred and seventy-five dollars here. Even when you and Rawls split it, you'll still have enough to buy grub for a drive."

"It's been split."

Bess's eyes fixed on Rawls's face. "You've got a like amount?"

"More or less." He nodded, thinking: *That damn' Marcus must have left ten dollars with Rose.* "We found a good market."

Bess lifted her hem, hurried in the house. "Clean up. I'm going to fry steaks. I want to hear all about your trip after dinner."

"Y'all go ahead. I'll be in directly," Rawls said. He found he needed space. He stuck his hand in his pocket, felt the bill of sale Darrow had signed last night. The paper had been signed before Marcus had showed himself at the top of the stairs with his pants around his knees and a pistol in his hand. The trip had taught him one thing. Big Brother was a fair hand in a fight only if women and booze were elsewhere. He wanted to see Patina, but, right now, it hurt too much to look at Bess.

Eventually he entered the house. Patina smiled at him, then burped. He tickled her chin and watched the grin return. Bess said it meant she was happy to see him. Marcus suggested that maybe she confused him with Rube. Rawls concentrated on fashioning a smoke. He worked slowly, deliberately, listening to Marcus bring Bess up to date on the trip.

They talked about money and gathering cattle, and their

87

spirits seemed to soar. Every obstacle to gathering a herd paled with available cash in hand.

Bess mentioned the need for Rawls to ride the outlying ranges to solicit partners able to consign cattle to the drive. Marcus argued against the idea, suggesting he handle that job since many of the newcomers to the area had not met Rawls. Bess changed the subject to the need for additional help.

Rawls's willpower deserted him, and he found himself sneaking hidden peeks at his sister-in-law. Still he avoided eye contact. He excused himself and spent the afternoon topping off three mustangs. Afterward, bruised, scraped, and exhausted, he nursed a bitten tongue and limped his way to the ditch's outdoor bathhouse.

Patina smiled again when he played with her while Bess put the finishing touches on supper. He turned, an unguarded moment, defenseless. His eyes met Bess's, and the longing he saw there tore at his innards. He could not mistake that look. She fought the same battle. Impossible, he must be crazy.

Marcus was on the porch, drying his face. He could hear him out there. Guiltily he quickly cast a glance at the door. Irresistibly his eyes returned to her face.

She paled, smoothed her apron, then blushed. He couldn't believe it. She came toward him. Put out her hand. Her fingers touched his face. They rested there. Palsy fought reflexes for the smallest of moments. For an instant, both were motionless. She nervously moved her hands to her own hair, then dropped them to her side and stepped to the door. She gathered her skirt tightly at either side and leaned out.

He put his hand to his face. His eyes followed her. Silhouetted by a dying sun, the curve of her hips, the V of her legs formed shapes and shadows through the threadbare material of her dress. The mirage vagueness created by the petticoat beneath only managed partially to obscure the vision and enhance the excitement of this moment.

"Marcus, you ready for supper?"

Her words snuffed the flame, and he looked away.

He ate little of the evening meal. He blamed the loss of appetite on his sore tongue and the mustang that gave it to him. He excused himself and retired to the barn. Later, he decided to return to the house and ask Marcus to put his coin in the hiding spot the fireplace held. The barn offered few choices. He walked barefoot, giving in tenderly to the sore-foot reminder of his toes' inability to support the weight of a mustang. He hoped all the snakes were holed up for the winter.

Near the porch, the sounds of an argument stopped him. At the sound of Bess's voice, he reached for the porch post. The jolting of the bronco was nothing compared to her words—plain, cold, harsh words, honed razor-sharp.

"I don't care what you say, I want him out of here. I mean now. Do you hear me? He takes the wide loop, Marcus. That's it."

"But, honey. . . ."

"No buts, Marcus. I want him out."

He'd been mistaken. It was a woman's ploy. She really hated him. She had just been being kind to her husband's brother. Well, he was damned glad he knew. They needn't worry. He'd have Baldy saddled and be out by daylight.

Chapter Twelve

Rawls wrote by lamplight. Finished, he looked around, wondering where to leave the note so Marcus would see it. He had a good mind to burn the thing and hit the saddle and just keep on riding. He reread it.

Marcus,

    I'm riding out fifty miles, will circle, see can I find folks willing to consign stock. Like we talked, I'll put the date for pulling out at March 1st. Will tell them to gather a week early, at the east edge of Buckthorn Mesa to road brand.

    Saying you the ramrod, and rules and condishions will be issued by you the day before we head out. Consignmutts: The first four dollars goes to owners. We'll figure the rest of the split for anything over that we get in Kansas. No cows sucking less than weanling calves and no smooth-mouths or sore-foots. I'll find hands, do I run across anybody so crazy. On the way back we'll bring in what we can gather. You and Ramón catch what you can handle. Don't take any wooden nickels. See you in two or three months.

Your brother

    He thought of the milk bucket. Marcus would see a note there, before breakfast, but if he stepped on that porch, they might wake. He'd decide where to leave the note in a while. In the meantime, he saddled the best of the mustangs he'd topped the day before, put a pack on Baldy, and a rope on Soot. He would lead them away from the barn before mounting the mustang. Odds were when he stepped aboard, the thing would cut a caper, and with an anvil for a gut he'd as soon not have anyone woke up for polite talk. He pulled the note from his pocket and reëntered the barn.

Outside again and after the short walk to gain distance, he mounted the new horse. To his surprise, the bronco only grunted and laid back an ear. He walked out, sort of stiff-like. The animal was a dandy.

Rawls looked back at the barn and smiled. The look on the old milk cow's face, when she had turned, trying to see the note tied with a horsehair string to her right front tit, would stay with him a while. Marcus would get a kick out of the new mailbox.

November turned to December the following week. Frost crackled frequently from the tarp covering his bedroll, and the wind held a bite. In morning shade, skim-ice hung to stream banks, and the mesquite foliage turned brown and spiraled to the ground. Cottonwood leaves yellowed, curled, and matted near trunks and roots. Feathery grass stems changed to hard straw with whiskers hiding hooks, and chaff lifted on the wind and swirled at the feet of the horses. Old Dandy learned to rein.

The middle of each day warmed, and the sun slowed his pace and drained his energy. At night, alone with his campfire, the Mackinaw and the piece of wagon sheet he slept under offered his only shelter. Sitting, with his hat pulled low, his back to the wind, facing the heat, and with his collar turned up, he stared into the fire. He smoked and drank coffee and studied the dancing flames.

Often a likeness of Bess rewarded him. She smiled. She

bent. She pouted. When happy, little wrinkles danced around the corners of her eyes and lips. The flames expressed her form bending over Patina, and again the material in her dress stretched tight over her hips. At these moments, ill at ease, and with guilt marring his contentment, tobacco or the coffee pot became his ally. The act of reaching for them interrupted his stupid brain.

Soon, curls of smoke would drift and roll, and from the haze her likeness would reappear. The sound of her voice drifted in the wind and whispered across the scrub. Whether soft or strong, the wind carried the same message. "I want him out of here."

At the sound Rawls shivered and pulled the coat's opening tighter. He struggled to abandon the wind's voices, the fire's visions. It helped to kick the partially burned wood back onto the fire and watch sparks fire at will into the ashes. Wrapped in his blankets, his defenses always melted. The scent of sage became confused with the household odors of spice and soap that drifted with Bess, and he jerked at the tarp over his bedroll.

Typically Bess's presence lingered with the dying coals. Tonight, he shut his eyes, and a freckle-shadowed face smiled knowingly from the darkness. *What was her name? The kid-whore at the Posey, what was it? Lil . . . Lilly, that was it.* On the loop back to the mesa he might just stop by the Posey. Old Snort was a corker. Rawls's eyes grew heavy, promised sleep. He embraced its void as a friend.

200 miles into the circle and a few days short of Christmas, Rawls took mental stock. He had agreements bound by handshakes from seven stockmen to bring at least 150 head each to the mesa camp. In addition, he drove fifteen two-year-old steers he'd caught and branded. An old-timer, a

widower named Sod Fedrick, fifty if a day, had said to count him in. Wages had not been discussed.

Later that day, he found himself facing the wrong end of a shotgun when he ran into a starved-out farmer. After Rawls explained who he was and what he was doing, the red-haired farmer finally lowered the gun, and then invited Rawls to share a mess of frostbitten turnips seasoned with months' old sow belly. The man introduced himself as Waldo P. Weathersby, late of Jeb Stuart's Confederate cavalry.

After they ate, they decided to remain as nearly motionless as possible while the vegetables fermented internally. They sat and visited. It turned out Waldo held claim to a couple of dozen cattle, a mule, and a love of conversation.

"You batch out here, do you?" Rawls asked.

"Do now." Waldo pointed to a slight rise behind the cabin. At its top stood a cross. Nearby was a smaller one. "Wife and baby girl are out there."

"Didn't mean to pry."

"No, it's OK. Just me and the dog now."

"Dog?"

"He's out there in the weeds somewhere," Waldo assured him. "He's half coyote. Don't take to strangers. Sorta shy, but he let me know about you and them stock two miles back. He'll probably show tomorrow. Reckon you'll be able to ketch that fifteen or so head I scared when I pulled down on you?"

"That's the reason I'm hanging around. I'll let 'em settle a few hours, then, come morning, they'll gather OK. As I said, my brother and I are gonna try trailing to Kansas."

"I'll help in the morning."

"I can loan you a hoss."

"Got a mule. Where'bouts in Kansas you driving to?"

"Abilene. The railroad's there."

"I'll swun. I could use the work. What kind of wages you pay?"

"Ain't shore. Marcus, he's my brother, will ramrod. I can pay twenty-five dollars a month and grub for the next two months. I need somebody to help me add to that little bunch I already got. Big Brother will announce the sign-on before we start the drive. Wages'll be better, but dependent."

"Dependent on what?"

"I don't know what all."

After a week of gastric upheaval, Rawls decided "Turnip" was a better fit as a name for his new friend and employee than Waldo. Turnip showed no fear of work. He woke the sun each morning. Allowed to complain a little, he'd stick to twenty-hour days. Now they watched forty-five head of cattle drop, shoulders first, to their bed ground. They were two miles west of Plum Grove. Turnip had agreed to ride night herd, while Rawls went into town. They needed supplies. Once the herd was settled at Indian Corners, Turnip would ride back for any personal items he needed.

Plum Grove's mongrel pack ignored Rawls's arrival. With the sun down and autumn coolness adding zest to the evening air, their interest seemed centered on more basic pursuits. Appearing and disappearing between buildings, their leader led the rounds, checking out trash pits behind the businesses.

Four bits rented a bath at the barbershop with a couple of fingers of whiskey added to boot. In the wooden tub, he alternated pulling on a cigar and the bottle. Warmed both inside and out, he dried, splashed on toilet water, then looked in the mirror and parted his hair into a cowlick to either side. He herded Bess from his mind and deliberately opened the mental gate to search for an image of the kid-whore with the knowing eyes.

Outside, the pale lamplight from the Posey's only window beckoned. The last of the ingredients from the barber's bottle warmed his stomach, but Bess's words nursed a chill that he was—by God—tired of. He'd made up his mind on the way into town that he'd thaw that frost if it took every ounce of whiskey Snort owned and every sporting woman from the Grove to El Paso. Marcus wasn't the only bad seed with a Slaton handle.

Inside, his eyes adjusted to the dim light. Lilly sat at the piano with her back and bare shoulders toward him. One hand held a glass, resting. The fingers of the other plinked a discordant tune—a sad tune. Somewhere a windowpane talked back to the rising wind. Snort smiled behind the bar. He raised his towel.

Rawls had worked up a smile and squared his hat prior to stepping through the door. He sensed the grin wash from his face. He left his hat on the rack and squared his shoulders. It had to be done. He was damned tired of being the good brother. He dredged up the smile again.

"Howdy, cowboy!" Snort announced. "Come, rest your funny bone. Might tickle up sumpin' better than that sick grin. Ain't seen you in a while. It's Rawls Slaton, Esquire, as I remember, hanger of renegades and master trader of mules. How you been?" The barman ran his eyes over his wares. "How's this? Best I got."

Rawls nodded, watched the amber liquid fill the glass two fingers high. The piano stopped.

"Where's your brother?" Snort asked.

"To home, I hope. That your only customer?" Rawls hooked a thumb over his shoulder at the drummer seated alone, dozing, near the wall. He downed his drink.

"Yep. Town's drying up."

Rawls sensed Lilly's presence. Her perfume didn't hit you in the face like Rose's. It sort of came at you like the coo of a dove. He turned, expecting to feel her arm encircling his waist or shoulder, expecting her body to touch his. Instead, she had stopped a couple of feet away.

"Hi, Rawls," she said. "It's good to see you." Little bird tracks formed at the edge of her eyes, her nose wrinkled, and there were the freckles, faint in the lamp's light. Her partially parted lips revealed traces of sparkling white and created suspicion of pleasures that Rawls found confusing.

"Can I buy you a drink?" he asked.

She nodded and led the way to a table.

Rawls, carrying the bottle, followed.

"You young 'uns enjoy," Snort advised. His ever-present smile had disappeared.

For a night of carousing, this one had sure gotten off to a slow start. "What's wrong with him?" Rawls asked.

"Snort's a good man," Lilly responded, "too good for his job. Pays us to push the snake oil, then seems saddened by our doing it."

"Us?"

"Me and Rose."

Rawls held out the girl's chair. She came near, smiling up at him. Maybe he was wrong about the night. They sat and he poured them each more whiskey and looked into her eyes—those knowing eyes. This girl must be the wisest woman in the world. She must know everything. And the hell of it, none of it seemed to bother her.

She put one hand over his and tilted her drink with the other. Her eyes continued to examine him over the glass.

He took a drink, clamped his jaw, and shuddered. "Shore is good, ain't it?"

She sipped and smiled. "Our best. Whatcha been doing?"

96

"Gathering beeves."

"What for?"

"They say there's a market in Kansas. We're gonna find out."

"I declare. You and your brother, I guess?"

"And some more."

"How many more? And where is Kansas?"

"True answer, I ain't for sure about either, but Kansas is somewheres north of the Red, on past the Nations."

"Snort told me you were in the war." She sort of lowered her head and tilted it, letting a twist of hair fall before her eyes. Her words drifted up at him. "You've traveled a lot, I guess. Wish I could."

"Traveled some, but I like it here best."

She gave him a look of disbelief. "That makes you a real maverick. You got strange taste."

"I like you."

"Proves my point."

Outside, the night aged, floated on updrafts of time aimlessly, slowly like a giant bird. The wind kicked higher, and other windowpanes joined the chorus of the first, and the building's eaves turned the wind, and it whispered back. Rawls took both Lilly's hands in his own. He slowly stroked her fingers, then rubbed her small knuckles. He gently tickled between her thumbs and fingers, and she smiled. The wicks on the lamps flickered and the globes blackened with smoke. The light dimmed and the shadows deepened.

Rose descended the stairs. She got a bottle from Snort and waved at Rawls and Lilly, then retraced her steps and disappeared.

He asked: "You wanna dance?"

"To what? There ain't no music."

"Oh!" For a moment he felt foolish, then thought: *What*

the hey, this is Lilly. "There's the wind," he said.

She chuckled, tossed her hair, leaned her head back, and laughed merrily, making her own music. "You wanna dance to the wind, cowboy, come on." She rose and held out her hand.

Then they stood swaying back and forth in each other arms, moving their feet only slightly. Rawls noticed the room had taken on a little roll of its own. Something like the rock of a lightly loaded stage, swinging in the leathers.

She felt good and warm and soft in his arms, and she leaned back and looked him in the eye. "Lil, call me Lil," she said, and put her face back against his chest. Her hair smelled fresh, and he was glad he'd bathed.

"Lil," he said. "Lil." The wind was making music. It had sort of a rhythm, and they were in perfect step, except those few times he stumbled. They returned to the table. Snort yawned loudly from the chair he'd retreated to behind the bar. Only the soles of his boots were visible above the mahogany.

Rawls dipped a couple of drops of whiskey on his finger and drew brands on the tabletop with the moisture. "We gotta come up with a road brand." He drew a lazy S for Slaton. He wiped out the S and drew a capital L, then put a small i beside it and placed another capital L upside down and backwards to its right to form a box around the i.

"What is it?" Lilly asked.

"The Open Box I or Lil."

"Isn't it a lot of trouble?" She smiled. Something about her brought Patina to mind.

"Not much. Only two irons."

The whiskey was thirty minutes below the halfway mark when she surprised him. "How's your sister-in-law?"

"What?"

"Your sister-in-law, how is she?"

"You don't know her."

"No, I'm just getting to know you."

"Oh, she's OK, the last I saw."

"When was that?"

"A couple of months back, I guess. I made a circle. Got about fifty head bedded down a couple of miles out of town."

"How much does she know about Marcus and Rose?"

"Beats me. How much is there?"

"You know as well as I do what there is. Know what I think? I think you care more for her . . . Bess, ain't it . . . than Marcus does."

"Damn it to hell, woman! I don't want to talk about her. That's why I'm here don'cha know." It just came out. He'd not intended to say anything like that. Damn whiskey, anyway.

Lilly's chin quivered. She reached for the bottle. Her hand shook. She poured a drink, downed it, then poured another. "So little Lil's supposed to fix everybody's problem, huh?" Her eyes blazed. "I may do it, but it'll cost you fifty head of steers."

Rawls knocked off another drink, tried to roll a smoke, but he spilled his tobacco. Lilly grabbed the makings and rolled them both perfect cigarettes. He lit the smokes and took the sack and papers.

"Baby," she said.

Rawls took a deep breath. Women! "Let's you and me take this bottle and go up to your room there," he said, pointing upstairs. "I'm about tuckered out."

"Just like that, huh?"

"Yes'um."

"Rawls, I don't think I can do that with you."

"Why not? I'm bathed."

"No, it ain't that. You got any idea how many brands Rose has on her undies?"

"How would I know a thing like that?"

"Well, I'm sure your brother knows."

"I ain't my brother."

"She's got 'em all, every 'puncher's outfit she's ever slept with. They're embroidered. Her petticoat's got more markings than the hide of the wildest mossyhorn ranging the Guadalupe. I don't do that, but I ain't no different. You, though, you're another matter. You're the only one I know can get next to me. There's something about you . . . like a brother. I want you to know the other side, but believe me, cowboy, it ain't a sisterly thing. You stir me plenty."

"I don't know what the hell you're talking about. You're the only thing I been thinking about."

"All?"

"Well, mostly."

She raised her eyes from the glass to his face. A wan smile crossed her features, then disappeared. She reached, placed her palm against his cheek. The wisdom returned and the mystery smoldered with it there, deep in her eyes. Her face grew solemn, and he looked long and hard. Whiskey unlatched reality. The deeper his gaze penetrated, the more he envisioned, and there were soldiers dying and babies crying. A fresh prairie of spring buffalo grass beckoned him to a new beginning. It was all there—there in her face.

Lilly nodded, and stood. He followed her up the stairs. His hands held her waist and her butt wiggled before him, up one step, then the other. He was glad for women like her.

She opened the door, entered the room, and sat on the side of the bed. She began to undress, then moved down a bit, patting the spot beside her, invitingly. The door latch clicked. The room swayed and Rawls stumbled to the other side of the bed. His face grew warm. He sat with his back to her. Little things told him she removed one garment after the other, and he yearned to peek, but could not bring himself to turn.

A bundle of clothing flew through the air and landed on a chair. He felt her squirm under the covers. She had to be naked. He couldn't get his boots off. He glanced at her and grinned. Only her face showed from beneath the bedding.

He spat on the palms of his hands, rubbed them together, and cursed the boots and the cobbler profession in general. Finally one of the rascals surrendered, then the other, and he fell backward on the bed, dressed, but barefoot. He could feel her legs beneath the spread, under his head.

Lilly raised from the covers and bent over him. Her finely shaped breasts filled his vision. A world of beauty surrounded him, and he buried his face between the mounds of pleasure hoping to sink forever in their softness. He struggled for breath, smothering, almost blacked out before breaking free to find her lips.

His fingers tripped over hers as he unbuttoned and discarded his garments, then they were together, under the covers, naked. Her body was warm, soft against his. Damn! He was in the corral. He didn't even remember opening the gate, but, by God, he was there, and the ride had started. It began, slow and gentle, then stampeded into a too brief cyclone of passion. Finally he sagged, spent and exhausted, unable to move. She struggled, giggled, gasped for breath, and finally extracted herself from beneath him.

Sometime later, Rawls awoke and dressed. Lilly opened her eyes and he bent and kissed her. He reached for money and she shook her head.

"Never," she said.

He continued to fumble at his tight pocket.

"Rawls, I said, no." He'd heard Bess use that tone. You didn't challenge it.

At the door, he glanced back. He wanted to wink, do something worldly, something to make her think he did this sort of thing all the time, but what? He closed the door, gently.

It didn't take the black gelding long to realize they were headed for the herd. The Milky Way hid, and the darkness before false light covered the plains. Rawls gave the horse free rein and let it work its own way to camp. He rode easily, drifting in that no-man's land of half awake and dreamland. He dragged one after the other of the night's events out to be examined.

He wondered about Lil. He didn't even know her last name. She sure tore up his ideas about the nature of females. She really sat him on his ear. Who would've thought women could find anything in bed besides pain and impatience. She hadn't said hurry up once. She'd sure never mentioned, was he through? Funny, she acted like she'd just been to a church social, and here he was feeling down in the mouth with all this guilt.

He wondered if there were others like her, other women that found fun in bed with a man. Probably not. Certainly those he'd encountered among the Army camp followers had not shown such a side. Neither did the prim and proper, long-suffering madams one encountered around the villages. He thought it unlikely they could muster that much energy.

One thing about Lil, she was easy on the eyes. Of course, he'd never inspected a lady that closely before. Damn, she didn't miss perfect far.

Chapter Thirteen

Marcus sat a long-legged roan. Around him, twenty men hunched in their saddles and tugged at their slickers or thumped water from hat brims. Behind the circle of men, 2,000 motley-colored longhorns milled, picked at grazed-over, trampled grass. This day had been slow coming. Mustangs had progressed to cow ponies, and the seasons had moved through fall and winter since Ned Slaughter had passed through peddling his flyers describing the market in Abilene, but now March had arrived, and with it the day of departure.

Moments earlier, Rawls had summoned the crew to gather around his older brother. Rawls stood in his stirrups beside Marcus, and raised his voice. "Men, I talked most of you into this. Like I said, Brother Marcus will captain this outfit from here on out. You all know him better'n you know me, anyway, and, in just a minute, I'll get off of my high horse and turn this over to him.

"First, though, there's two, maybe three things. One is that jug in the wagon . . . a fellow gets snake bit, near drowned, or hurt bad, cook will give him a swig. Other than that, a man touches it, he's on his way home, without wages. Period! The same goes for gambling . . . there won't be none. If a man turns a gun on a bunkie before Abilene, he hangs on the spot. Fist fighters draw a double watch of night herd. That's all I got. It's Marcus's play from here on in."

Marcus glared. Tracks of anger showed on his face. He opened his mouth, then closed it. He turned to the men, and his features brightened. "We get back with all that money, Little Brother's gonna get him a frock coat and sign on as a circuit rider. Better'n that, maybe we can build him a brush arbor behind the Posey to hold services in."

Chuckles mixed with low murmurs flowed around the circle. Relieved to be done with the branding, although still carrying the sore backs and scent of burned hair that accompanied it, even the weather failed to dampen their spirits. Wounds and scratches from brush popping were yet to heal. But now there was hope, just maybe they could change a worthless herd of snaky, mean-eyed cattle from a yoke of poverty to a real cash crop.

Marcus continued: "Till we get him set up as a sin-buster, though, I reckon what he said I'll enforce. All that stuff is part of the rules. The rest goes like this." Marcus carefully explained the consignee's four-dollar base draw per head, cowboy wages of thirty dollar a month, and the hoped for percentage split for everyone if prices beat the base price. He pointed out two exceptions. "The wrangler, that'd be Ramón's boy, Amando . . . he gets a straight twenty dollars. Sod Fedrick's gonna cook. He gets thirty-five a month, plus his share of the percentage.

"Rawls will scout and help with the herd when he can. We draw regular cowboy wages. You understand if we get over four dollars a head, a big chunk of all them fractions stays with us Slatons for getting this thing together and bankrolling the supplies. Money is payable as received after the herd sales. Anybody got a problem?"

"Your part would come to half of all over four dollars after wages and bonuses, wouldn't it?" Sam Meadows asked.

"Exactly, plus our own stock's four bucks," Marcus said.

"Seems fair," the Slatons' neighbor said, looking at his nodding companions.

"Half of something beats hell out of nothing," another added.

The men had taken to the moniker of Turnip for Waldo. The young Reb showed no offence. He raised his hand and waved vigorously, careful to keep the elbow bent to avoid water finding a route inside his sleeve. He caught Marcus's attention.

"Yeah, Turnip, what?"

"Marcus, you know I'm going, lessen y'all run me off. But how do percent work?" At the sound of Turnip's voice, his coyote's ears and upper head appeared from a clump of nearby brush.

Marcus pointed. "Leo, would you go through it with him?"

Leo nodded and rode up next to Turnip. A moment later he hollered: "Marcus, that ten-percent bonus, is that per hand or ten percent split amongst all us?"

"Hell, no! It's ten percent for the lot of us." Marcus laughed. "They ain't that many percents in a poke. OK, you boys ride out here with me as I call your name. You already signed on as hands. We got eleven, counting ourselves. There's room for two more. Leo, Mark, and you, Todd, get that clean shirt over here. Ramón, your son Amando, Miguel . . . our Comanchero fighter . . . Turnip, Yates, and Mister Fedrick, y'all come on."

"Marcus," spoke up Fedrick, "you can drop that mister. I ain't never been much for handles. It's just Sod."

Marcus nodded. "We'll take two more."

Six hands shot skyward. Marcus studied the men. "Tankersley, Wells, you're hired. The rest of you, well, we'll be back with your share soon as we can make it. I ain't got the foggiest of when. Today, we're gonna drift this bunch up to Dixie Springs on the stage road. Ain't but four miles, and they's good grass and water there. Besides, some of us got people driving out to see us off. You hands, throw your war bags on the wagon and let's mosey. Miguel, you and Yates take the lead. Turnip, Leo, you'll drift back and bring up the drag."

At Marcus's mention of "people", Rawls had stiffened. He'd said "us", so "people" could only mean Bess and Patina. Excluding present company, Marcus had no other kin.

The smell of whiskey and scent of Lil kept stabbing at Rawls's conscience. It was enough to make a fellow's head sore. He'd been fighting the feeling since that night at the Grove. Seeing Bess with that on his mind was scary. Such thinking made no sense. Mixing and mating didn't leave a mark. Some of the best bronco riders he knew weren't bow-legged. Bess, Rose, Lilly, they all proved that. Well, Bess did have Patina, but Marcus, it didn't show on him. And Lil, there was no way just looking at her one would know. He carried no brand.

The men lifted reins, ready to move out. Marcus raised his voice. "Boys, I don't have to tell you how rank this bunch is! You collected 'em. You know. By my count, over a dozen have their eyelids stitched open to keep 'em from sneaking away in the brush. These first days, we're gonna move slow and easy. Best we can tally, they's a thousand, nine hundred, and eighty-six head out there. Our first want is to get every head to Abilene. You know, and I know, somewhere, some-time these next few days, they're gonna run. Be ready. OK, go get 'em!"

When Marcus turned to Rawls, the younger brother tried to sound casual. "Bess and Patina gonna be at the Springs?"

"Supposed to be," Marcus replied. "They're riding out in the Meadowses' rig. They'll see 'em home safe."

Sod Fedrick moved the chuck wagon a few yards ahead. Moments later, Yates and Miguel funneled a few leaders into a thin line behind it. Others followed the first. The bawling, milling mass showed little semblance to a trail herd.

Amando's remuda flashed by to the left of the cattle. They moved with tails high, leaping brush and gullies, traveling at a broken lope. A light-footed gray mare sporting a cowbell attached to a leather neckband led them.

"Reckon we'll ever see that bunch again?" Marcus asked.

"Yeah," Rawls said, "and, when we do, that boy will be with 'em. Marcus, about that jug, it ain't personal. Just seen too many dying men crawling in the wake of drunken leaders and others let down by whiskey-blinded bunkmates. When we get money back to these men, then what you do is your business. Right now, I'm obliged with promises and harnessed tighter than a Missouri mule to what ifs. Most of them questions concern other men's stock."

"Know what you mean, Little Brother. We get back from this, I ain't taking on nothing of nobody else's long as I live." Marcus's last words trailed over his shoulder as he spurred his horse to cut off a bolting steer.

Pride welled inside Rawls. Marcus had handled himself well this morning. Rawls had always respected the load Marcus had accepted after their dad's death, even though they'd had their spats. He'd forgotten how comfortable following Big Brother's shadow could be. If only it wasn't for that damned streak, that urge to fight the bit that seemed to grab him every once in a while.

Rawls reined Baldy toward a half dozen longhorns near the edge of the herd. Behind the drag, the remaining stockmen raised their hats and waved. He lifted his own second-hand headgear. These men, on the verge of starvation and economic disaster, had put their trust in the Slatons.

Their only hope rode with this herd. They'd lost a war and now faced hard times, asking no quarter. Well, he'd see they didn't get let-down.

The drizzle had stopped. A bright sun fought the chill, and far to the northwest dark skies marked the front's retreat. The air warmed and lay heavily, laden with moisture. The cattle worked better, although still as jerky as a freight train. More outlaw and renegade than trail-broke, only time would settle them. Even a drummer could see the run in them.

Rawls breathed deeply and pointed Baldy north. The route to Dixie Springs was gentle and well known, but he might as well scout beyond there. North of the stage road they would travel Indian Corners country. Some of that land was flinty. Sore hoofs were to be avoided.

Besides, maybe Bess and Patina would have arrived early for the rendezvous. He gave Baldy slack, nudged him into a slow lope. Right now, he didn't care if Bess liked him or not, he had a thirst that only sight of her would quench.

Dixie Springs seeped from beneath a rock outcropping hidden by horseshoe-shaped higher ground on three sides. It fed a clump of trees, then braved the arid land a few miles, before seeping back into the earth. The tops of the cottonwoods were visible from higher ground for miles. Buggies or wagons parked there stayed hidden till a rider's final approach over the ridge line.

Warmed up, Baldy worked himself into single-foot, and they crested the spring's high ground two hours shy of noon. Three rigs appeared, their teams staked. Other buggies dotted the stage road from the direction of Plum Grove. Looked like the ladies were out to send their men off in style.

Rawls pulled the horse to a stop and reached for the makings. Relaxed, he surveyed the camp below. He stroked and licked the cigarette into acceptable shape and cupped a light. Flame gnawed at the dry, twisted paper and smoke filled his lungs.

The lady dipping water at the springs was Mrs. Meadows. He'd never forget that determined manner or the straightness in her back. Especially after the way she had scrubbed Marcus's face with that plucked chicken. One of those buggy horses over there looked familiar, too. The surrey with the canvas covering must be their rig, but where was Bess? The thought had barely formed when the rig's canvas lifted at the tailgate, and she backed out. She reached with a toe for the foot rail, then stepped to the ground. A turn positioned her toward him. Her hand raised to the brim of the faded bonnet. Her fingers held the limp stays of the headgear to shade her eyes while she gazed in his direction. No question, she had him in her sights.

He sat there, feeling dumb. It would take more than sight of her to put out his fire. This helped about as much as the time he tried to slack a thirst by drinking up all the dregs of Rohondo's alkali sump over by the Pecos. He nervously checked all his buttons and tugged at the tail of his shirt. Sometimes scratching just made an itch worse.

A bobwhite whistled nearby, the note sharp and demanding. Another responded, grew silent, then started up again, moving nearer.

Time froze, Rawls forgot to exhale, choked. Smoke clogged his lungs and he coughed, tears streaming down his cheek. He wiped them with the back of his hand, stood in the stirrups, leaned forward, and raised his hand.

Her voice, calling his name, drifted on the moist air. She moved quickly up the slope toward him. He dismounted, waited. She didn't sound like she hated him. He detected no anger in her voice. Bess called his name again, only feet away.

He reached and helped her up the edge of the slope, then quickly released her hand.

She grasped each of his arms above the elbow and shook him. She smiled, her head tilted up, looking into his face. He sensed a growing grin of his own. She breathed rapidly, and light danced from her eyes. "You rascal! Where have you been? Why didn't you come home Christmas?"

"You know where I been . . . nursing them beeves, that's where. Besides, you and Marcus are entitled to be shut of me hanging around."

The smile left her face, but she didn't release him. He hoped she never did.

"Where'd you get such an idea?" she asked.

"What idea?"

"About you not being part of that home place. Not being welcome there."

He examined the toe of his boot. It seemed there ought to be something to do with his hands. They were just sort of dangling. She still gripped him there, above his elbows.

"Rawls, if I said anything . . . whatever you think you heard. I want you to know that's as much your house as anybody's. You helped build it. Your daddy left it to both his boys. You got a right." She released one arm and her hand moved to the point of his chin and tilted his head up till their eyes met.

The birds were silent.

Her face blocked his view, surged forward. A moment of warm, firm lips, the familiar scent that screamed her name, and he realized he was going to kiss his brother's wife. His hands found a mission. They pulled her closer. He tasted her, then again, but, sensing her moving back, he released her.

Her eyes no longer reflected light. They smoldered—deep

110

pools of green and shadows of gray, body-aching beauty. Then that wisdom thing showed itself, that *I know you better than you know yourself* woman thing. It lasted but a moment, then faded. Lil wasn't the only one that had it. Funny, he had not noticed it with others.

Bess's hand rested on his chest, her arm straight, holding him back. Her words rushed nervously: "Rawls, forget that, please. It never happened . . . it didn't. What must you think? I'm sorry. Just excited at seeing you, I suppose . . . well, say something."

"Thanks! Marcus always had the durn' luck." Her arm didn't seem too steady. She wasn't pushing too hard. He believed he could kiss her again. The good Lord knew he wanted to. Given a choice, brother or not, that's what he would do.

Mrs. Meadows stood at the spring, hand on hips, watching. Rawls saw her and tipped his hat.

"How's our girl?" he asked Bess.

"She's fine, asleep there in the rig. You gonna be here for supper?"

"Yeah, Marcus is bringing up the herd. I better scout ahead, but I'll be back, come dark." He gathered Baldy's reins. "Don't guess you got a biscuit down there." *It wouldn't need sweetening,* he thought.

"Just a minute." Bess turned and skipped down the slope to the surrey.

Rawls mounted, letting Baldy pick his way down the slope to the campground.

Bess emerged from inside the canvas, bringing a cup towel wrapped around a piece of chicken and a biscuit. "How about a pulley bone?" She handed it to him, smiling.

She knew only too well how he and Marcus fought over the white meat. He needed to say something. "Bess, you're a sight for sore eyes. And what you said a while ago, you mean that?"

"I meant what I said Rawls. I think you know what's happening. Sometimes a wind is so strong you can't stand it. Times are a person has to go inside, has to hide. I hide a lot." She stopped. "You got any idea what I'm talking about?"

"No-oo, but I got pretty keen eyes. Finding stuff is what I'm best at. Besides, I'd know you were about, even with my eyes shut. . . . I better go." He nudged Baldy forward, then stopped him and reined about. "Bess, about hiding, I done my best, but you seem to find me no matter how far away I pitch my roll."

Bess's face brightened. She took a half step toward him, seeming to straighten, grow taller. She stopped, smiled. "Be careful."

"My middle name. Be back shortly." That last smile of hers seemed sort of sad. He gave Baldy slack and clucked him into movement. *Damn Marcus,* he thought, *he doesn't deserve that woman. Big Brother better cut a straight trail from here on out. Husband or not, he better cut a straight trail.*

Thunder rumbled in the northwest. Faint lightning played along low, dark clouds, drifting more purposefully now. And the sky—somehow, it appeared less grouchy. What did the Good Book say about coveting? He was going to have to look that up sometime.

Chapter Fourteen

Near mid-afternoon, Rawls found a stream with good grazing suitable for the next night's camp. He drank from the stream, and weighed the urge to head back to the spring. Bess's presence there drew him like a bee to honeysuckle. Besides, he'd not even seen Patina.

That kiss had put a damper on his scouting skills. Likely it didn't mean as much to her as to him. Women tended to want to be kind. Could be she thought she had hurt his feelings and wanted to make up for it, feeling sorry for him. Still, she had seemed serious. He turned back for the Springs.

He found the crew loose herding the cattle north of the watercourse. Miles down the stage road a speck grew, moving nearer. The eastbound coach took form. Approaching the camp, he saw Marcus holding Patina near the Meadowses' wagon. Rawls raised his hand and rode past them, dismounting near a rope corral.

Yates, Miguel, and two other cowpunchers sprawled in the tree's shade. Bess and Mrs. Meadows worked near the fire. Across the way, Sod kneaded dough while Turnip stoked coals near the chuck wagon's tailgate.

Sounds of rattling chains, the creak of leather, and muffled hoof beats announced the stage's arrival. The team left the trail with eyes rolling and mouths agape. The driver sawed backward on his six reins while the guard cracked his whip, opposite the turn. Combined, they changed the leader's course. Veins bulged in the driver's forehead, and his voice carried like thunder. "Yeah, hey, yea sons-a-bitches!

Crazy bastards! Whoa!" The stage continued in decreasing circles with the driver's curses overriding the racket.

Yates and Miguel scrambled to opposite sides of the coach's course, both leaping and grabbing the bridle of a lead animal as they passed. Their boot heels plowed furrows, then bounced free of the hard ground. Slowly their combined efforts stopped the mules. Rawls recognized the crew from Plum Grove.

The driver spoke, his voice breaking over gulps of air: "Zeb, believe young Slaton over there's got the right idea when it comes to mules . . . just plug the damn' things in the ear. They. . . ." His view traveled to Bess and another woman near the wagons. He looked at Mrs. Meadows. " 'Scuse me, daughters. The good Lord knows a dirty mouth is my worst weakness, and me with a parson for a passenger." The big man finished with a lift of his whip toward Marcus and Rawls. "Howdy, Slatons. After we water this bunch, you reckon you could give us a hand chaining the rear axle of this thing to that cottonwood?"

"Just holler when," Marcus said. "Hard to get them things still, ain't it? They ever learn whoa?" His eyes fixed on several cattle scampering for the herd with tails swishing skyward.

The driver ignored Marcus's attempt at conversation, and addressed his passengers: "OK, folks, if you're quick about it, you can jump off. We're gonna be here thirty minutes."

The coach's door opened and Rake Darrow, crouching sideways, placed a boot on the stage's foot rail. He touched the brim of his big hat, bowing slightly to the ladies and nodding at Mr. Meadows and Marcus. The sideways look he cast at Rawls said he'd watched him from inside the stagecoach. "Still standing, I see."

Rawls reached for his tobacco, and asked: "That mule work yet?"

114

Without answering, Darrow moved toward the cat tails and salt cedars near the Springs.

Rawls stepped near Yates to give him a hand with one of the mules he was fighting. He liked working with the man. The only thing quicker than the handsome cowboy's smile was the way he moved around stock. The shine on his legging's silver ornaments paled beside his nature. Particular about his rigging and the garb on his back, he was at home in the lead and proud of his shadow. His outfit had a few patches and splices, but it was top drawer and fit. His high-creased Stetson was the envy of the crew.

Yates stayed a split second ahead of the mule's flashing teeth. "Watch him, pard. The onery son-of-a-gun'll take yore arm off. Ya reckon the Butterfield mixes gunpowder with their oats?"

"Might be," Rawls answered.

A black-garbed, hollow-eyed young man wearing a Lincoln-style stovepipe hat stepped from the coach. Like the mules, he was a cross—part handsome, part comical. The scarecrow appearance aided by the headgear tended to tilt the balance to the comical side. He carried a Bible and headed straight for the ladies without a glance at the men.

Halfway to the women, the stranger doffed his hat. "Ladies, I am the Reverend Jules Lamb, late of Saint Louis, on my way to the community of Plum Grove to gather a congregation and form a brotherhood to worship our Lord and Savior."

The mule left little time for a mind to wander, still Rawls noticed the preacher had a hungry look when he took Bess's hand. Why would a preacher, of all people, hold on so long and use so much energy pumping a handshake. He tried, but couldn't remember ever shaking hands with a preacher. Jules Lamb didn't look nearly so out of place with his hat off. He had sort of a square jaw, and, although he wasn't a dandy like Yates, he was a cut above Turnip, maybe himself, too.

Rawls lost sight of the parson while watering the mules, then, after they'd helped secure the stage to a cottonwood, he and Yates drifted toward the crowd gathered around Lamb.

Yates whispered: "Ain't so sure Plum Grove's ripe for preaching."

Rawls nodded.

Marcus introduced them. "Reverend Lamb, this here's my brother Rawls Slaton and with him is Lartheum Able Yates. Over there's Miguel."

"Brother Slaton, Brother Yates, and Mister Miguel, I'm pleased."

Rawls thought Lamb put a bit more weight on "brother" than "mister". Maybe he just didn't brother-up to Catholics. A man, even a preacher, shouldn't be so forward in shaking a woman's hand. This *hombre* allowed too much difference in his manner of greeting folks.

"Pleased to meet you, Preacher. What faith you peddle?" Rawls asked.

"Baptist, Brother Rawls. Are you acquainted with John the Baptist?"

"No, no, I'm not. Knew a John Oglesby once. He from around here?"

A smile brightened the parson's face, but then he noticed Rawls's .45 and immediately grew more somber. "I'm sorry, Mister Slaton. I refer to the Biblical John the Baptist, of course."

Rawls saw Bess frown, and assumed the look was for him. "Oh, you mean that John. Had a cousin named after him. In the early days, Uncle Will took the scriptures serious. Named his boys Paul, James, John, and Luke. Fifth kid was a girl, and Aunt Matilda wanted to name her Mary. But, by this time,

116

the old man had developed a taste for the hard stuff, and he kept on till they named her Bourbon. Said it had a ring to it. They put that in the Bible, but Mama and Matilda nicknamed her Bon-Bon before she got out of the cradle. Far as I know, that was all she ever knew." Rawls crossed his arms over his chest and nodded. "You remember Bon-Bon, don't you, Marcus?"

Lamb looked a bit disconcerted.

"Rawls," Mrs. Meadows interrupted, pointing at the chuck wagon, "looks to me like Mister Fedrick needs help with that fire over yonder."

"Aw, him and Turnip can handle it."

Lamb turned from Rawls. "Brother Yates, with a name like Able you must come from a family that studies the Word, also."

"I suspect. Most just know me as L.A. or Yates, though. You going to the Grove?"

"For a fact. I have a letter written by a good lady of that town named Rose Velure. Do you know Miss Velure, Mister Able?"

"Know a Rose, but probably a different lady." Suddenly Yates seemed interested in the cloud bank north of them. "Ain't shore the one I know does much writing." A little pink showed around Yates's cheeks.

"How'd Rose come to know you, Brother Lamb?" Rawls asked, noticing Marcus had lost the color Yates had found.

"Oh, we've not met. She wrote an open-hearted letter addressed to any Protestant man of the cloth, care of general delivery, El Paso, Texas. The clerk said I was the first one by. He'd had it near two months. Sister Rose wrote it right after Christmas. She said something about having passed the Savior's birthday without the Word, she felt the need for spiritual help. She must be a good woman."

Again, Mrs. Meadows interrupted: "Where you planning on staying in Plum Grove, Preacher?"

"Sister Velure mentioned her employer let rooms above his business establishment."

"And what business is that man in? Did she say?" Rawls asked.

"No, he may run an opera house or something. She mentioned entertainment. I'd have thought some of you good people would know, close as it is and all."

No one acknowledged knowing Rose. No one met the preacher's eyes.

"Daddy," Mrs. Meadows addressed her husband, "I think we better invite Brother Lamb to our place. He might be more comfortable till he's had a chance to look around."

Mr. Meadows seemed sort of grim, like he had coiled an empty lariat while a maverick made a beeline over the hill. "They's room, all right."

"That's it, then! Preacher, that's our rig." Mrs. Meadows indicated the surrey. "We live just a ways from the Grove. There'll be three, well, four counting the baby. We'll be leaving, come light. Missus Slaton lives just down the way. Her men are moving this herd. Won't be no trouble. It'd be best. I don't think you'd find comfort suitable in Plum Grove. You get your things offen that stage. Yes, that's it. You get your things."

The preacher's face had a moment's look of bewilderment, but then he glanced at Bess. And when she smiled, Lamb said—"Yes, ma'am."—and headed for the stage.

At the end of the thirty minutes, the driver waved the guard and Darrow toward the coach. They climbed aboard, then Miguel and Yates unlashed the stage and it jerked into motion. The only passenger now, Darrow showed he preferred company to the comfort of the inside seat. He sat cross-legged on top of the stage, behind the driver and guard. At the stage's first lurch, his hand streaked for the support of the rail.

When Rawls, standing near the chuck wagon, saw the movement, he reacted automatically, learning forward and grabbing for his pistol. Halfway through the draw he realized the agent's move was innocent. Self-consciously he allowed his hand to continue beyond the butt of his revolver and raise to pass his sleeve across his mouth.

The cook eyed him, puzzled.

Rawls mumbled: "Must be the heat . . . nerves a little raw."

"Nose raw, what's wrong? You catching the drips?"

"Not my nose . . . nerves!"

"Oh!" Sod said. "Didn't know you had any. Probably hungry. Just be a minute."

Rawls ate with Miguel and Turnip, keeping his back to Bess who ate with Patina, Marcus, and Lamb. Somehow, it was easier that way. He mulled over the chances of Ramón's converting the parson to a priest, since he didn't think they took wives.

All the while they ate, Mrs. Meadows talked rapidly to her husband in whispers. One could almost see the man's ear bend. The lady was just an old busy-body. She just kept sticking her nose in things.

Rawls, tired with the fussing, dumped his utensils in the tub and mounted. He rode toward the herd with the others to relieve the crew. Lightning flashed in the north, and a furnace-like breath of moist air touched his face. He cast his eyes northward. Dark clouds rose high.

His group drove the herd to mill on to the selected bed ground. One by one the herd dropped, shoulders first, to rest. Rawls figured they'd be all right. Even though they were rank, their bellies were full. Too full to run, he hoped.

Yates said: "Marcus wanted 'em put down on high ground."

Rawls nodded. "Good. They're on it. Mean-looking cloud."

"I don't like storms," Turnip said. "Make me think of them old dug-out cellars. Next, I'm seeing snakes lolling around, trying to get out of the sun. My momma was afraid of storms. Everywhere we moved, first thing, Daddy had to dig a hole. Me, I was afraid of cellars."

"Storms I can take," Todd Raines announced. "It's lightning makes me suck up my milk. If that thing gets any closer, you boys stay away from trees."

"Trees," Yates scoffed. "Only tree in miles is back at the springs. Don't worry, Mister Raines, lightning gets you, we got a regular parson back there to say your words, and we won't have to even change that shirt you're wearing."

"Cleanliness is next to Godliness," Turnip put in.

"How'd you know?" Yates laughed.

Clouds surged higher and closer. Darkness gathered and shadows worked slowly up the slopes. The cattle chewed their cuds, apparently full and content. Occasionally an animal would raise its head toward the north and sniff. Rawls noticed the sign. The plan was to leave Turnip, Todd Raines, and Miguel to ride the first shift on night herd.

Rawls rode opposite the circling hands. Passing them, he commented: "Whatcha think? 'Pears to me we better all hang around with these old outlaws a bit. That storm's coming fast. It's gonna be darker'n pitch here in a minute. They seem a little spooked." Each man nodded agreement.

Marcus was at the wagon, two miles back, with Bess and Patina. He'd have issued the order had he been with the herd. Rawls reached for his saddle strings and untied his slicker. It wasn't long before he wished that his hat was a tent.

Chapter Fifteen

Thunder crashed, rolled, and the world lit. Rawls's ears tingled and his skin felt dry. The air held a peculiar odor. Fringe on his chaps stiffened. Rapid-fire flashes lighted the herd. Five men circled the startled stock. Lightning struck, sending balls of fire bouncing across the prairie. Spears of light darted in the sky, and forked bolts stretched to the earth. Rawls blinked, jerked. Miguel charged toward him in the eerie glow of unreal strangeness.

"Ride for the wagon!" Rawls yelled above the roar. "Get the others. Tell Marcus hell's a-popping out here. This bunch won't hold. Ride out!"

The mustanger veered without hesitation toward the camp. The storm drowned all sound of the sorrel's hoof beats. Blue-green, bright blindness followed the flashes of light, and the storm swallowed the rider.

Rawls's roan slung his head and stopped, and then put his muzzle to the ground between his legs as punishing hail pelted them. The flashes dimmed, and to Rawls's right a black-spotted steer sprang to its feet. Small blue-white balls of fire played about its ears and horns and ran down its back. More balls of fire rolled on the ground and ricocheted off the horns of hundreds of startled, bawling animals. The cattle were on their feet, heads high, tails raised. White showed in their bulging eyes.

Opposite Rawls, an even brighter flash dimmed all others. Its source was Todd Raines, astride his bay. Sitting tall, his arms stretched upward, he cast that strange, popping, wavering light. The glowing rays from both man and horse were too intense for more than a glance. Rawls caught a glimpse and turned away, unbelieving, sick. The world shuddered, and a terrible stench of burned animal fat and hair and sulphur assaulted Rawls. The cattle swayed like a mighty wave and bolted away from the aberration on their flank.

The roan reacted at the same time. Thrown back from the saddle, Rawls clawed desperately, stretched for the horn, and finally struggled back into leather. The quivering flesh of the horse beneath him told, plainer than words, that he rode in the lead of nearly 2,000 crazed and stampeding longhorns.

Darkness engulfed them, and the thunder's roll weakened and gave way to the roar of almost 8,000 hoofs almost on the roan's tail. The sound tore at Rawls's gut. He could feel the horse's heartbeat pounding through the saddle's fenders, and the animal stretched low.

"Dear, God," Rawls moaned, hardly hearing his own voice.

The storm and this red roan's quick hoofs owned this night. He hoped he'd picked a good one. He'd know when it ended. The hail stopped, the flashes slowed, and he rode blind. He stretched low over the horse, thanked God for the stock's grass-filled bellies.

A mile slipped behind them, then another. A flash showed other riders on either flank. One—probably Marcus—rode a gray. He was sure it was Yates waving a slicker on the right flank, and someone just behind that rider fired a six-shooter. Slowly, a step at a time, he eased the horse toward Yates's side of the herd. How could anything stay erect moving at this speed and in the dark?

"Rawls, is that you?" Yates yelled from his right.

"Yeah! How far am I from the flank, L.A.?"

"Twenty feet, maybe more."

Rawls unbuttoned his slicker, wadded the neck in his hand. "Next flash of light shoot that front son-of-a-bitch! Keep shooting. Let's see can we turn 'em. If we don't get 'em circling, we'll lose the bunch!"

"Wait till the second flash. I need to make up a foot or so!" Yates hollered.

The next flash of lightning showed the roan had bought another yard of separation from the herd. He'd also gained precious inches toward the right flank. Rawls placed the reins in his teeth, switched the slicker to his left hand, and filled his right with the colt.

Lightning flashed. He popped the slicker inches in front of the closest animal's nose. He bellowed through clenched teeth and fired, emptying his revolver into the ground toward the stock's hoofs. Yates dropped the lead steer and more flashes spouted from his pistol.

The heads of the front animals dodged to the left, and slowly the wave angled, turning. Behind them, others took their cue, and gradually the mass was changing direction. The shift grew sharper. A glimmer of hope formed somewhere in Rawls's chest. The chill in his gut warmed.

The herd's turn sharpened, then slowly straightened, and the stampeding animals plunged on, heading south, arrow straight, and fast as death. They refused to circle. Hope melted, and ice returned. Dixie Springs and the camp, Bess and Patina were directly in their path. Too late, Rawls realized he'd turned this plunging fury straight toward the innocent. A horse's stride from safety on the wing of the herd, he had never felt more hopeless. An empty gun, a spent horse, and flying beyond control through a black void, what could he do?

As the herd moved back over the land it had covered in the opposite direction not that many minutes earlier, Rawls moved to the right. Yates pulled beside him. A flash revealed him working with both hands, trying to load his pistol. "Dumbest things in the damn' world!" Yates yelled. "Rawls, ain't camp up ahead?"

"Straight ahead!" he confirmed. "Yates, my God! We gonna kill 'em all."

"We got a chance, can I get this old pistol primed. You loaded?"

"Empty! They're crazy anyway . . . it ain't gonna work." The sounds of their voices tore from their mouths, barely reaching the other before being plowed under by the thunder of hoof beats.

"Get back in their face with that slicker," Yates snapped. "This old revolver blows a bunch of cylinders at once if it's jolted about the time it fires. Gonna try hitting her with my fist when I drop the hammer. Might do it. Scary . . . makes hell of a show."

Lightning popped, and ahead the site near the cotton-woods lighted. Vehicles sat directly in the center of the herd's path. Forms scurried for the trees, dimmed, and their images fixed in Rawls's memory fed the fear that bucked in his gut.

A second flash revealed Bess's flour-white face reflecting the pale light. She was perched on a limb of the nearest cottonwood. She was bent, reaching for Patina, who was in the hands of a man on the ground below.

Rawls swept past the wagons, and again lightning showed the man jumping, trying to hand Patina up to Bess. But he was almost out of time. The lead steer was nearly upon him. A blast, second only to the thunder, shook Rawls. It was a huge explosion from Yates's pistol. The revolver spiraled above Yates's waving hand. The roan and the nearest cattle veered from the blast. They turned.

Rawls reined the roan into the shoulder of the nearest

stock. He sensed an animal fall beneath the horse's hoofs. The roan struggled. With his neck and head on the back of a large cow, the gelding lurched and fought to regain balance and straighten. In an instant the pony was erect and running free.

A glow illuminated the preacher just as he heaved Patina to Bess. A huge shape ran only inches ahead of Yates's horse, hiding Lamb for a moment, then the preacher was catapulted skyward. He dangled like loose bagging on the horns of a monstrous steer. The berserk brute slung his head, barely slowed.

Yates stood in his stirrups, and his horse brought him beside the steer. He leaned over the animal's shoulder, then lunged from the saddle, and Rawls saw both of the cowboy's hands grab a horn before darkness returned.

Rawls whisked past the tree, the sound of Patina's wails catching his ears. He pulled the roan to a halt. Stragglers from the herd lumbered past. The main herd had veered a few yards to his left. Rawls realized from the sounds around him that Yates with a little help from himself and perhaps the rise behind the springs had finally succeeded.

A horse approached, hoofs pounding the mud, and came to a halt. A flash of lightning showed Marcus, erect and wild-eyed, sitting on the gray. "Bess?" he asked, looking around desperately at the churned-up earth.

"Up there," Rawls answered, pointing his finger at the cottonwood, even though unsure whether Marcus could see anything in the dark. But he had, for he smiled, his white teeth glowing through his mud-spattered face at sight of his family. Rawls turned the roan in the direction he'd last seen Yates and the longhorn.

If Yates was OK, Rawls thought, *he'd be signaling . . . except he has no pistol.* He hustled his horse forward and had only traveled a short distance when he heard his name called. He turned the roan toward the sound and let the gelding pick his way.

"Rawls! Over here, me and the parson . . . we're here! Don't step on us! Hell, we're messed up enough."

Rawls pulled up the roan, dismounted, and followed the parson's groans to the two men. Lamb lay stretched on his back in the mud. "How bad is the preacher?"

Yates knelt on both knees, facing the downed man. "I don't think he's too bad," Yates answered. "Thought he was hooked at first, but that horn was only between him and his old wide belt. Leg's busted, though."

"Parson, you hurt bad?" Rawls asked.

"Who's there? That you, Brother . . . Brother Slaton? Oh, I hurt, but I'll come around. Don't know how it happened. The good Lord sure showed His wrath tonight, wouldn't you say?"

"Yeah, it's me the younger Slaton. You showed a little stuff tonight yourself, Preacher. I'll go back and get help and a lantern. See can somebody set that leg, before we move you."

Marcus and Mr. and Mrs. Meadows returned with Rawls, followed by others. Marcus offered the whiskey jug while Rawls and Yates held the parson.

The preacher shook his head. "I've stomped the devil and refused his brew till now. I'll not weaken on this muddy ground."

"It'll ease the pain, Parson," Marcus advised. He wanted to take a swig himself, but knew Bess hadn't been far behind the Meadowses.

"I'll lighten it for you, boss," quipped Yates. "It's been a long night." A smile worked at his lips. His eyes looked haunted, unusually large in the lantern light.

Marcus glanced again at the ashen preacher. "You sure?"

Lamb groaned and nodded. Marcus put the stopper back in the jug, set it to the side, and offered his assistance to Meadows, who was working at removing a trouser leg from the parson's pants.

That accomplished and at his wife's instructions, Sam Meadows along with Marcus grasped the bared leg. The parson screamed, jerked, and fought for escape. Mrs. Meadows patted the injured man and interjected—"There, there, now."—without slowing her directions in guiding her husband's efforts. She added a running dialogue, explaining how she had learned her skills from her father, a doctor in Fort Smith. Her voice was rapid, but showed no panic.

Rawls struggled with Lamb's flailing left arm. The man's shoulders and head twisted and thrashed, and Bess stepped forward and wrapped her arm about the preacher's forehead. Rawls wished Meadows's old lady would just be quiet. Even though she was helping the parson, she was driving him crazy. When Sam Meadows seemed satisfied that the bone was right, she sent Sod to fetch three boards for a splint from one of the wagons that had been smashed by the stampede.

At the task's completion, the parson fell back, exhausted. Marcus stood and picked up the jug from where he had set it. He slumped, wet, allowing the whiskey to dangle loosely in his hand.

"Marcus, Rawls, I know what y'all said this morning, but I could sure use a slug of them spirits." Yates's voice had a whipped sound to it. "What do you think?"

Marcus looked at Rawls. "That's his rule. I just enforce it."

Rawls nodded. "He deserves it. He saved the whole lot of us. Cows, folks . . . all of us."

Marcus handed the bottle to Yates. "Seems fair. Good work."

"Naw! What it's about is . . . I'm low. I kilt Todd Raines. I talked it. Now, he's dead, deader than stone." Yates pulled the cork and took a long drink. "I more or less said . . . 'Todd when lightning gets you, we won't even have to change your shirt.' I ought to be horsewhipped. C'mon, let's go find him."

"Marcus, how about it. You want us with you?" Rawls asked.

"Naw, go ahead. See if Ramón needs any help. From the sounds off there, I believe they got them cattle milling. You sure Todd's dead?"

"Yeah, he's gone," Rawls confirmed. "Tell you what, Brother, one of us may have to stay with him till the rest of you get there to help bury him tomorrow. I think we're gonna have to put his horse down with him. Think they're about one now, after that lightning burned them."

"It was lightning then, not the stampede?" Marcus commented. "Well, stay with him." He looked at Sam Meadows. "I'll use the surrey to bring the parson to say words, come morning."

Meadows nodded, and said: "We'll make sure someone tells his mother."

Rawls motioned for Yates to follow him. As they walked toward their horses, he put his arm over Yates's shoulder. "Easy, pal. I think even that old crippled preacher's gonna tell you to drop a little of that load you're packing. Some things're just bigger'n us."

Behind them the preacher's weak voice whispered: "Brother Slaton, you don't mind, maybe just a little sip of that medicine would help."

Chapter Sixteen

Rawls lay on his slicker, his saddle blanket between him and the rain gear. His canvas and blanket covered his body, and his head rested on his saddle. Gray light turned darkness to shadows and the outlines of objects began to take form. Trickles of water wound under his hips and shoulders, and mud smeared him. His hat covered his face. Rain seeped through its bullet hole. A neck wrinkle formed a rivulet that irrigated the inside of his shirt. He was not asleep.

Ten yards away, Todd Raines's mounted corpse guarded an absent herd. He sat erect, an apparition astride the rigid carcass of his once bay horse. Charred black, both man and beast appeared to be from another time, petrified, a foreign landmark on a forbidding scene. The rancher's ripped, scorched, and torn clothing fluttered. A foul odor wafted near the ground.

Yates had ridden for the herd shortly after they had found Todd. Rawls had stayed behind. His heavy eyelids and fatigue said it had been a short night.

Dressed, he rolled his bedding, saddled, and then burned a couple of smokes. He saw Marcus riding toward him, leading a procession of vehicles and a number of mounted men. The group included those who had been at the campsite. Turnip, Yates, and Sod Fedrick represented the crew. Bess with Patina rode in the surrey's front with Mrs. Meadows. The parson occupied the rear. His leg lay stiffly across the back seat. He seemed asleep. Mr. Meadows sat a horse beside Marcus.

Those on horseback dismounted and with sidelong glances approached the dead. Yates and Turnip each carried a shovel. Mr. Meadows had a pick. They began to dig.

"We gonna put 'em both underground?" Sod asked.

Marcus studied the erect remains. He loaded his pipe and struck a match while walking around the stiffened animal. He blew smoke. "I don't see no other way." He walked to Rawls's side. "You look like hell."

"Feel like it," he muttered.

Bess walked over to them. She handed Rawls two biscuits with strips of bacon dangling from each. A canteen was slung over her shoulder. "There's coffee in here." She removed the container and handed it to Rawls.

"Marcus, case I never told you, you don't deserve this woman." He smiled at Bess, turned back to his brother. "How many head did we lose?"

"We found eight carcasses, most with broke legs and trampled, but three were killed by lightning. That old coyote of Turnip's was knocked silly by it. He let Leo catch him this morning. His right eye had been blown out, all scorched and everything. Ramón and a couple of the boys are holding about sixty that broke off and hit the brakes along that last creek. Once they bring them in, they'll be moving the lot of them this way."

"What about the horses. I never saw hide nor hair of them last night."

"That boy brought 'em in before daylight."

"All of them?" Rawls formed the words while chewing.

"All."

"Except for Todd and the preacher, we got lucky."

"Guess so. Don't feel much like it, though," Marcus admitted.

Rawls finished his biscuit, then relieved Turnip. "Sorry

about your coyote, Turnip."

"You hear . . . he let Leo catch him? Think he's gonna be all right. We had a one-eyed mare once. Daddy knocked it out with a singletree. . . . What's holding them up?" Turnip almost whispered it while tilting his head toward the aberration beside them.

"Ain't sure. It's just like all the juice is boiled out. They're sort of crisp." A secondhand taste of bacon filled his throat and he wished he'd thought of another comparison.

Marcus reached for Yates's shovel. The cowboy handed it over, then shook his right hand and flexed his fingers. Black powder burns covered the skin up to his wrist. Yates shrugged and walked to his horse. He reached into a saddlebag, pulled out a garment, remounted, and rode up beside Todd Raines. Sitting sideways in the saddle, he slowly slipped the clean shirt onto the charred corpse. Unable to stuff in the shirttail, he looked about helplessly. Then Mrs. Meadows brought him a shawl, and he neatly tied it about the body's waist and tucked in the shirt.

A couple of feet down in the hard earth, the diggers had to resort to the pick. The men took turns using the pick. It was hard work, but slowly the hole grew large enough to accommodate horse and rider. As the men worked, the women sung in low voices. Their musical words told of the saving of a blind wretch and then moved on to a gathering at the river. The parson continued to sleep. Marcus and Rawls stood beside Sod.

Marcus pointed at the preacher. "Sod, you reckon that man is ever gonna wake?"

"Cap'n," Sod replied, "I'd never question a man's calling, but that ole boy got pretty cozy with that jug after you all went back to the herd." Sod shifted his gaze to Todd and his horse. "How we gonna lay them two over?"

131

"We'll wrap a rope in front of the bay's shoulder and bring the other end over the top and behind that old burnt-up saddle," Marcus replied. "A little tug ought to do it. We better wake the preacher soon and get on with it. I imagine the herd's probably hard to handle this morning."

"Maybe we better ask the womenfolk to leave till we're done with this part," Rawls suggested.

"Why?" Marcus asked.

"Marcus, spilling those two into the grave ain't gonna look too good. Not to mention how it'll sound."

When the grave was ready, Marcus instructed: "Mister Meadows, pull that buggy up right in front of that grave, so's the parson can put the word on us from his seat. And if you ladies don't mind, would you walk off a ways. What we got to do ain't gonna be a pretty sight." Marcus directed the surrey to the grave while the women moved slowly away.

Rawls nodded to Yates and Turnip, and Yates handed him his rope, then mounted his horse. Turnip mounted and moved beside Yates. The two men sat quietly, a few feet beyond the grave and the blackened remains.

Marcus gently touched the preacher's shoulder, saying: "Brother Lamb, I'm sorry, sir, but we need you." When he got no response, he shook harder, raising his voice. "Preacher, you got work to do!"

Rawls tied his rope to the one Yates had given him and placed it around the horse's carcass. He handed one end to Turnip and one to Yates.

In the meantime, Marcus was shaking the preacher with two hands. Finally Lamb came alive, grunting and rubbing his eyes. He looked around for his hat, and for the first time saw the mounted mass above him. He screamed and jerked, grabbing for his leg and hollering all the louder.

Rawls looked over his shoulder, relieved that the herd was

out of earshot. He moved to the buggy. "It's OK, Preacher," he reassured Lamb. "Maybe we should have waked you before you got so close." He nodded at the source of Lamb's horror. "They ain't parlor dressed, but see can you think of fit scripture. We're all a ragged bunch this morning. The ladies especially have a need for comfort. We're counting on you, Preacher. You're all we got."

Marcus nodded at the mounted pair. Yates and Turnip took a wrap around their saddle horns with the ends of the ropes, and nudged their cow ponies forward. The rope had barely straightened when the charred bodies tilted and fell into the hole with a sickening, thudding sound.

Brother Lamb's gut-wrenching heave must have gathered power from somewhere below the navel, for it grew as it rose. It accompanied the crash of horse and rider, and covered the surrey with a liquid no one could bear looking at. Lamb straightened, mumbling undecipherable sounds—perhaps words of apology—from behind his hand.

It was Mrs. Meadows who grabbed her skirts and went running toward the stricken man while Bess and the others stayed some distance, their backs to the grave site. "Oh, you poor man," Mrs. Meadows uttered over and over as she panted her way to the surrey. She held the parson's shoulders and gave Marcus a look of disgust. "Why didn't you just drive him right into that terrible hole?"

Marcus ducked his head, and kicked at a soggy clod of dirt.

"We'll cover them," Rawls said, nodding at Lamb, "then you can preach."

The tools were brought out again, and the covering took far less time than had the digging. Sod fetched water from the chuck wagon's barrel and dumped several buckets' worth into the surrey. The women gathered. Mrs. Meadows wiped the preacher's hands and face with a rag she'd wet in Sod's bucket. The men removed their hats.

Brother Lamb cleared his throat and raised a hand. His face took on a peaceful expression, although he still looked ill. "Let us pray. Dear Father in heaven, be with us your children. Help me find a way to do justice to this man's life and these people's needs at this sorrowful time. Dear God, forgive my weakness, for I have sinned this very night past. I am reminded of Acts Two, Thirteen, when Peter and the apostles were accused of drinking the 'sweet wine'. Well, let me tell You, Lord, there was nothing sweet in the vile stuff that crossed my lips yonder evening, and it was past the third hour. In my pain and weakness I failed the test and looked to foul spirits for strength. Forgive me. I am ashamed. These good people deserve better." He paused but briefly, and went on.

"Brethren, prepare yourselves for the day when we, like this good man here, will ride into eternity to be with our Savior. You know the words of prophet Joel . . . 'I will grant wonders in the sky above, and signs on the earth beneath, blood and fire and vapor of smoke. The sun will be turned into darkness and the moon into blood.' We saw that last night, and Joel said it would come to pass shortly before the Lord returns for us. He also promised . . . 'And it shall be that everyone who calls on the Lord shall be saved.' Are you ready?"

Rawls felt Lamb was backsliding to his original sentiments. It seemed the man should spend a little more energy getting Todd into heaven and maybe less time meddling in other folk's doings. But still, hard as he might try, he could find no serious flaw in the man's words. After all, the preacher didn't even know the cowboy they'd just put under. Lamb continued for only a few more words, and Rawls thought the preacher ended his remarks sort of abruptly. Then everyone lined up, single file, and walked past the surrey to shake hands with the preacher. That done, the men donned their hats and moved to their horses. Rawls shook Lamb's hand last. With his free hand, he squeezed the preacher's shoulder. "I want to say thanks for what you did for our women there, at the tree. I saw the last of it. Thanks! And this other stuff you was talking about, in your prayer there, ease off on yourself, man. I reckon if old demon rum ran a little rough shod on you . . . you was entitled."

"Thank you Brother Rawls. Would you tell Brother Yates thanks, also? I know he saved my life. I ain't good for much today. I let him get away without telling him."

Rawls nodded and moved to the roan. He noted that Bess stood with Marcus. How she turned her cheek to his light peck. How they hugged self-consciously, and Marcus lifted the blanket from the sleeping Patina's face, before turning to his horse.

Rawls led the roan toward Bess. He stopped a few feet away. A whirlwind worked inside. He hoped he hid it.

Bess took his hand. A light-hearted, infant smile started, crawled part way across her face, but then vanished. That haunted look came into her eyes. "Take care," she said.

He stammered: "You . . . you, too."

She turned and stepped rapidly to the buggy. Marcus had mounted and was riding toward the herd. The cowpunchers rode beside him, all but Rawls. He worked at manufacturing a smoke. He worked by feel, because it was hard to handle tobacco and papers with your eyes on a disappearing surrey. He watched as Bess turned in her seat, talking to Lamb.

When he had finished rolling the smoke, he nodded at the freshly turned pile of dirt and self-consciously touched his hat. He lit the cigarette and took a deep drag. One fluid

135

motion carried his foot to the stirrup and seated him in the saddle. The roan turned to follow the remuda. Like the damned disappearing preacher, it seemed to know where the good life beckoned.

Chapter Seventeen

From Dixie Springs the Open-Box-I herd moved north. They put the Leon River behind them before the grass improved, and the stock gained weight. With each pound their tendency to run lessened. In the next month they moved beyond the Guadalupe, the Blanco, the Pedernales, and the Lampasas. The Colorado, the Leon, then the Bosque followed. They lost ten head of good steers to the quicksand of the Brazos.

Later that day, they moved from the prairie into rougher country. Since entering the broken land, distant riders had appeared and vanished. Turnip advised that Indians scouted them now that they were near the Nations. Rawls tended to agree. Whoever it was, they were stealthy as his friend's one-eyed coyote. That scamp had fattened on Sod's scraps. The riders proved equally harmless.

Rawls rode miles in front of the herd. His eyes worked the land, looking always for the easiest and straightest trail. He crested a rise, sensed a presence, finally sighting an aging Indian astride a bony pony.

The Indian watched him from the shade of a post oak. He raised a hand, palm outward. "How!" he said.

Rawls made a similar gesture.

The old brave pointed south. "Have cows?"

Rawls nodded. He rested his right hand on his saddle horn, inches from the butt of his belt gun.

The Indian's body was threaded through his bow, its string over the front of a white man's shirt. He wore no pants, only a loincloth. A tomahawk fitted through his belt on one

137

side, and a knife was sheathed on the other. He held a long lance. It rested with its butt on the ground. The point aimed at the sky.

Rawls glanced quickly in all directions, spotted no others. He nudged the chestnut forward, pulling to a stop only a few feet in front of the brave. "Where's your young men?" he asked several times before the Indian answered.

"No got young men, only me and old squaws. All purty much hungry. You got crippled cow?" The old man's voice rattled over the broken words like a dry gourd.

The Indian's face resembled saddle leather, his eyes pebbles in a dry creekbed. Perhaps a hundred warriors surrounded them. *Perhaps,* Rawls thought, *grandpa spoke the gospel. He looked hungry enough to eat stove wood.*

The Indian's cracking voice rose again. "Me watch. You lead cows. You got cripples? Indians hungry." Fire flashed from those cold, stone eyes. "You cross Indian country. Squaws heap hungry. You trade cripple, ride across these lands. Let tomorrow smile on you."

Well, there it was, plain as it could be put. "I got lots of friends back there." Rawls tilted his head toward his back trail.

"You not back there. We here."

"Old man, you don't look all that mean. Suppose, I tell you to go somewhere else for your beef?"

The Indian sneered: "Old panther most dangerous. Nothing to live for. Lose all fear. Just bad."

Rawls couldn't fault the man's logic. "Tell you what, chief, you and your squaws come to camp when the herd stops. I'll see does the cook have something he can spare. Then we'll talk. Maybe we got an old lame steer, or something. Savvy?"

"No chief." He pointed at his chest. "No call on visions,

138

no chant big medicine, talk with straight tongue, just old brave." The old man raised and shifted his lance, appearing to grip it harder.

Rawls whipped out his pistol and pointed it at the Indian's chest, cocked. He motioned with the revolver's barrel for the Indian to lower his weapon.

The old arm relaxed, hung loosely with the lance at his side.

Words alone were dangerous with this old wolf. Rawls pointed at the sun.

The wrinkled warrior smiled. "Good, eat, take cow. White man pass. Good!" He lifted his rein and kicked the mount into life. As he rode away, Rawls was left with a sense of tragedy resting on his shoulders. He shivered and remembered what it was like to fight for a losing cause. He wondered if the old man really traveled with squaws.

At camp that evening, the appearance of the old brave with three females answered the question.

Sod Fedrick set down his stirring spoon and took a rifle from the end of the chuck wagon. "Those your red men?" he said.

Rawls nodded. Marcus stood with his brother, ready to greet the four as they arrived. Half the crew ranged behind them. In keeping with Marcus's standing order after crossing the Red, they were all armed.

The ponies the women rode were even more used up than the man's. Yet, compared to their riders, they were mere colts. Rawls reflected on the women's ages. One squaw in particular looked like Old Testament material. He'd bet the stars called her mama. She sat stooped, squinting from slits in her wrinkled face. Her breath whistled around a single tooth in a half-opened mouth.

Again the brave raised his arm in salute. "How, white

friends." He pointed at his chest. "Me called Poor Medicine. These my squaws." He pointed at the nearest, an old woman that looked to be near 100. "This one Walks-In-Rain, my youngest." He pointed at the next squaw. "White name, Singing Bird." Poor Medicine looked at the oldest of the three. He paused a long moment, seemed in deep thought. "Forget her name. She come one night. Dogs make big racket. No matter, she answers Grandmother."

Marcus followed Rawls's lead and raised his arm. "Welcome, Poor Medicine. My brother told me you'd come. Get down. Have a seat. Like coffee?"

The Indians looked blank.

"Go slower, Marcus," Rawls whispered. "This ain't the Posey."

Yates helped Rawls carry plates of stew to each of the newcomers. Poor Medicine sat cross-legged. The three squaws kept an undercurrent of excited talk streaming back and forth. Their tattered garments dragged, spilled out across the ground, when they sat down.

The crew, seldom distracted from their food-laden plates, seemed fascinated with the new arrivals. They ate hurriedly, gulping their food without taking their eyes off the Indians.

Yates handed the last helping to Grandmother, and she burst into a hen-like cackle and took the food with one hand. She motioned for Yates to sit beside her.

Yates shook his head.

Grandmother reached. Her fingers caught the cowboy's leggings, and he jerked away. " 'Scuse me, ma'am. I need to see about my horse." Yates rushed toward the tethered mounts.

Leo and Turnip burst into laughter. "Where's yore manners, Yates," Leo chortled. "Get back here."

After Yates departed, Grandmother turned her attention

to the stew. Like the others she ignored her spoon and plucked the meat and vegetables with her fingers. She moved the tin plate to her mouth and tilted it, drinking with noisy gulps.

Sod proclaimed: "Ain't no damn' more food!" He looked at Marcus. "You Slatons ever hear of the fellow that let a camel get his nose in their tent? Yuh better be careful that don't happen here. You liable to find this bunch sleeping with you."

Grandmother's eyes again settled on Yates, who had returned to finish his meal. He sat behind the rest of the hands. The old squaw spoke excitedly to Poor Medicine.

Rawls handed the old Indian a rolled cigarette and watched as he lit it from a burning stick.

Poor Medicine blew smoke. He spoke slowly. "Grandmother wants him." He pointed at Yates.

A smile came to Marcus's face and he coughed, then reached for his pipe, obviously enjoying himself. "How about it, partner?" Marcus asked Yates. "You doing anything the rest of the night?"

Yates surged upward, erect. His plate fell at his feet. "I've had enough! This ain't funny. You sons-a-bitches, have your laugh."

"Take it easy, Yates," Marcus said. "We'll protect you." Marcus's struggle to keep a straight face showed.

"Marcus, don't push this. I've had enough!" There was no mirth in Yates's tone. His face echoed his seriousness.

The old woman harangued Poor Medicine with an urgent tone, her voice brittle.

The old brave turned to Rawls, again speaking slowly. "Squaw have half-breed little one . . . got lost in fight with Tejas Rangers many years ago."

Rawls took a short breath. He knew little of Yates's past,

but he'd heard his father had served with the Rangers in the early days.

Yates paled. His lips compressed and a vein appeared in his forehead. His eyes flashed wildly.

Poor Medicine stood.

Yates strode right up to the Indian's chest. He raised his arms and pushed with the flat of his hands against the old man's chest. He screamed: "I ain't no filthy Injun! I'm a white man! Take that damn' old squaw and get the hell out of here!"

Poor Medicine stumbled, tried to regain his balance, but fell sideways. He threw out his hand to catch himself before hitting the ground. His right hand closed on the lance. He shoved and regained his feet. He thrust the lance into and through Yates's upper belly before anyone could move to stop him.

Grandmother screamed. Her ancient voice was loud in the stillness. Sounds of her raw and long-strangled emotions filled the air. She screamed again and again. Her loud cry shattered against Rawls's ears. It blanketed him and held him immobile.

Turnip's six-gun roared. Poor Medicine's head jerked. Brains and blood rained to his rear. The Indian spun, took a step, and fell face down.

Walks-In-Rain and Singing Bird grabbed Grandmother and half dragged, half carried her to their ponies. They had difficulty mounting, trying to handle the old squaw, so gave up and led the ponies away, scrambling frantically.

The crew stood motionlessly, silently. With guns in hand, they watched the squaws disappear into the evening. Yates coughed, vomited blood, and lay still. His lifeless eyes seemed darker against his pale skin. His face wore a twisted look.

The night was dark, the stars pale. Rawls organized a group, headed up by Ramón, to dig a grave for their partner. No one said anything. Yates's death brought back the death of every friend Rawls had buried. When the hole was dug, Marcus asked if anyone had a word he wanted to say, if anyone had known Yates for any length of time.

The tall cowboy named Tankersley raised his hand. "Don't guess they's anything I want to say 'cept I knowed him for years. Daddy knew his old man when he brought the boy in from the prairie. The old squaw was right. He's part Indian. Story I got was he fought ever' kid in school till he quit. The last one he whipped was the man hired to teach. Don't think he learned much numbers, but he learned to not like being Indian. Far as I know, it mattered only to him. I'd as soon ride with him as any man I ever met."

Chapter Eighteen

The next morning, Turnip motioned for Rawls to follow him. He rode to the drag and roped a fat, but sore-footed, steer. He tied the animal to a blackjack oak with Yates's rope. "Way that thing's bawling, them squaws are bound to hear. You tell Marcus to take him out of my wages in Abilene, if you want." Turnip's chin quivered, and he looked away, silent a long moment before turning back to face Rawls. "You reckon that old Injun thought he had a chance against all of us?"

"Don't know. Just figured it was time to go, most likely. He made his play . . . paid his price."

"Who would 'a' thought old Yates would 'a' been done in by a rusty ole worn-out Injun?"

"Does seem queer," Rawls agreed. "I mean, 'cause he had so much juice and all."

"Why, yeah, being around him you would 'a' thought he'd live forever. Hold up, Rawls. I need a smoke." Turnip pulled up his roan, hunched his back to the wind, and protected the makings against his chest. He rolled the cigarette into shape, struck a match on his saddle, cupped the fire with his hands, and took a deep draw. Smoke rolled out with his next words. "Tell you one thing, when this drive's over, I ain't never sitting another durn' horse long as I live. I'm tard of a sore butt and raw . . . raw . . . well, you know, just being chapped all the time."

"It does seem a smart man could find a better way. Then, I've had it worse."

"That's just it!" Turnip exclaimed. "I've been faced with

deep-rutted dirt roads and old, shallow women all my life. I'm ready for cobblestone streets and something young and frisky that ain't trying to throw or hook me."

"Where you planning on finding this good life?"

"Don't know. I was born down on the Nueces. I'm sorta drawn to good strong rivers, maybe New Orleans. Get me a black frock coat, a stovepipe hat, like the parson's, and a deck of marked cards and squat on some riverboat till my days is up."

"New Orleans got cobblestone streets?"

"Don't know, but it's got to beat this Indian Nations country, and nothing's worse than Texas."

"Sounds to me like all the good country's lost its appeal to you, Turnip."

"Appeal! New whiskey, old women, and warm beer, where's the appeal in any of that?" Turnip wagged his head. "Damn! That old squaw was a ugly thing. I'll have bad dreams about her for the rest of my days."

Rawls wrapped his reins around the saddle horn and worked at his own makings. He chuckled softly. "Turnip, every outfit needs a waddie like you on the payroll." He held his formed paper and tobacco between two fingers of one hand and pointed the index finger of the other hand upward. "Not two, just one."

"Rawls, you want, you're welcome along with me."

"Wal, thanks, old pard, but somebody's got to work on that warm beer." He put a match to his finished cigarette and touched spurs to his horse.

Turnip raised his voice as they parted. "Rawls, you reckon Injuns count against them commandants?"

Rawls turned in his saddle to say: "Simple answer . . . I don't know. I wondered some about Yanks. We just play what's dealt. I'll tell you what, though, when we get to Abilene, we'll tilt one to old Yates." He reined away from the herd, raised his hand in parting.

With the passing days the sun drifted higher, more directly overhead. Flatter country put the horizon more distant as the herd inched along. One day trailed the next, and the freshness and hope of the drive aged like leftovers under a hot tablecloth. Days dragged, their pace resembling the sore-footed stragglers. Friendliness became a chore.

Rawls rode into camp and Sod handed him an empty plate and coffee. He tilted his head beyond the bean pot and Dutch oven. "That big brother of yourn's down in the mouth tonight."

"Where is he?"

"He's coming in from the herd, edgy as an old wider woman."

"What'd he do, gripe about your grub again?"

"Naw, hell, I expect that. He damn' near shot old Turnip's coyote . . . that's what! Said he bet he had lice."

"Probably does."

"Hell, he'd have to shoot us all, that being the case."

Marcus arrived in camp a few minutes later and followed Rawls to the dish tub.

"Ride out with me a ways, Little Brother," he said. "Got some things on my mind."

"Fair enough," Rawls said, and picked up two biscuits and a fistful of bacon and wrapped them in a flour-sack cloth while heading to the horses. "You ain't gonna put me back on drag with Leo, are you?"

"No." A few yards from the wagon Marcus stopped and pulled out tobacco. He packed his pipe, took a draw, then used his pocketknife to loosen the load. Seemingly satisfied, he repacked and lit it. Then he mounted. Smoke rolled around the stem as he spoke. "Rawls, I didn't sleep much last night."

"Most don't on a trail drive," Rawls said, climbing into his saddle, and the two headed toward the herd.

"Naw, it ain't that. Hell, I didn't even pull a shift at night hawk. No, even in my roll, I couldn't get easy. I been thinking."

Rawls waited, enjoying his own smoke. When Marcus was like this, things took a while to come out. He thought to ease the conversation, and pointed at his brother's head. "No wonder you're tired. They must be a lot of dust up there."

"Hear me out, Bubba. This is wringing me tight."

"Must be, when you call me that. Well, what's up?"

"I want you to take over this captain business. I ain't much 'count at responsibility."

"What're you talking about?" He reached for his own makings; this showed sign of taking longer than one cigarette. "You know cows good as any man alive, Marcus."

"It ain't that. It's being in charge of folks. Responsibility's what it is. It's responsibility."

He'd seen every mood his brother could muster. He recognized serious when he saw it. "Maybe, we better go back some. What's eating on you? Is it Yates?"

"That and Todd . . . that stampede. I should have been with the herd when you boys got hit that first night. Where was I? Back at camp, that's where. Playing tiddledly-winks with wife and baby."

"You been there . . . don't think there's a lot you could've done. You're gonna start turning lightning, are you?"

"Might 'a' had you boys dismounted. If not that, at least I could have had more riders out there. And I picked that bed ground too close to Dixie Springs with the women there."

"Let's have the rest of it." Rawls lit the second smoke.

"Then there's old Yates. I was taking part in the nonsense that got that poor cowboy killed. I was joshing him right along with the rest of them. A real ramrod wouldn't have been doing that. I'm supposed to keep that kind of horseplay down, tend to business. Everybody knows stuff like that leads to trouble. I was just wanting to have some fun. You know me. Having a good time always came first with me."

"Marcus, there's spells on a hard trail ain't nothing but long faces and grit teeth. Sometime them spells are weighed in years."

"Yeah, see, you're used to all that. Me, I ain't cut out for it. We'll tell the boys. This bunch is handling good now. I'll turn back in a couple of days, and head south. Y'all will be in Abilene 'fore you know. Everybody will be better off that way."

"You thinking of stopping by Fort Worth on the home trail?"

"Yeah, I might do that. Who knows y'all might beat me back to the ranch."

"Marcus, I'll tell you something. You always had me digging the hardest dirt, carrying the heavier rocks. Started when I was little, and you could talk me into or out of whatever pleased you. Well, not this time. You're the straw boss. You're it!" When he started this conversation, he was worried, not mad. Now that he had thought about it, they should have had this out long ago. He went on. "You just take a tight grip on your ass, 'cause you're taking this bunch to Abilene. I'm the scout. You're the captain. Say it over and over. Roll it on your tongue. Belly up to the bar, Big Brother. It's time for the boys to stay home. The men got work to do. The Slatons gave their word, and, by God, we stick to it. Anything else you want to talk about?"

"Well, look at you! You've got awful damn' righteous,

ain't yuh? Something's changed. What's going on? Snort said you came by the Posey when you was out on that loop. Said he thought you had a good time. How good a time did you have? You ain't falling for that whore over there, are you?"

"What? Who you talking about?"

"Rose. You know who I'm talking about. You seemed mighty interested questioning that preacher about her. You got the fuzzy ass for her?"

"Rose ain't my flavor. I'm just a serious old boy. Like you say, you're the fun lover." Rawls turned the sorrel and headed north. He sensed anger burning his face. *The crazy bastard,* he thought. *An angel at home, and him worrying about a whore . . . a cheap ugly whore.*

Uneasiness rode Rawls through the next day. His older brother worried his mind. Marcus read like a pup. Brag on him and he wiggled all over. If he'd grown a tail, a couple of pats would set it to wagging. Scold him and he sulked. But it had never been his nature to stay mad. All his life he'd angered fast, laughed easily, and recovered to something in between, while, for his own part, Rawls had drifted one or two moods back. Now things were different. Marcus's remoteness extended beyond Rawls to the other hands as well.

Weeks passed and the days became hotter, water more scarce. Sod ran out of bacon, and the hands grumbled. Three days later they were out of coffee. All grew sullen. Rawls chewed sticks and sucked on pebbles to conserve his smokes. His last sack of tobacco rested in his pocket, but its bulk made no bulge.

He rode into camp late. He tethered his horse with three others near the wagon. The day crew, like their gear, was scattered about the fire. No one broke the silence.

Sod spit tobacco at orange coals. The spittle hissed back at him.

"Somebody dead?" Rawls asked.

"Nope," Sod answered, and nodded at the bean pot. "They's cornbread in that pan yonder," he added, and tilted his head back, indicating the tailgate area of the wagon.

"No meat tonight?"

"Got raw coyote."

"What?"

"Got raw coyote," Sod repeated.

"That ain't even funny, the way I feel."

"Never cracked a funny in my life. That sour-ass brother of yours kilt old Turnip's dawg at noon." The cook spoke low, spat the words.

"Why'd he do that?"

"Your brother's gray stepped on his toe. While he's jumping around cussing, that old biscuit thief got scared and ran past. He was about twenty yards away. Dernedest handgun shot I ever saw. Old coyote's luck played out."

"What'd Turnip say?"

"Didn't say nothing. Thought he might reach for his iron, but he didn't. Smart man. You don't kill a man over a dawg. Leo was there, but I ain't sure he felt that way. Thought he might take it up for a minute or two. Seemed like he wanted some of your brother. This whole outfit's running on raw nerve and gunpowder. We need coffee."

"Well, cheer up," Rawls advised. "Sign is we're getting close to where we can maybe get some."

Rawls ate quickly, rolled a smoke, and rode out to see Marcus, who sat his horse alone, away from the camp. "Marcus, you trying to ruin it?" he asked.

"What's bothering you?"

"Turnip's dog, that's what."

150

"That damn' thing was a coyote. You upset about a damn' slinking, one-eyed coyote?"

"Not me, you. You're the one upset . . . shooting upset. Damn, Marcus where's your smarts?"

"Hell, it was just a sneaking damn' coyote."

"Dog . . . coyote, he weren't yours to kill."

"He was with my herd."

"Whose herd?"

"Leave me to hell alone!" Marcus snapped.

Rawls wheeled the gelding and rode to night herd. He allowed the roan to pick his way to the herd's edge. A shadow of a mounted rider, whistling, moved toward him through the dark. He stopped and waited.

Leo stopped whistling when he pulled up his horse. "Rawls, that you?"

"Finally. Thanks for hanging around till I got here. Next time I'm your relief, you got an extra half hour sleep coming. Who follows me tonight?"

"Tankersley."

"This bunch is about as quiet as that chuck wagon crew," Rawls observed.

"They tell you about today?"

"They did."

"Rawls, you and I always got along, so I want you to know, when we get to Abilene and settle up, I'm gonna give your brother a licking. I'd like to know where you stand."

"You mean with fists?" Rawls asked.

"Fists, no-holds wrestling . . . whatever Marcus wants. He knew that ole mangy coyote meant something to Turnip. Hell, shy like the way it was, it sort of reminded me of myself. Turnip's been in the dumps since shooting that ole Indian. And Yates's passing tore him up. They was close. Hadn't been for that, I believe he'd 'a' drawn on your brother right then."

"After we're through with business," Rawls said, "and, as long as it's square and from the front, that's between the two of you."

"I work from the front," Leo said, and clucked his horse toward camp. "See you come morning." He pulled up after a couple of steps. "I still got a half a sack of tobacco, Rawls. You want some?"

"Thanks, Leo. I got a little."

Chapter Nineteen

Beyond the Meadowses' barn, mesquite beans had long since fallen. Here at the edge of the front porch, wild roses, so diligently cared for by Mrs. Meadows, wilted in surrender to the late summer heat. Only the flowers' seedpods clung to the bushes, and Bess studied them, occasionally glancing through the window at her sleeping daughter. She thought of life's cycle. The security the neighbors' porch provided reminded her of her mother's embrace.

"God bless you, Brother and Sister Warren!" the preacher shouted at the last wagonload of Sunday-dressed families.

Bess mused over his earlier sermon, decided it had been the best she'd heard Jules deliver. She found it strange that she thought of a parson in the intimacy of a first name acquaintanceship.

The preacher's walking stick stabbed the earth like an angry third leg as he energetically returned to the porch. He mounted the first step and seated himself with his back against a post. He stretched out his bad leg alongside the cane. The Meadowses entered the house.

"Five couples today, besides you and Patina. It's our best gathering yet." The parson's face showed eagerness she recognized as a quest for praise.

"You had a good sermon, Brother Lamb. We were all moved."

"I do hope so. I believe these weeks of study here on this porch, confined to that rocker, gave my messages a depth they'd long missed. But tell me about you. You and Patina must be terrible lonely. Have you heard from your husband? Any mail?"

"I had that one letter from Fort Worth, but nothing since. They expected to be into the Nations a couple of days later. It frightens me, how wild that country must be."

"They seem capable. And you . . . how are you holding up out there with only your child?"

"Me, bosh! Patina and I are doing great."

Lamb removed his hat and leaned his head against the post. "It felt good, preaching here in the shade this morning."

Bess smiled. From inside the house came the sound of Mr. Meadows snoring. It sounded like he'd taken to the floor just inside the door. She looked at the preacher and smiled. His grin was nice, not stiff like you'd expect from a minister, just a boyish grin. Marcus used to grin like that.

"Brother Merle works hard," he said.

"Pastor, do you think grownups ever change?"

"Jules, please Missus Slaton . . . call me Jules."

"Oh, I couldn't. Pastor or Brother Lamb seems more proper." *Please, God, forgive me,* she thought.

"To answer your question, of course. It's basic. All is possible under God's love."

"And divorce. You know Sam Houston was married before coming to Texas. Do you think a person is lost if they break their marriage vows and lie to God?"

Lamb seemed taken aback. Obviously her frankness surprised him. He remained silent for a long moment, before he spoke. "Some seem to think our brothers and sisters in Catholicism promote that view. Most Protestants struggle with the issue. I would certainly try to lead my flock away from breaking up a home for any reason. However, if a spouse abandons the home, after a decent time, some cases might warrant such a move. Your question is philosophical, of course?"

"What?"

"Divorce, it's not a personal issue with you?"

"Oh, no. Oh, my goodness, no! I had Mister Houston on my mind." Why had she asked such a stupid thing? How could she get out of this? "I understand you've visited our town . . . even met Miss Velure?" She'd not known the whore's name till it had been voiced at the Springs

The pastor's face reddened. "I must have sounded such a fool." He laughed.

Bess couldn't help laughing, too. She caught her breath. "I'm sorry, Reverend. The laughter is not aimed at you."

"It's OK. I should have known. The men got a good laugh at my expense. A good preacher ministers to all, you know. I conducted services . . . shall we say in Miss Velure's side of town in Saint Louis. I believe your brother-in-law . . . Brother Rawls . . . tried to warn me of my folly. I owe him for that, and the kind words he left me with concerning my overuse of those spirits that night. He seems a warm man, though, I must confess, I don't believe he likes me."

Bess groped for the fan on her lap and rocked faster. She turned her face, fanning vigorously, having sensed the flush's heat on her cheeks. She wondered if Jules had noticed. Just the mention of Rawls's name, and she fell apart. She glanced covertly at the preacher. He studied the distant horizon.

She lowered her guard and allowed her thoughts free rein. *Rawls . . . Rawls. Dear Rawls, where are you? God, ride beside him.* One thing about it, curiosity and loneliness might encourage a first name intimacy, but she couldn't, in a thousand years, imagine this preacher mustering up enough raw manliness to cause that flip in her stomach like the animalism of Rawls. No matter, Rawls rode a thousand miles north, and the magnet that pricked her insides followed him like a star.

The Nations had long since passed beneath plodding hoofs. For days the herd struggled through Kansas. Today Abilene sprawled before Rawls. Marcus and Turnip sat their horses beside him.

Cabins, shanties, and assorted structures spread across the Kansas plain like a drunken nightmare. Most had sod roofs. New rails gleamed in the morning sun. West of town, the tracks surrendered to the prairie. Gathering pens and loading chutes crowded the rails.

"Look at them pens." Marcus pointed. "There's McCoy's office, remember, Slaughter said he had built one."

"Burg's not as big as I thought," Turnip put in. "Didn't think it would be."

Rawls looked at his friend while smoothing a cigarette paper. "Ain't sure I follow all that. That mean you had her figured or not."

"Towns always disappoint me."

"Not me, never saw one I didn't like," Marcus said. "I'll meet you back with the herd this afternoon," he added as he left the two and headed into town.

True to his word, not long after noon, Marcus returned with the buyer, McCoy. Rawls and Ramón joined the pair, and they spent the next hour riding around and through the herd. They rousted cattle to their feet, and Rawls noted with pride the ease with which the animals rose. They had cut daily travel in half the last week, and the stock carried extra flesh.

McCoy knew cattle and nodded approvingly each time one of the resting animals rose to its feet while they were still a good distance away. "No sign of fever in this bunch," he said.

"Clean as the day they were born," Marcus offered.

This man obviously wanted beef. Rawls envisioned being buried alive by thousands of gold dollars. He did his best to act unconcerned. He recalled Bess's excitement the night after Ned Slaughter's visit. If this deal went through, he'd get that girl something nice. He'd see Marcus did the same.

McCoy said: "The three of you come to my office at nine in the morning. I'd like to have your cattle. I'll make you an offer then. I believe you'll be pleased. You going back to town, Marcus?"

"Yes, sir."

"Good day, Ramón, Rawls. See you tomorrow."

Rawls headed for Sod's coffee pot. He bet the best three horses in his string could put him in sight of Bess by—*What was this, early September?*—by the end of the month.

Marcus had told Rawls to distribute $3 to each of the hands and free half the crew to go into town for the afternoon, which he had. At dusk, Tankersley held the lead as four hands straggled in from town. Behind them Abilene's lights winked. Leo brought up the rear. Even his horse seemed to stagger.

Tankersley stopped in front of Rawls and Turnip. "Sorry, we're a little late. Them's awful friendly folks back there."

"What's wrong with your horse, Leo?" Rawls asked.

Leo looked surprised. "Him, oh, nothing. He just ain't got a wooden leg like me. May have been brought up by a Baptist. He ain't much for rotgut, but the fool's a glutton for keg beer," he said from behind his hand and in whispers, as though the cow pony might be offended.

"Any of you men bring a bottle back to camp?" Rawls looked carefully for bulges in the men's clothing.

Leo sucked in his breath and produced a small bottle from the belt area behind his back. It held slightly more than a good drink. He held the bottle aloft. "Snakes still crawling."

Rawls nodded at Turnip and pointed toward the bottle.

157

"Leo, Turnip's first drink is on you. We're going to town. You think you can stay ahorseback and nursemaid them beeves till we get back?"

Leo made a pretense of pulling the bottle back when Turnip reached for it, then laughed and let him take it. "Shore, boss, think I'll change hosses, though."

Tankersley giggled, and then announced: "Boys, they's sort of a shack of a honky-tonk on the flat this side of the tracks. There's two in there ain't bad on the eyes. One's called Annie. Sometimes she answers to Woodpile." He started to giggle again but managed to get out the rest. "Don't rub the back of her dress. You might get splinters. The stack's out back. The other one's called Mattie. You be careful, Turnip. Them two like Texas boys."

In town, Rawls stopped at the barbershop. After a shave and a bath and a thorough dusting of his clothes, he crossed the street to a self-described general store. He bought tobacco, crackers, cheese, a pickle, and a dozen cartridges. He noted Turnip's horse swatting flies at a hitch rack in front of a saloon. Munching a cracker, Rawls patted Turnip's horse's rump and moved inside. Miguel sunned himself under a dim kerosene lamp. He held a bottle in one hand and spun a coin on a tabletop with the other. His booted feet rested on a chair.

Rawls approached the table. Miguel pointed the bottle at Rawls, spun the coin again, and spoke above laughter clamoring from around the bar. *"Amigo."*

Rawls hooked his thumb at the woman singing to three men at the bar. "Annie?" he said, sat, and poured a drink from Miguel's bottle.

"No, ees Mattie! Turnip and Annie, they are out back . . . stacking wood. It ees maybe the beginning of a great . . . how you say? . . . romance."

"We're a long ways from Indian Corners, old partner." Rawls turned up the bottle, made a face. "Turnip gets back, I'm buying a round. We'll drink to Yates. You ain't seen my brother, have you?"

"His horse ees tied north of the tracks at one of them places."

"I missed it. Well, what the hell, he's a big boy."

They finished Miguel's bottle, and Rawls bought another. Turnip returned and they toasted to Yates's memory, bragged on his meticulous dress and kind manners. A tear came in Turnip's eye and he called Annie over and bent her sympathetic ear to the finer points of the companion they had left behind on the trail. Miguel found a poker game, and Turnip and Annie made another trip into the warm night.

Rawls stood, stretched, and headed for the door. He soon nudged his roan into a ground-eating lope and thought, with excitement, of pushing for Texas—just a few more days.

The next morning, Sod served a breakfast of biscuits with honey. The pot on the fire smelled of real coffee. The second crew was back in camp and most of the first. A bashful sun showed half its face and worked its way upward. Miguel and Leo supported Turnip and helped him wash last night from his face.

Turnip blubbered. "I dern' near shot him." He grabbed his friend. "Leo, what if I'd shot him? Killed a man over . . . over that!"

"Who? Over what?" Leo asked.

"That's it, I don't know. I just heard her hollering. Blood all over . . . her crying . . . all that noise, and me pulling my hogleg on that poor drummer! Thought I was womanhood's last defender. I remember her saying . . . 'The busted nose don't matter, but he called me a whore.' What if I'd shot that man? Hell, that's what she is."

Leo burst into laughter and let go of Turnip, who slid to his knees. Miguel got both arms under him, grinned, then sat Turnip down and handed him a plate. Leo continued laughing, joined by Miguel, and then others. Occasional groans cut into the amusement, indicating others, besides Turnip, carried sore heads.

Tankersley mounted and rode toward the herd. He dropped his reins and made motions of playing an imaginary fiddle. He tilted his face skyward and roared in his loudest voice.

> **Oh I'm ragged and tattered**
> **And grubby I know,**
> **But you orta see the**
> **Bloomers on Mattie Marlow.**
> **Oh, Turnip, my champion,**
> **Turnip, my love,**
> **The black eye don't matter,**
> **The bloody nose's just a boar,**
> **But why'd the son-of-a-bitch**
> **Call me a bawdy-house whore?**

Marcus grinned at the men and turned, saying: "Come on Rawls, Ramón, let's go see can we find us one Mister J. H. McCoy."

Chapter Twenty

"How's thirteen dollars a head sound?" McCoy's words flowed around the thick cigar bobbing up and down in his mouth. His eyes moved slowly from Rawls, past Ramón, and settled on Marcus. They sat in the buyer's office.

Rawls had the numbers worked out now. Last night he'd borrowed the barber's pencil and found numbers worked easier when soothed by a tub of bath water. He'd mustered enough spit and wrapping paper to extend the totals. He'd herded them all the way from five to twenty dollars a head. Thirteen meant roughly $6,000 in his pockets. It was all the money in the world. His head reeled. Bess would do cartwheels.

Marcus's words grated like a mouthful of sand. "Well, I dunno. Met a fellow on the trail who said good stuff might go as high as fifteen or twenty dollars. What do you think, boys?" He looked at Ramón.

"Fifteen ees better than thirteen, but a chick that walks ees better than an egg that smells," Ramón said.

McCoy's eyes brightened, but his face remained expressionless.

Rawls had visions of Marcus swinging by his neck from a tree limb with his foot sticking from his mouth. *Don't mess around, you fool,* he thought. He did his best to hide his emotions. "If we make a deal," he asked, "how do you pay off, Mister McCoy?"

"Gold eagles, singles and doubles . . . half when the cattle are counted and aboard the train, the other half will come in on the weekly in three days."

Rawls forced himself to concentrate on the cigarette he worked at. He smoothed the tobacco without spilling a grain. Three days—he could be on his way to Texas in three days.

"Fifteen!" Marcus rolled out, part statement, part question.

It didn't work. "Mister Slaton, there's another herd three days back of you. They'll fill the next cars as well as yours. I'd like to do business with you boys, but thirteen's as high as I go. By the way, that's conditional on two men, you or Rawls here and another, riding them cars to Chicago. We gotta have somebody dependable to keep those animals prodded up on their feet. First load out we lost ten percent . . . trampled. 'Course, the two going north get free fare and meals. Whoever goes, their responsibility ends when Rankin signs the papers at the Chicago yards."

Shit, Rawls thought, *with the thirst Marcus has built, there's no chance of dragging him out of sight of a saloon for a week. Chicago . . . hell-fire . . . I could be halfway to the Grove before I get back here from Chicago. Damn!*

"OK, thirteen it is then," Marcus agreed. "Let's count cattle. Rawls, looks like you and Turnip are heading for the city."

"You're the one likes towns," Rawls reminded Marcus. "I don't see no broke legs on your carcass. Maybe you'd be happier in Chicago than me."

Marcus stood and shook hands with McCoy, and responded to Rawls: "No sir-ee. You made me stay in charge to the bitter end, Little Brother, remember. Besides, I'm a family man. I gotta get back to Texas. You better tell Turnip."

Rawls shook hands with McCoy. "When does the train pull out?"

162

"Soon as you've loaded them. You're the one going?"

"Looks like . . . me and a fellow named Turnip will see them there. Guess, it's a far piece, ain't it?"

McCoy nodded. "I'll get the papers ready. We'll count them in the pens, soon as you get 'em shut in."

Rawls stepped outside to a beaming Marcus and Ramón.

"How's being rich feel?" Marcus poked at Rawls's ribs.

Rawls dodged the jab and put one arm around Ramón's shoulder and the other over his brother's. "By God, we did it!"

The day moved like a whirlwind. The next hours spun by while they penned and counted the herd. Next they crowded them up the chutes and into the waiting rail cars. After that, Rawls and Turnip had another hour to get their pay, buy what they needed, and throw their war bags aboard the train's caboose. McCoy showed them the long poles tied to the slated cars to be used for punching downed stock through the panels.

"The train will stop often enough to take on water," McCoy explained. "That'll give you a chance to work them lazy ones up. You may want to walk the top of them cars and take a peek down inside on some of them long stretches. But these trains are dangerous, so be careful. Good cowboys're about as scarce as beef."

McCoy shook hands with Turnip and Rawls. "So long, boys. Rawls, I'll see your brother has the balance paid to him before you get back. You boys ain't hauling all that coin with you, are you?"

"I bought these duds and asked Marcus to keep the rest of mine," Turnip said.

"Nope," Rawls added. "Most of mine from that first draw is hid in a safe place. When the rest comes in, Marcus'll ask you to hold onto my part of it."

"That's good," McCoy said, and again warned them: "Watch yourselves in Chicago. You see anybody too friendly, look out. Here's your tickets and bill of lading."

Four days later, they stood in front of a three-story frame structure in Chicago. It carried the name Stockman's Parlor. Below the name the sign read: **Two-Bit Bunks.** The clerk took their money before leading them up narrow stairs to a second floor lined with three rows of single beds. They dropped off their bedrolls and sauntered back to the streets.

Turnip pulled out his train ticket and checked the departure time. It had become a ritual. "Nine-thirty tomorrow morning," he said, then pointed at nearby saloon doors. "Buy you a drink."

"If you're gonna be here a while, I think I'll check this burg out a little."

"If I can find a game of seven card draw, think I'll be good."

As Rawls proceeded down a number of streets, he began bumping elbows and dodging people, like a mule hunting cover, as the sidewalks filled. The street sign read: **Michigan Avenue.** He had gone no more than a few steps when a small boy tugged at his sleeve. The kid's tangled red hair fell over his eyes. It was apparent that he wasted little time on soap and water. He carried a canvas sack and a three-sectioned board hinged in two places. The urchin's face wore an expression of contempt as if judging Rawls equal to the street matter one stepped over. "Bub, I'll shine them boots fer a three-cent piece," he said.

Rawls carried two of the suggested coin in his pocket. "Whereabouts?"

The kid pointed to the sidewalk near the wall. An empty vendor's pushcart rested nearby. It protected a space of four or five feet from traffic.

Rawls moved to the wall, leaned against the brick. He raised his pants leg from his right boot and placed his foot on the rest the boy had fashioned from the hinged boards. He watched the kid's nose wrinkle as he pulled out a knife to scrape away remnants from the stockyards.

The kid took a rag and a container of polish from his sack. He patted the boots and replaced the contempt on his face with an angelic smile. "Double or nothing says I can tell you the date and where you got these rascals."

The boy's eyes reminded Rawls of Marcus when his big brother drew to an inside straight. "Where?" He fingered the three-cent piece.

"You got 'em right here on Michigan Avenue, Chicago, and the date is September Thirteenth, Eighteen Sixty-Seven. That's where and when you got 'em, now."

Rawls remembered that upon delivery Rankin had dated the papers the 13th. The fact that he had bought the boots as well as a new hat in Abilene mattered not. The kid had him cold. He'd been suckered. He laughed and fished out two coins and handed them to the boy. "Make sure you do a good job, bub."

Rawls's attention was attracted to a number of passengers arriving and departing in elegant coaches across the street. The conveyances delivered and picked up beautifully dressed ladies. Nearby an awning topped a carpeted walkway that extended from the street to a recessed doorway. A brightly uniformed doorman assisted the ladies from and into their carriages. When free of that duty, the doorman stood at attention at the awning's mouth. The canvas carried the words **The Parisian.**

The splendor of the women's dresses brought Bess's words back from that long ago evening when she had dropped

165

her guard and spoke of an adolescent fascination with elegant ladies, and a certain bonnet.

Rawls glanced at his boots and the boy's bobbing head. "Good enough, son. I gotta go."

He dodged a number of draft animals to cross the street, then stood beneath the awning. A huge display window wrapped around the recessed entryway. Dresses draped lifelike over full-figured, but headless, wooden and wire hangers. Soft-looking material—silk, satin, or velvet—covered little steps and raised areas of the floor. Shoes and handbags rested upon the fabric, and its obvious softness reminded him of Lilly's room above Snort's bar. Rawls sniffed the air, anticipating the fragrance he'd found so overpowering in the upstairs room where Lilly plied her business. Then an object in the back of the display caught his eye. *What had Bess said when she spoke of the bonnet?* Rawls thought. *"Time stood still" . . . ? No. She said . . . "There are moments when time stops." Well, them people on that street are still bouncing along, but that bonnet is a dead ringer for what she described that evening. The sash, the bow, the ruffles, they're all there. The color . . . is it the same? Had she said a deep blue velvet or green? This one was blue. The ribbon yellow.* He could see it on her and that soft look in her eyes. He rushed for the door.

A hand grabbed his shoulder. "Sir, you can't go in there."

Rawls turned and looked up. Above his face the doorman's broad features blocked the sun. "Why not? I got money," Rawls said.

"You can't pack any gun in there, buster. This is a genteel place . . . a place for ladies."

Rawls squirmed. The man's strong fingers were thorns of pain. His arm was separating from his shoulder. At least, it felt that way. "What can I do with it? I need to buy a . . . buy something."

"I'll hold it for you till your business is done."

"How do I know you'll be here when I come back?"

"You gotta trust me. I work here."

Rawls shoved his elbow upward and jerked his shoulder free. He offered the pistol and watched the huge man tuck it in his waistband. The man opened the door to the store. Rawls peered inside. A thin lady with eyes buried in deep shadows and enough hair to bale stared back. She held a long pin in her mouth, and a pencil rested over her ear. She talked through clamped teeth.

"May I help you?"

Rawls opened the door a little wider. "This gent out here work with you folks?" He motioned with his thumb at the doorman. "Is it safe to leave my stuff with him?"

The lady took the hairpin from her mouth. "Who, Henry? Why, yes, of course. Your property is safe with Mister Edwards. Won't you come in?'

Rawls smiled at Henry, then eased inside. "You got a lady's bonnet . . . there in the window . . . with yellow ribbons. I'll take it."

The woman opened a panel that revealed the interior of the window display. She picked up the bonnet, gently, like one might a baby or, perhaps, a featherless bird. "This one?"

Rawls nodded.

The clerk carried the bonnet behind the counter, bent, then straightened holding a large, round, brown and yellow hatbox. Blue bordered the lid of the box. Large oval blobs of the same color dotted the brown and yellow sides.

"That'll be one seventy-six, please."

"A dollar seventy-six cents?"

The woman stopped tying the string. "One *hundred* and seventy-six . . . dollars, sir." The lady straightened her shoulders, seemed to grow in height. "I'll have you know this is a

167

De Maupassant, popularized by Madam Bovary. There are only three in the United States. We have two. Is the price a problem?"

"No, no, that's all right," he answered. Maybe he should have studied Marcus's bargaining efforts more. The beeves seemed cheap in this place. "It's just that I've been on the train the last week. My ears are sort of dim. In other words, I can have two, if I want?"

"You want two?"

"No, guess one will do it. Just a minute." Rawls pulled a knotted neckerchief from his inside coat pocket. He undid the knot and counted out nine double eagles.

The lady tied the string around the box after handing him his change.

He pocketed the money, picked up the box, and walked to the door. He opened the door, but turned back at the clerk to ask: "How many of them Pie Saints you say this was?"

The lady's chalky face blushed ever so slightly. She shook her head. Her mouth opened as though to speak, then closed. She held up three fingers and smiled.

Rawls thought it a sort of weak smile as Henry handed him his pistol. He took the revolver, slapped the big man on the back, and flipped him a quarter. He'd gotten loose with his money the last hour. He'd never done that before. He'd never floated on air before, either, but he barely touched earth as he crossed the street. That bonnet fit the description Bess had painted that night on the porch to a T. She would be one happy gal!

Later, with the hatbox under his arm, Rawls studied the framework of the bridge he'd crossed earlier. He whistled as he walked, made an effort to meet eyes with folks, and touched his hat brim to Yankees of all descriptions. *This Chicago has a lot going for it,* he thought to himself. These people had energy, and that breeze from the lake just spurred the blood. This place would stay penned in his memory. Here he'd found the answer to at least a part of Bess's dream. Money in his pocket, a bonnet for the prettiest girl in Texas— it had been a good trip. Even Marcus had pulled his weight.

Marcus! The truth dawned on Rawls. What the hell was wrong with him? He couldn't give Bess that bonnet. Husbands bought presents for their wives, not brothers-in-law. Rawls set the hatbox on the walkway between his feet and leaned on the bridge's railing. He wanted a smoke, but hadn't the energy to build one. Reality drained him. Somehow he'd drifted out of himself. He'd turned into a cowardly, nest-robbing crow. The hell of it was, he had justified what he had done by blaming Marcus for not doing right. You'd think, by now, he'd have it in his head that Bess wasn't his.

Below, water rippled around bridge supports. Its gentle murmur staged a background for the street's excited voices and the energy that faded into a moody din of busy uncaring. He'd give the bonnet to Marcus, make him swear to take full credit for the idea.

He hurried to meet up with Turnip, storing his hatbox at the flophouse and paying the caretaker four bits to guard it. He retraced his steps to the saloon and watched Turnip play a couple of hands of poker. Two drinks later, he roused himself enough to look around. He bought a third drink and noticed double doors leading to an adjoining room. Above the doors a sign read: **Hurdy-Gurdy Girls.** After that, watching poker seemed pretty slow entertainment, especially with those big doors to the other room opening and that music blasting through the place. He moved toward the doors.

Rawls spent the next hours puzzling over the energy of the dancing girls. Whiskey failed to solve the puzzle. Sometime after midnight, he and Turnip helped each other to the flophouse. A flickering oil lamp beckoned them toward the stairs.

Rawls woke to gray rumors of dawn framed by the window at the end of the long room. Turnip's snores mixed with dozens of others. When Rawls nudged him, he woke, blinked, and began dressing with closed eyes. A little man, tracked by untold years, watched them. The man sat three bunks away with a large valise near his feet. He wore buckled shoes, a tie, and a black derby hat.

Rawls completed his dressing with a final tug at his boots. Their shine was the only bright thing about the morning. That boy did good work.

The man smiled. "You waddies strayed a bit, ain't you?"

Turnip held his head with both hands. Rawls looked at the man, sensed friendliness, and replied: "Yeah, but I thought we'd hid our tracks. Been holding our cards close to our chest. What gave us away?"

The little man chuckled. "Son, it's plain you two ain't used to no roof. First thing you covered was your head. Genteel folks, spoiled by soft living, come out of the blankets and dress bottom up. Cow nurses and wolf hunters, used to spending their days under a leaky sky, come off the bed ground and cover their head first thing before moving down. I'd say Kansas, maybe even Texas."

Rawls stuck out his hand. "You got good eyes, mister. Name's Slaton. Texas it is. The big guy over there doing all the whining is Turnip. What do you sell?"

"Laces, lotions, implements to clothes! Dudley Warner's the name. Glad to meetcha, Slaton . . . Turnip. How do Texans get to Chicago?"

"Howdy," Turnip mumbled, then asked: "Where's a man wash this town off his face?"

"Basin and water pitcher's on the back porch. You boys come upriver to Saint Louis?"

"No, Texas beef is driving to Abilene. Railhead is out there."

"You don't say. Texas to Kansas, huh? Believe I'll head for Abilene."

Rawls looked at light coming through the window. "That's where we're pointing in a couple of hours."

The man stood, picked up his valise. "See you on board."

Chapter Twenty-One

Rawls, Turnip, and Dudley Warner, the salesman from the flophouse, occupied a bench on the St. Louis depot platform. The sun shortened the evening shade, moved it closer to their feet. Somewhere across that river was Abilene. Two hours earlier, they had bid farewell to the seats they'd occupied across Illinois. Bess's hatbox rested on the wooden floor.

"So, Rawls, from that box you're toting, I suppose you have a missus back in Texas."

Rawls squinted into the distance, answering—"Nope, single is all I've known. My brother asked me to get his wife something different, thought Chicago might be the place."—and lying like that old river gnawing at the banks, spreading all the time.

"Looks like a hat."

"Bonnet . . . from France."

"Marcus, that's his brother, he's a lucky man," Turnip commented while whittling a small piece of pine.

"I carry a line from Boston. Mind showing her to me?" Dudley asked.

Rawls hesitated. "You know about Paris stuff, do you? Well, there's something bothering me. Come to think of it . . . I'd like for you to look at this thing. Maybe tell me, if it's naughty. Woman had it some madam wore 'em."

"I doubt it's ugly that way, Rawls. There are other kinds of madams."

"Good!" Rawls breathed the word with gusto.

"Go on, untie it. I'd like to see it, too," Turnip added.

"We got another hour to kill."

Funny how, in a way, he didn't want these guys gawking at Bess's bonnet. He'd rather even Marcus didn't see it. Might as well show it, though. He had to get a grip sometime. He slowly lifted the box and untied the string. The lip of the lid fit tightly, required use of his fingernails.

"That's a pretty box," Turnip offered. Dudley nodded.

Rawls folded back thin white paper. A crumpled newspaper lay beneath. Something wasn't right! That woman hadn't used newspaper. The buzz of a thousand rattlers sounded. He lifted the paper and tore at it. A raggedy cut-off leg of red long handles fell in his lap. The knee area was frayed and ripped.

"Son-of-a-bitch!" Rawls hollered.

"You been robbed." Genuine concern rode Turnip's voice. "Sure as my name's Weathersby, you been robbed."

Dudley wagged his head. "Welcome to the Chicago switch, young man."

"That damned, flophouse clerk!" Rawls hissed. He stood, kicked the hatbox, then followed its flight across the platform and picked it up. He entered the depot and bought a round trip ticket back to Chicago. The man handed him change, then looked at the crushed hatbox and pointed at a wooden trash barrel nearby. Rawls deposited the box and returned to the bench.

"Tell them in Abilene, I'll be along in a few days."

"You going back to Chicago?" Turnip nodded knowingly. "Need help?"

Rawls shook his head.

"He won't be there," Dudley said. "Knew he was leaving or he'd 'a' been afraid to pull it off."

"Probably right, but, hell, the woman said she had two of them Pie Saints."

Rawls watched the Abilene train pull out, then nearly chewed off the edge of his lip awaiting his return connection. Aboard the coach, he slouched, deep in his chair, and pulled his loneliness around him like a cloak. He tipped his hat, low over his eyes. He'd miss Turnip's company on the long trek back to Texas. But then, who knew? If Annie didn't run out of firewood, the chef of Texas turnips might still be there when he showed up.

The morning after his arrival, Henry, the doorman, stuck his hand out for the six-shooter when Rawls approached. The remaining bonnet was green velvet, instead of blue, and it was two dollars higher. The shadow-faced woman with bales of hair had smiled sweetly at him when he entered. Strange, she seemed much friendlier. Women beat all.

"Don't tell me you want the other one?" she said.

"Yes'um," he answered.

The woman retrieved the bonnet from the display case and twirled it on the tips of her fingers while returning. She continued to smile. As limber as a willow in high wind, she walked to his side of the counter. She placed the bonnet in the box. It was probably an accident, but her hip sort of nestled there against his and moved ever so slightly. She tied the string around the lid.

"Just how many ladies you buying for, honey?" she asked.

"Just the one." Rawls sighed. "She's partial to Pie Saints, 'specially them threes." He paid and moved for the door.

" 'Bye, dear. Come again," the saleswoman cooed.

Outside, Rawls took his six-gun from Henry. He crossed the street, thinking of the weight of advice he'd gathered over the years concerning the danger of the crosscurrents of female behavior. An amount of wariness around that one would probably be good. It must be the money, he decided.

$354 didn't just ride by every week, he bet.

Walking, with plenty of time before the train left, something tugged at his sleeve. He looked down.

The tear-streaked face of the shine boy looked up at him. He had a cut lip and a swollen eye. "Hey, Boots, mind if I walk a ways wif yuh?"

"Sure, always good for company." Rawls glanced away from the boy's face, tried to show no concern. He felt a small hand wiggling into his and opened his fingers and gripped the hand firmly. "Changing pastures?"

"Thought I'd move down a block or two. Money's drying up this side of the river." The boy shifted his sack.

"Failed to get your handle the other day, bub. What do they call you?"

"Deuce." The boy glanced quickly behind and to the right.

"That's it . . . just Deuce?" Rawls spotted four boys shadowing them on the other side of the street.

"Well, Father Ruebin had it on the register as Horatio Galliger, but here, on the street, Deuce sort of does it. Think it's that double or nothing line."

"I see. Deuce, I'm Rawls. That bunch over there account for that eye? They put you to looking for new pickings?"

"Yeah, I'm tired of this neighborhood, anyway. Where you from, Boots?"

"Texas."

"What's that?"

"Where I hail from. It's a place, like Illinois."

"That mean you're new here?"

"Was when you shined them boots. I'm getting the hang of her, though."

"I'll show you around some. It's OK, I won't charge yuh, just sort of hang around, show you the ropes till morning."

They walked in silence for a couple of blocks. Rawls stopped and looked in all directions. Only adults filled the streets.

"Deuce, how old are you?"

"Thirteen, why?"

"How old?"

"Well, eleven. Least, I think eleven."

"You on your own?"

"Yep, lone as a kid left on a doorstep can get."

Rawls spit. It was something to do. Nothing came out, just dry air and acres of hurt. He turned and put a hand on each of Deuce's shoulders. "Boy, I ain't gonna be here tonight. I'm catching the twelve o'clock to Saint Louis. But, I sure need company till then."

An idea seemed to be swirling around in Deuce's head. "I'm sorry, Boots," he said excitedly. "Can't help you after all." He spun on his heels and hit a run in two steps. He hollered over his shoulder: "Some things I got to gather!" He dodged a pushcart and flew around a corner.

Rawls shoved the hatbox tighter under his elbow and tilted to the left while making a cigarette. He lit up, then scratched his head. Smoke curled around him. He stared down the crowded but now lonely street. He sighed.

Halfway across Illinois, the noon train to St. Louis stopped for water. Rawls stepped to the ground to stretch. He raised a foot, one at a time, and shook each pant leg down. He tucked in his shirt, yawned, then spread his arms heavenward.

"Don't stray off. We'll be under way in a minute," said a passing railroad man in a flat-topped cap. He continued on to the office.

Rawls rocked on his heels.

"*P-s-s-t*, Boots, is that you?" a voice hissed.

Rawls looked both ways, up and down the track, then turned and looked up the street behind him.

"Under here, I'm under here. Anybody around?" A wad of clothing partially covered and tied in a red bandanna fell to the cinders and cross-ties of the roadbed.

"Nobody here, but me," Rawls answered, bending low enough to see under the train. "What are you doing down there?"

"Getting out of down here, that's what." Deuce crawled out from beneath the train, dusted himself off, and pushed his belongings clear of the rails with a toe. "I ain't never doing that again. Never!"

"What are you doing under there? Ain't there better places?"

"Them bulls are too lazy to bend over to find you there. They'll whack you, if they find you." Deuce picked up his things and turned to walk away.

"Where're you going?" Rawls asked.

"Down the track . . . to that flat car . . . going to find somewhere I can't fall off."

"And after that?"

"Texas, I guess. That where you're going?"

"That's the thought," Rawls answered, trying to figure out what to do. "Tell you what. You come with me. We'll talk to that railroad man with the flat-crowned cap. You keep climbing around on this thing, we're liable to soak you up with a rag."

Chapter Twenty-Two

Deuce rubbed sleep from his eyes. Rawls placed his bedroll and the hatbox on the bench of the St. Louis depot. It was here he'd first discovered the theft of Bess's bonnet.

Earlier, on the train, a stout lady passenger had crocheted rapidly, pretending not to be eavesdropping while Rawls settled Deuce's fare to St. Louis. Her movements had slowed when Deuce had begun arguing that Abilene, not Chicago, should be his destination. At a lull in the argument, the lady had pulled two boiled eggs and a piece of cornbread from a basket beneath her seat, and offered them to Deuce.

Sight of the food had brought a sparkle to the boy's eyes, but her reference to him as "sonny boy" had dulled the shine. Nevertheless, the food had vanished quickly, and then Deuce had leaned back and gone to sleep.

Rawls's lap, for the first time in his life, served as a pillow. His resolve to return his new friend to Chicago was weakening as the boy slept. Still the question loomed as big as life, as unstoppable as that river—what was he going to do with this boy?

Deuce stretched as he woke, shifting his curled-up body.

"Pardner," Rawls began, turning the boy's shoulders so he could look him in the face, "that Abilene ain't much of a place. I bet a feller'd starve to death there, shining boots. They mostly wear 'em out with the dust and cow . . . cow stuff on 'em." He noticed the kid's bruised eye had blackened considerably over the last hours.

"You ain't staying in Abilene, are you?" Deuce asked.

"Naw, I'm Texas bound, fast as good horseflesh can make it."

"I can ride. Old man Snelson has the garbage route. When I was a kid, he let me poke along with him . . . sitting behind the hames on old Nell."

"Outgrew that, did you?"

Deuce stared after a departing train. "Outgrew everything back there. Think I'll be a cattle drover like you. I wanna go to Texas."

"Boy, I ain't fixed up for no kid. Besides, I got bad manners."

The kid jumped up and stomped to the door of the depot. Holding the knob, he turned, yelling: "You said you'd help pay my way back!" His voice was brittle, his chin quivered.

Rawls followed slowly. What could he do? An eleven-year-old needed a mother not a saddle tramp. What would Bess think?

Deuce marched up to the ticket counter, his eyes almost level with the top of the counter. He reached and gripped its edge, telling the trainman: "That gent"—he hooked his thumb backward—"says he's good for a one-way back to Chicago. He's probably got a saddle in soak somewheres."

The ticket man's eye caught Rawls's. "One way to Chicago for a less than twelve-year-old?" The statement came out as a question.

"How much would that be?" Rawls asked.

"Two dollars, eighty-six cents," the man answered, studying Rawls's face. "Didn't you turn around and go back without ever leaving that platform a couple of days ago?"

Rawls nodded. "I did. We're looking at both ends of them bridges. Give him his ticket."

Deuce took his ticket and whirled and headed for the door. Rawls thought he caught a tremor in those, otherwise, stiff shoulders. Outside, the air had warmed, hung heavily with moisture. Trees had dulled, lost their summer lushness, had yet to gain fall's rich colors. The in-between season matched his mood.

Deuce slowed and turned to face him. "I'll tell you one thing, Boots. I wouldn't've been no damn' bother to yuh."

Dammit to hell! Rawls thought. A dirty-mouthed eleven-year-old. He stared back at the bright eyes shining at him. "Know you gamble, do you chew tobacco?"

"No."

"Smoke."

"Some."

"Like girls."

"Hate 'em."

"If I take you to Texas, there's a lady there. Would you do exactly as she says, till you're sixteen . . . on most things reasonable, that is?"

"Yes, sir."

"C'mon. Give me that ticket." They returned to the counter.

Rawls waved the ticket at the man. "If I give you this back, how much boot to make out another for this kid to Abilene?"

The clerk looked from Rawls to the boy, saw the youth's grin spreading. He glanced back at Rawls and reached for the ticket. "Only another dollar and. . . ." He stopped and gazed at Rawls. "Aw, hell, we'll just call her even, cowboy." He smiled.

At the door, Deuce turned, raised his right hand, touched the tips of his fingers to his forehead, then flipped his palm outward in a salute to the clerk and winked.

"Give 'em hell, buster," the clerk said, grinning back, wondering what the wife had cooking for supper.

Deuce caught up on his sleep crossing Kansas. Each turn of the train's wheels strengthened Rawls's belief he'd been right in agreeing to bring the boy along. Bess would be pleased, and Marcus liked kids. It wasn't the same as it would have been a month or two back. They had a little money now, as a matter-of-fact a lot of money. There'd be a place for the kid at the ranch. Sight of Abilene's new buildings pulled him from his thoughts.

Deuce leaned out the window behind him. "Now that we're here, what we do first?"

"Find somewhere to borrow a shovel," Rawls replied. "The livery has three of my horses. In fact, maybe we can get a shovel at the stables."

"Why do we want a shovel?" The kid's head dropped back inside.

Rawls tossed the boy's bandanna-wrapped clothes at him. "You ask a lot of questions."

The train hissed and screeched its way to a halt near a partially constructed depot. The last blast of its whistle cleared the nearest hitch rack of two horses. Deuce laughed at the cowboy who ran out of a building, shaking his fist at the departing animals. He ducked when the man turned and pointed a revolver in the train's direction. A companion grabbed the man before he pulled the trigger.

Deuce's disappointment showed. "You're right about this place. Looks like cows're the only thing could scrounge a living here."

At the livery stomp lot, Rawls's three horses stood apart from the balance of the herd. "There they are." He pointed. "Looks like they don't trust the rest of that bunch yet."

"You got smart horses," Deuce said.

Satisfied his animals had been well cared for, Rawls borrowed a shovel from the stableman, and then looked around for a spot to leave his bedroll.

"You want, just drop her on that hay in the corner," suggested the hostler. "Probably'll end up sleeping there tonight, anyway."

Rawls tied a string around the hatbox and hung it from a rafter, out of sight, behind the hay.

Deuce walked by Rawls's side through the town. That was good. The kid had manly ways. A lot of boys sort of tagged behind, but not this one. The town's buildings behind them, fresh mounds of dirt appeared ahead. At their approach, a number of small animals vanished underground.

Deuce stopped. The shovel rested on his shoulder. "What are they . . . rats?"

The colony had grown during Rawls's trip to Chicago. "They're called prairie dogs," Rawls explained, reaching for the shovel. "Watch your step. There're rattlers all around. Here they're close to dinner, and those holes make a good place to get out of the sun." Rawls stepped around a number of burrows toward the center of the earthen mounds.

Deuce skipped gingerly, stopped, and, balancing on one foot, examined a mound, leaning toward its outer edge. "If they's snakes out here, why are we? We ain't gonna catch and cook a batch of these little dogs are we? You out of money? I got a dollar and six bits."

"No, ain't that hungry yet." Rawls found the hole he had been looking for and kicked the bent horseshoe to one side. "Here we are," he announced, then continued on about prairie dogs: "They ain't that tasty, you know." He sank the shovel in the dirt, enlarging the opening. "I don't like them that good."

"What are they good for then? What're we doing out here?"

182

"They're good bankers. . . ." The *buzz,* even though expected, jolted Rawls's nerves. His reflexes carried him backward.

Deuce danced back and forth near the colony's perimeter, yelling: "Dammit, Boots! Let's go back to town." Then he stopped bouncing, bent forward, his hands on his knees. His black eye stood out like coal on powder snow. The rattler buzzed again, then was joined by another. "You gonna get your ass bit," Deuce warned Rawls.

"Boy, if you're going to Texas, you gonna have to clean up that dirty mouth."

"I will, but what the hell you doing in them holes? C'mon!"

"Told you, I got banking to do. Just got to get rid of the guards first." Rawls jabbed the blade of the shovel at a diamondback slithering from a nearby hole. The shovel severed all but a fragment of the reptile's body inches behind the triangular head. Its body coiled, rattled, twisted, and continued to thrash about for some time.

Deuce jumped up and down. "I'm going!" he yelled.

The rattling sound inside the hole Rawls had opened stopped. Rawls tossed the dying snake several yards away with the shovel, then returned to his digging.

"You about ready?" Deuce yelled.

"Just a minute."

Several inches down, the burrow turned parallel to the surface and Rawls found his double eagles. He counted them once and a second time before he was satisfied they were all there, then he stuffed them in both of his pockets. He shouldered the shovel, dodged holes to the edge of the colony, and walked up to the boy.

"You had money hid in them holes?" Deuce said, adding: "Let me borrow that shovel."

Rawls laughed. "That's all. There're ain't no more."

"You sure?"

"Here." Rawls handed him one of the heavy gold coins.

Deuce rubbed dirt from it with his thumb and finger, then bit it. He removed the coin from his mouth and grinned. "She's real, all right. Think I'm gonna like working wif you. They any more of them dog towns between here and Texas?"

"No, but see that little building with all them fresh planks on her? Well, there's a gent over there, name of Joseph H. McCoy. He's supposed to be holding more of this stuff for me."

"He don't use them guards?" Deuce stuck the coin in Rawls's pocket.

"No, he's got a safe."

"OK."

Chapter Twenty-Three

Rawls knocked on McCoy's office door.

"Who's there?"

"Rawls Slaton."

Footsteps sounded. A moment later the door opened. "Rawls, come in. Saw Turnip when he rolled in, and he said you'd been delayed." McCoy's eyes traveled down to Deuce. Recognition flashed in his eyes. A smile lifted his mouth. "Hey, bub!" he said. "Did you get him to double or nothing?" He tilted his head toward Rawls, his grin showing teeth. "Y'all sit."

"First I did," Deuce admitted. "We're kind of partners now."

"You two know each other?" Rawls asked as he pulled up a chair.

"Bub, here, gives me a shine every time I go to Chicago. I don't gamble with him, though. You two running together?"

"We sort of hooked double for a while," Rawls confirmed. "He looks out for me, like a brother. Speaking of . . . did Marcus leave something with you for me?"

McCoy's face clouded. He became visibly uncomfortable, squirming in his chair, and drumming the table with his fingers. "Mister Slaton, I assume you mean money?"

Rawls sensed a storm brewing. Maybe those rattlers were buzzing again. McCoy's features, even his manner, beat out the message. It spelled trouble. He nodded.

"You ain't heard about your brother, then?"

Rawls shook his head, saw Deuce look from him to the

stricken face of the cattle buyer.

"Damn, I didn't want to be the one to tell you. The second half of the payment came in . . . just as planned. I settled up with Marcus that same day. Paid him off in full. He asked if I'd hold your part, saying he'd be back about eight, after he'd paid off the hands and such. He asked would I be here, and I told him I would, but he never came back."

"He never came back?"

"Last I saw of him. Now the rest of this is secondhand. There's one of your men over in that hoosegow. He can tell you this is straight, but you better see him tonight. He's Mexican . . . think they said Miguel . . . don't recall the last name."

"Why tonight?"

"What happened, way I hear it, your brother found a poker game and a bottle. Ain't sure which came first. Anyway, he got the wages paid out, then lost every dime after that."

Rawls slammed his fist on the table top. The noise drowned the sound of bawling cattle.

Deuce left his chair, running for the door.

Rawls reached and grabbed the boy's arm. "Deuce, I'm sorry. It's OK. Nobody's upset with you. It's just my damn' brother. Excuse me. See, you don't ever want to get like me."

"It's OK, Boots. I been mad before."

McCoy stood. "Slaton, that ain't the worst."

"How could he do that?" Rawls lamented. "I ain't sure you can top that."

"Rawls, the next day he broke one of your men's leg with a branding iron, then. . . ."

"Which one?"

"Said his name was Leo. They had a hell of a fight. Leo had him beat, till he grabbed that iron. Of course, your brother was still hitting the panther juice. The following day, he and this Miguel stopped the overland stage to Denver. There's some question as to whether they held it up or just stopped it and took back what they lost from one of the passengers. Either way a guard died."

Rawls sat, his face buried in his hands. *Damned bawling cattle.* He pressed his fingers against his ears, trying to close out the sound. He sat for a moment, his eyes closed. A small hand gripped his shoulder.

"Where's Leo?" Rawls asked McCoy.

The hand relaxed, moved away.

"The barber tied splints on his leg, and they loaded him on the train to Kansas City."

"And Miguel, what about Miguel? You said something about tonight."

"He's gonna hang come morning," McCoy replied soberly.

Rawls stood, feeling like he'd been punched in the stomach. "Where's that jail?" he said.

"Marshal's got a desk in the barber shop. When he's in town, that's his headquarters. Jail's a little rock building out behind. It's across the alley. There's a guard."

Rawls heard the door close behind Deuce.

"Mister Slaton," McCoy said, "I got a telegram from Rankin in Chicago. You boys did a good job keeping them cattle on their feet. They figured less than two percent loss." He rose, stuck out his hand. "It's been a pleasure. You bring more cattle this way, we'll do it again."

Rawls shook the buyer's hand, muttering: "Thanks."

McCoy looked at his feet, started to say something, then scratched his head. "You don't mind my sticking my nose in, I'd like to tell you something. You ain't responsible for that brother of yours. Son, I'm afraid he soured." He paused before he added: "And that boy out there, I'm glad

187

you got him out of Chicago."

"Yeah, me, too," Rawls responded.

Outside, Rawls found Deuce watching two cowboys ride toward the saloon. "What am I gonna ride to Texas?" he asked.

Anger and pain mixed inside Rawls, pounding in his head and boiling in his stomach. He wanted to cuss and kick things. All the work, all the hopes washed away in a shot of rotgut and the turn of a card. Neighbors had placed their trust in the Slatons, and that worthless, fiddle-footed, good-for-nothing brother of his had dallied it all away.

Again a question: "Am I gonna ride one of them three at the livery?"

"What?" The present gained his attention as they walked down the street along the building's lengthening shadows. "How's that?"

"To Texas, what am I gonna ride?"

All that Rawls could think about Deuce was that the boy had had enough trouble in his short life. He needed to be spared as much of this as possible. "That red roan's good," he stated. "He'll do for starters, but we'll pick you up a second before we leave tomorrow."

"Tomorrow? We're going tomorrow?"

"Come first light," Rawls said, noticing the barbershop door hung ajar. Rawls angled toward the alley behind it. "Why don't you wait here till I see this man." He looked around. "There on that bench is a good place." He pointed. "Soon as I have this talk, you and I'll see what this burg offers in the way of food."

"I'd rather go. He the one they're gonna hang?"

Rawls pointed a second time. "Wait over there. I won't be long."

Deuce ducked his head, put his hands in his pockets,

kicking dust as he moved to the bench.

A bewhiskered, scarecrow figure of a man leaned in a ladder-back chair against the front of the rock jail. A Spencer carbine lay across his lap. At sight of Rawls, he pointed the weapon at him. "You're about close enough, pilgrim," he said.

Rawls agreed. Either the man's body, his greasy buckskin garments, or the slop jar sitting nearby sent an odor testifying to the wisdom of the advice. Rawls halted and asked: "You got a Texas man in there by the name of Miguel?"

"Don't know if he's Texan or not, just a Mexican thief with a bullet in him. Him and me's gittin' on pretty good, though, but not too cozy. What's your business here?"

"You don't mind, I'd like a few words with him."

"And if I do?"

"Don't think they pay you that good. It'd be a long night, wondering which one of them shadows I'm in." The guard seemed to ponder the truth of the statement while Rawls went on: "Besides, one of the things I wanna ask him is what brand of hootch he wants to suck on till morning. Maybe he'll pass it around . . . y'all being such good friends. They tell me even a man waiting on the gallows hates to drink alone."

"Let me have that pistol," the guard said, standing and sticking out his hand. "You can talk from the doorway."

Rawls eased the six-gun from its holster and handed it over, butt first. He walked to the door and leaned inside. The room was dark with shadows, but slowly his eyes picked out a man's form.

"*Amigo.*" The word came out weak, slightly louder than a whisper. Rawls turned to the guard. "Can't I go inside?"

"This is the best you get. Don't worry, he'll live to hang at sunup."

189

Rawls turned back to the doorway. "Miguel, it's Rawls. You hurt bad?"

"Pretty much. Don' know good hurt. Eet ees my shoulder . . . lots of blood."

"What happened? What can I do?"

The sound of Miguel's labored breathing filled the air before he answered. "That brother of yours, he ess a rooster. Heem and me, we get pretty drunk."

"A damn' fool's what he is," Rawls interjected.

"Maybe so, but we get a fistful of our *dinero* back."

"Your money? Robbing a stage? Way I hear it, your money chased bad cards."

"Thees cards . . . they were mostly held by thees agent . . . of Butterfield . . . thees one we see at the Springs . . . back in Texas."

"You mean Rake Darrow? What was he doing in Kansas?"

"Came in on the train . . . headed for Denver on the stage. What for, I do not know, only that he has *dinero*, lots of eet, especially after he cheated us out of ours. Never saw so many face cards." Coughing seized Miguel. "Damn thees . . . I leak too much blood." Silence followed.

Rake Darrow's cold, hard face drifted across Rawls's mind, slid like a snake, from one dark corner to the next. "I should have killed the son-of-a-bitch at the Grove," he stated.

"You see heem . . . be careful. He ees fast."

"Miguel, you want anything . . . food or something?"

"No, not hungry. Maybe a bottle. You know about to-morrow. *Si*, a bottle. Tequila." Miguel's words came slower. "You find a *padre* . . . you send him. I got lots to get rid of. But no, nothing else." Rawls began building a smoke while coughing racked Miguel's body before he could continue. "*Amigo*, I must tell you, eet ees true we were wrong, but

Darrow . . . you need to know . . . he ees poison. We had eet pulled off clean . . . nobody hurt . . . no hurt to the team. We left money with thees cheater . . . only took what we had lost to heem. Then we let the stage pull away, but thees devil Darrow, he sneak a boot gun out and he fire. The guard, he caught a stray, and die. I caught thees bullet . . . I could not ride. Darrow, he rode to the next station, I guess, and then he come back. He finds me, and he brings me back, belly down, over a horse. That ees when this cough lock up my chest."

"I'm sorry, Miguel," Rawls said. "You're a hell of an *hombre*."

What sounded like a gasp broke the quiet of the darkened jail. "She ees no matter, my friend. You know, in here, I theenk of El Grande Comanchero, how he cussed when we strung heem up. I hate to go in such company. But, no matter, I don' sleep so much anyway. The face of the girl . . . you remember? . . . I keep seeing the face of that leettle girl down at the mesa." Again he paused. "*Si*, Rawls, breeng me tequila, can you find it. And, Rawls, I know you. You want to free me from this place. Even now, you build a plan. You could do eet, maybe, but I cannot ride, not even een a wagon. Eet ees no use." He shifted and groaned, his voice no more than a whisper now. "But get me your knife. You know . . . the long one that folds and you carry een your pocket. I will cheat them yet. I weel not hang. Were that door and guard gone . . . were I free . . . I would sit in the street and die."

Listening to Miguel's weakening voice, Rawls knew there was nothing he could do to save Miguel.

"Rawls, one last theeng," Miguel said. "You weel catch up to Marcus. Tell him, Miguel said eet was a good run. Tell heem, Darrow ees on hees trail . . . headed for Texas." There was a long silence. "And say . . . for me . . . say . . . *adiós*."

Rawls turned, took his pistol, and walked away. He had to

go or embarrass himself. *God, what a dark and dirty place to die!*

In front of the barbershop, he pointed at Deuce, saying—"Just one more minute."—and moved on to a saloon down the street.

Friendliness showed in the guard's eyes at sight of the bottle. Rawls leaned with his back to the makeshift jail's door and scratched the back of his neck. He locked eyes with the guard, handing him the bottle. "I'll be back later," he advised the man. "If that cowboy's sober and you're drunk, I'll kill you. Understand?"

The guard held the bottle up to the light. "Don't worry, we'll work her down together. No need you checking back."

While he was holding the bottle up and talking, the guard had failed to see or hear Rawls toss the knife into the cell where it landed quietly on the dirt floor. Rawls shuddered. The world was coming down around him. Everything in him screamed to take action. But it was hopeless, and there was an orphan kid out there—a kid that had a life before him. Beyond this, he could do no more for Miguel. At least he'd given him a way to avoid the hangman's noose.

Miguel's words came from the dark at his back. *"Gracias, amigo. Vaya con Dios."*

Rawls gave the guard a threatening glance, and headed out of the alley. When he rounded the building, Deuce met him with a grin. "Come on, let's eat," Rawls announced, attempting to shed his dark mood. "Then me and you're mounting up and heading for Texas."

"Tonight?"

"Yeah, I've had enough of Kansas."

"What about my second horse?"

"When we shake that old boy up to get Bess's bonnet, we'll dicker for that hoss then. We'll make camp a few miles south of here."

"Bess . . . so that's her name."

Chapter Twenty-Four

The sign on the first building they passed read: **Butterfield Station—Gainsville, Texas.** The second—**General Merchandise.** Rawls and Deuce knotted their horses' bridle reins in front of the store before they entered. A few minutes later they stepped back outside. Deuce toted a half-gallon metal bucket under his arm. Scrawled across its top was the word **sorghum.** Rawls ate a pickle. It had looked lonely, floating alone in the brine of a gallon crock sitting near the cracker barrel.

A stagecoach blocked the view into the open door of the station. Rake Darrow crossed Rawls's mind. He glanced up and down the street. "Think you can pack that syrup? I'm gonna have a drink. See what the world's doing."

"Sure," Deuce replied happily. "Hey, you know what day it is?"

"No, but that storekeeper likely knows. You ain't going back to that old game . . . back to them Chicago ways, are you?"

"You ain't quick, I will." Deuce moved toward the horses.

Rawls crossed the street and entered the saloon. Inside, two card players sat near a window. He met the bartender's eye, held up two fingers, and said: "Whiskey."

The barman reached for a bottle, opined the days were shortening.

Rawls agreed, then described both Marcus, as well as his gray, asking if he'd been through. "My brother," he explained.

The bartender studied Rawls's face a moment. "Yeah, the

forehead's about the same. Came through about a week ago . . . two of 'em. Said they wuz from Fort Smith. Remember the gray, he'd been pushed hard. They only had one drink. Stopped in the store, and gone before you knew it. Next day the marshal asked about 'im."

"Marshal?" Rawls leaned forward, studying the whiskey's color and allowing the weight of the trail's miles to drain from his elbows to the bar. "Your law got a deputy?"

"We ain't got two of nuthin' but carpetbaggers an' polecats."

Rawls responded to the bartender's questions about the market in Abilene, but made no connection between the questions and his own search for Marcus.

One of the poker players walked to the window and looked out. He spoke loudly over his shoulder: "Hey, Sam, we got a new business starting out here. Looks like a kid setting up to shine boots between here and the station. Saw that in New Orleans once. We're getting civilized."

"Good," the bartender stated, "maybe he'll get some of that stuff raked off before it gets to my bar rail." Sam used the bar rag to brush away a fly.

Rawls lifted his glass toward the picture above the mirror. "To the ladies," he toasted. The liquid burned his throat as he swallowed. He shut his watering eyes.

"Gets better with every drink, don't it?" the bartender said, smiling.

Rawls chuckled, then said: "Notice you got a Butterfield line. Know a division agent name of Darrow . . . Rake Darrow?"

"Who don't? You got peculiar luck tracking folks. He ain't your brother, is he?" The barman answered his own question. "No, he's a son- . . . I'll let others fill in the rest . . . but, anyway, he just came in on that stage. He's over at the station now."

"Thanks," said Rawls, and wheeled for the door. He stopped midway, undecided about what he could do. Much as he thought of Miguel, he couldn't call Darrow out for shooting at two men stopping a stage with guns in hand. It may not have been intended as a hold-up, but the world saw it that way, especially with a dead guard.

He moved to the window, spotted Deuce. The boy's face was looking up at a customer. A disarming smile broke across the boy's face. Rawls didn't have to read his lips to know the spiel. Then Rawls's heart skipped a beat—the customer being offered the double or nothing deal was Rake Darrow. Rawls watched the transaction. The agent nodded his head, turned to a nearby man, and said something. They both laughed. Deuce snapped his cloth. He spoke, pointed at the newly shined boots, then swung his arm to encompass the town. He held out his hand.

Rawls was headed out the door when he saw Darrow's face darken. He exited in time to see Darrow raise his boot and swing it viciously. It landed on the boy's thigh. Deuce fell, rolled, and came to his feet without stopping, while Darrow turned and walked toward the saloon with the other man. He looked over his shoulder once, and waved his fist at Deuce.

At the same moment, across the street a couple came out the general store. The man wore a pistol, and sunlight reflected from a shiny star on his vest. The bulk of the woman with him suggested a weakness for her own skills in the kitchen. One arm was hooked through the man's arm. Her other arm clasped a gallon crock against her body.

As Deuce darted for the syrup bucket, Rawls thought— *The little shit's going to throw that bucket!*—and stepped into the street.

Darrow saw Rawls just as Deuce managed to loosen the sorghum bucket's lid. Darrow stopped as recognition spread

196

across his face. He glanced to his sides and back.

Running for Darrow, Deuce stopped just out of reach, behind the man, and threw the bucket. It sailed toward Darrow's shoulders, dropping short of its target, but the can's contents splashed Darrow's pants and newly polished boots. "You owe me!" Deuce hollered.

Darrow leaped sideways. In the street now, he spun, tripped, and staggered farther from the walkway. With each step, the syrup formed puddles of gooey mud. "You little bastard!" Darrow shouted, and gathered himself to rush the boy.

The man with Darrow bent, laughing and pointing at his friend's feet.

Rawls's voice knifed the stillness: "Darrow, that's enough!"

The agent stopped and wheeled. His eyes locked on Rawls, and the rage left his face. Cold calculation replaced it. Both hands opened and inched closer to the butts of his holstered six-shooters.

Without turning, Rawls knew the saloon had emptied. Someone behind him cleared his throat. The man with Darrow backed against the saloon wall. His hands were spread, digging into the clapboard.

Deuce stared wide-eyed, pale, then bent and pressed the lid onto the bucket.

He shouldn't see this, Rawls thought. He knew what effect violent death could have on a boy, how it could break him. No, there was a bigger need here than Darrow's blood. "Get your stuff, Deuce," he ordered, "hang it on the pack, and take the horses on down the street. I'll be along."

Deuce grabbed his shine sack and trotted away. His footsteps sounded on the wooden sidewalk, moving on behind Rawls.

Rawls kept his eyes on Darrow and waited. Somewhere a crow cawed.

The smile grew on Darrow's face. "Well, I'll be damned, if it ain't the Slaton pup!" he announced to no one in particular. "Kid brother to the dumbest thief to ever heist a stage? You're partners in the shine business now, are you?"

"That's right, Darrow. You might say I'm district agent for the Shoeshine Express. You dunned me once. It's my turn today. Pay up. You owe us two cents. Fork it over or take down your colors and scat." He stepped sideways, arching toward the center of the street.

"Had that pepper swung before you left Abilene?" Darrow taunted, and leaned slightly forward, balanced, ready.

Rawls remained silent.

"I asked had they strung up that frijole yet?" Darrow's lips barely moved.

"No, he was having a drink when I left," Rawls answered softly. "Said I was to give you a message."

"What's that?"

"He said to tell you, you're an egg-sucking whelp of a Yankee whore and he pisses on you and your ancestors, too."

Darrow stiffened right before his hands streaked for his weapons. The revolvers cleared leather. Their barrels swung upward.

Rawls felt the walnut butt of his own weapon. He squeezed the trigger—timed the release of the hammer to the alignment of the sights on Darrow's shirt. The wind fluttered near his ear. From behind, a woman's scream mixed with the roar of the agent's weapons.

Rawls's revolver bucked and thundered loudly. A spot appeared on Darrow's shirt, turned red. The feared Butterfield man took a step, then fell forward. His second pistol fired. A single puff of dust exploded in the street. He coughed, knotted into a ball, and lay still.

The crow squawked rapidly. Down the street, a farmer's wagon rattled to a faster pace.

Behind Rawls a male voice cried: "Leta, are you hurt?"

"For God's sake, Wilbur, do something!" answered a woman's voice. "That drunken agent's trying to kill us."

Rawls moved toward Darrow's downed body, kicked his guns from lifeless hands, and turned in the direction of the general store.

The marshal knelt on a knee beside his struggling wife. He worked to sheath his pistol, missed, then succeeded on the second try. "Are you hit, dear?" he said.

Leta crouched on the boardwalk, trying to rise but slipping on the wet boards. The container lay shattered around her. "I'm OK, but he shot my crock. Them cucumbers will toughen before Henry can get me another one."

Rawls shifted his gaze to the man who had been walking with Darrow. The man still stood against the wall, looking frightened, hands raised with his palms out. "I ain't no part of this," he said.

Deuce arrived at Rawls's side. "Boots, are you OK?"

"My God, Deuce," he chastised the boy, "you could 'a' been shot. Thought you was with the horses."

"I . . . I stepped off. They kept going. I'm after 'em, though." Looking sheepish, Deuce turned and ran.

Rawls spotted the bartender, and approached him, shrugging his head in the direction of the couple on the board walkway. "Guess, that's your law?" he said.

"That's him and his missus. Looks like you're fixing to meet them both. They saw it all, just like we did. So your name's Slaton, huh?" the bartender said. "I heard Darrow call it out."

"Yeah, Slaton . . . Rawls Slaton. Hang my hat out west

from San Antonio, toward the Guadalupe." He shook the bartender's hand, and strode toward the marshal and his wife.

The marshal was using a bandanna to absorb the pickle brine that covered his wife's clothing.

"Ma'am, are you hurt?" Rawls asked.

The lady shook her head, smiled from a pale face.

"Marshal, do we need to talk?" Rawls said.

"Not so far as I'm concerned. Seems you saved me a bullet. Thanks."

Deuce held his roan close for the next hour. Rawls sensed the boy studying him, but, when he glanced in his direction, the boy turned away.

"That bullet hit him, his mouth opened, but he never made a sound," Deuce blurted, tapping his chest and mimicking the bullet's impact. "Was he a gunfighter?"

"Some would say."

"You done that before."

"Kill, you mean?"

Deuce nodded.

"In the war . . . some. Then there was a pack of mean ones that had a young girl captive we had to fight once, when we were getting horses."

"Weren't you scared?"

"I was scared."

"You're quick, though. How'd you get so quick with a pistol?"

"Quick helps, but the trick is being quick and straight. Poppa had a history with pistols, the Rangers, and such. He taught us . . . my brother and me. Seems speed comes natural to the Slaton bunch. Then, later, I honed all that learning with Colonel John Mosby. Rode with his raiders in Virginia.

We fought ahorseback."

There was a little paleness around the boy's mouth. Looked like he had seen enough today.

"Thing for you to remember is, gun play is bad business. The knots tied by guns stay tied," Rawls warned, and added: "Sorry you saw that back there."

"But he wasn't fair, and he bullied a kid."

"It would 'a' cost him two cents to live. He died because he went for a gun. But the same time, you're right, boy, a feller has to mark his own borders. It's a tight call. You stood up for yourself. No fault in that."

They rode in silence a few moments. "Try putting it behind you. I know a lady we're gonna see before long makes a biscuit you wouldn't believe, an' she keeps plum jelly the year around."

"She the one getting that bonnet?"

"That's the one. Tell you something I am proud of, boy, and you ain't gonna believe it."

"What?"

"One time I delivered a baby."

"You didn't do no such thing."

"Did too. It was this lady's . . . my sister-in-law. Well, I almost delivered it . . . the baby was there before I was, but I helped put the finishing touches on her."

"Ugh!"

Rawls laughed. "Not interested, huh?"

Deuce shook his head. "Sister-in-laws . . . they like them chippies? Just have to spend money on them."

"Naw, not exactly."

"Like mothers? They take care of you and such?"

"No, that neither. Maybe, a little like sisters, you know . . . family."

"Wouldn't know about that." Deuce turned his eyes skyward and watched a flight of geese for a moment. "Think I got it. They is somebody you don't want to be mushy with, but having 'em around ain't a big deal."

"Think it's supposed to work that way," Rawls said, thinking: *The kid understands it better'n me.*

Chapter Twenty-Five

Rawls knew, riding in, that the ranch was deserted. He and Deuce passed the spring. No dog barked. The milk cow, with her calf at her side, grazed nearby. Chickens pecked far from the barn. It was then that the meaning of the three or four scatterings of feathers hit him. Those pullets had paid a price for freedom. That many chicken dinners for coyotes meant Bess had been absent for some time. He spurred across the yard and sat Baldy on his haunches as he sprang to the porch.

A note on the front door read: **Patina's at the Meadowses. I have word Marcus is in San Antonio. I've gone there. Bess**

Rawls avoided going in the house. Her absence rode too heavily even outside. In minutes they rode for town.

They dropped off the two horses at Plum Grove's livery and entered the Posey. Rawls looked around, uncomfortable. He wanted to take his hat off, but the boy had one hand and the hatbox filled the other. Lilly sat alone at a table. Her gaze wandered from the window to Deuce. No customers were present.

Deuce tugged at his hand. "OK for me in here?"

"If you're hungry."

"I'm hungry."

"Then it's OK." Rawls removed his hand from Deuce's, placing it on his shoulder instead. "Want you to meet a couple of friends. Behind the bar . . . there's Snort. He runs the place." Rawls guided the kid to the table where Lilly sat, saying: "This is Lilly . . . she's a good friend. Folks this here's

Horatio Galliger, better known as Deuce. He's from Chicago."

Lilly put out her hand, shaking with Deuce. "My daddy and brother got manly-like hair that color. You're a good-looking lad, Mister Deuce." She leaned near Rawls's ear. "You shouldn't have the boy in here." Then she noticed the hatbox. Her face brightened.

Rawls handed it to her. "Wondered, would you keep this for me for a while. It's for Bess. Down the road, if anybody asks, Marcus got it for her. It's a surprise."

The light disappeared from Lilly's face. The little wrinkle across her nose smoothed and the small splotch of freckles intensified as her color drained. She brushed the knuckle of her right hand quickly across her cheek, beneath her eye, and forced a smile. "I'll take it up right now and put it away." She hurried toward the stairs.

Rawls mentally kicked himself. *Stupid, you hurt her,* he thought. *I should have brought her something, anything. Damn.* He led Deuce to the bar.

Snort leaned over and shook the boy's hand. "Welcome to the Posey, young man. You traveling with this one, are you?"

"Yes, sir," Deuce said.

"How about two of them pickled sausages," Rawls said, "and maybe a couple of boiled eggs tossed on a biscuit. We're hungry," he added, smiling down at Deuce. "Got any sweet milk?"

"No."

"Sarsaparilla?"

"No, got buttermilk."

"I like buttermilk," Deuce said.

"Buttermilk and a beer, then," Rawls said.

Snort placed the food on two pieces of brown paper spread on the bar. He was friendly enough with the boy, but, otherwise, seemed to have a little edge. "See you outgrew my generosity."

"How's that?"

"You changed hats."

"She was getting a little airy, what with winter coming and all."

"Come into money, did you?" Snort observed, raising an eyebrow. "What I hear that brother of yours is a marked man. Don't know if any of that's spilled on you or not."

Rawls stiffened; caution gripped him. He didn't want to give anything away. How much did Snort know? If word had spread that Marcus had robbed a stage, every lawman in Texas would be hounding him. "How's that?"

"How's that is . . . there's a bunch of ranchers around here ready to be paid for risking their herds with the Slatons. But between you and me, the real mark on him is the one the law's likely got by now. Waldo rode in a few days ago. He got rip-roaring drunk. Rawls, that boy's tongue got pretty loose, and, if his is, there're others. You know the word's out."

Lilly came down the steps. She had added color to her face—a little rouge along her cheek bones. She smiled, walked over, and took Deuce to a table to finish eating.

Rawls returned to his conversation with Snort, lowering his voice. "Snort, he's put the whole bunch of us in a mess. You do me a favor?"

"Maybe."

"You know about the gambling, him losing everything?" Snort nodded.

"Well, I got paid about half of what I had coming. There's one hundred double eagles stitched in this vest. I've made up a list of people we owed and what I can pay out of the money I've got. If you don't mind, see they get it. Likely it's all they'll ever see, and, while it's a far cry from fair, it's all there is. Maybe it'll ease the winter some."

"A hundred double eagles! That's two thousand dollars!"

"Snort, we made it work. Then that damn' Marcus. . . ." Rawls shook his shoulders from the vest and handed it to Snort. "Tell them folks, I'm on my way to San Antonio. Bess left a note, saying Marcus was there."

Lilly cleared her throat to get the two men's attention. "Rawls, Rose is in San Antonio with Marcus. Just thought I'd throw that in, case you're interested."

"I ain't," he snapped.

"Didn't think so," Lilly responded, and turned her chair so her back was to the bar.

Snort met Rawls's eyes and shook his head.

"When's the stage?" Rawls asked.

Snort hefted the vest, made a face acknowledging its weight. "Nine in the morning. You boys are welcome to Rose's room tonight. Least I can do. I'm gonna get a lot of bar bills paid out of what's in here." He grinned.

Two days later, the eastbound coach raised a cloud of dust in the streets of San Antonio. At the river, the stage turned and traveled a short distance through the shade of a stand of cottonwood trees. Throngs moved at a far slower pace than that in Chicago. White clad *peones*, wearing sombreros, prodded burros laden with firewood from the river's bank.

Deuce hung out the door's window, taking in the scene. "Half these people are barefoot."

"Not a good sign for a fellow in the shine business," Rawls acknowledged.

From the station, Rawls led the way toward the Menger Hotel. He reached to open large doors just as a man came through.

The man stopped. "Brother Slaton, is that you?"

"Parson?" Rawls extended his hand.

Lamb took the hand, shaking it.

"Preacher," Rawls began, "like for you to meet my friend. He's thinking of going into business in these parts. Name's Deuce."

Deuce followed Rawls's lead and took the parson's offered hand.

"I was gonna ask about my sister-in-law," Rawls explained. "She left a note, saying she was on her way here."

"Yes, she's here," Lamb confirmed. "Has a room. I'm on my way to meet her. I escorted her from Plum Grove. Missus Meadows thought I should. I'm down the street at Reverend Blankenship's. He has a guest room."

"What about Marcus? Is he here?"

"We've been told he has been. We've not found him as yet, though. A terrible thing. How a man could have such a flower and not worship her . . . I can't understand. You know Rose is here?" Lamb paused, then added: "Excuse me, Rawls, I shouldn't have said that."

Deuce peered through a window into the hotel. "Boots, there's a lady," he said excitedly, pointing. "Is that her?"

Rawls stepped into the hotel's lobby. A huge clock chimed, the sound reverberating near the ceiling. The splendor of the place reminded him of the window in the Parisian shop. He saw Bess then, and time, even breathing, no longer had meaning. She stood out like a flower in a garden of thorns. She saw him and ran toward him. He threw open his arms, stepping forward awkwardly.

The force of her motion stopped him, and she was in his arms, her body against his, warm and real, and the world was right. She cried quietly, trembling, and he held her head against his chest and repeated—"It's OK."—over and over. People turned and looked and passed on, in and out the door.

He sensed the warmth creep from his neck into his face, but no matter. They were together.

Bess raised her tear-streaked face, and for a moment her lips touched his cheek, before she stepped back. "Thank God, you're home," she said. Her hand rested in his. They stood apart and each allowed their gaze to examine the other.

"Yep, I'm here," he said. "Oh, excuse me." He reached, put his hand on Deuce's shoulder, guiding him forward. "Deuce, this is the lady I told you about. Bess, this here's a pal of mine. He may put up with us for a while. If it's OK with you, that is."

Deuce touched the brim of his cap. "He's told me about you, ma'am."

Bess bent, took Deuce's hands. She stooped down, so her face, still bearing a teardrop, was level with the boy's. She looked up at Rawls, questions on her face. She engulfed Deuce in a strong embrace. Somewhere, deep in Rawls's heart, a meadowlark sang.

Bess released Deuce. "You'll stay with us as long as you want, young man," she said.

Looking ill at ease, the boy from Chicago started to back away, but Bess reached out and pulled him back by her side, nestling him against her hip. Deuce's expression showed surrender, then he seemed to relax and stood easily beside her.

"Rawls, can you believe this?" Bess said, obviously recalling why they were all in San Antonio. "What are we going to do?"

"We've got to find him, get him to leave the country . . . maybe go to California, Oregon, somewheres like that. There're lots of places. He gets set up, straightens himself out, he can send for you and Patina. Who knows, maybe in a couple of years he can drift back this way, depending on us finding a way to ease the hurt he's put on folks around here."

"Folks around here?" Bess looked puzzled.

Rawls looked at Lamb.

The preacher nodded. "She knows. Ramón was in Plum Grove, pretty mad. He told Mister Meadows and he told us . . . the poker, the drinking, about the stage, all of it."

"Bess," Rawls said, trying to reassure her, keep her spirits up, "I know it looks bad, and it is, but, maybe, not as bad as it looks. I saw Miguel and he told me that card game was crooked. The money they went after on the stage was Darrow's . . . stolen from them."

"Rawls, stop it! They killed a man," Bess challenged. "Quit making excuses. It's too late. A man's dead . . . another one likely hanged because of your brother, my husband. The worst is he had everything and still risked it, and more, for a few laughs and a night of fun. It's time to stop the lying."

Rawls felt deflated. "Guess you're right, Bess. Deuce and I are gonna see can we find a room. Then I'll mosey around, see what I can sniff out." Rawls turned to leave.

Bess put her hand on his arm. "You're right, though, about getting him out of the state. We've got to do that. The law will hang him for sure. And that man . . . did you say Darrow? . . . given the chance, he'll shoot him down like a dog."

"You can forget Rake Darrow. Some badman planted him about six foot deep in a little place called Gainsville up on the Red." He grasped Deuce's shoulder to silence the open-mouthed youth. He avoided the boy's accusing eyes.

Lamb took Bess's arm. "Why don't you go back in and rest, Sister Slaton? I, too, will scout about." He looked at Rawls questioningly. "We'll meet back here and dine this evening?"

Rawls nodded, and he and Deuce left the hotel.

"Boots, you lied!" Deuce protested as soon as they were out of earshot. "Badman, my eye."

Rawls shrugged. "Time for her to worry about that later."

"You still lied."

Chapter Twenty-Six

Rawls knew San Antonio offered a number of places for Marcus to kill that lonesome feeling—cock and dog fights, saloons, and more. As he headed for a place called the River *Cantina,* Rawls passed Deuce a block from the saloon and tipped his hat. The boy worked on a pair of knee-high shotgun boots while bragging up the wonders of Chicago.

At the end of the street an unsaddled bay mare stood hip shot on the end of a hitch rack in front of the whitewashed adobe saloon sporting a flat roof and a tilted sign. Additional horses, tied with the bay, caught Rawls's attention. Among them Marcus's gray caused a pause in his step.

From inside the *Cantina,* sad notes from a guitar drifted out on the evening air. Rawls moved closer, listened as the Mexican music melded with buttery and cooing notes of a *señorita*'s love song. He opened the heavy wooden doors and slipped into the dim interior. His eyes adjusted. Across the room, an upside down wagon bed supported by two wooden beer kegs served for a bar. The floor was dirt, the ceiling low, and the odor stale. He removed his hat. Five men sat at a poker table. Marcus was one of them.

Alcohol and fatigue tempered the recognition that flashed on Marcus's face upon seeing his brother. He threw chips at the pot. "Raise you three dollars," he spat. His cards made a little swatting sound as they followed the chips, face down, to the table. "Howdy, Little Brother!" he called out, and leaned back in his chair.

Rawls nodded, mumbled—"Marcus."—and took in the

room as he approached the poker game.

The huge bartender tempted gravity by leaning heavily on the improvised bar. The man's neat beard contradicted his remaining shabbiness and failed to hide his frown. *Mean*, Rawls thought.

The guitar was played by a slender Mexican with nervous eyes and sure fingers. The *señorita*'s accompanying voice played second fiddle to her beauty. Rawls doubted she ever received complaints. Her elbows rested on the shoulder of a clean-cut cowboy seated to Marcus's left. Rose sat alone at the next table.

Tough, described the poker group. Still, one stood out. Although slender, size was not this rider's measure. He sat on Marcus's right. An air of impending doom cloaked the man. His eyes were cold and emotionless above an eagle-like look of cruelty that curled his mouth. He wore a buckskin shirt with heavy, leather cuffs. On his right hip, over duckin cloth britches and batwing chaps, rode a bone-handled Colt. The handle of a large knife nestled near his belly. His face and hands were scarred. Everything about him spelled brush country.

"I saw Miguel in Abilene," Rawls said.

"You know the story, then." Marcus leaned forward, picked up his cards. He frowned at the two players who had called his bet. He slapped the cards on the table face up. Three tens showed. One of the callers dumped his cards. The brush-country man took the pot with three queens.

"You boys meet my brother, Rawls Slaton," Marcus began. "Rawls, this gent on my left hails from north o' here, up Denton way. Name's Sam Bass. Owns the fastest mare in Texas. Don't believe it, check his pocket. You'll find three hundred of my dollars in there." Sam leaned forward and shook hands with Rawls over the table.

"Next to him's Jackson. This old boy on my right's Dickens. Blister Dickens! He came down from Kansas with me, but hails from the Neuces country. That other *hombre* is Jim Crow." He looked across to the next table. "You know Rose." The named men all nodded. Rose paid no attention. Marcus dropped his hands to his side, let out a long breath. "You ain't gonna preach, are yuh?"

"We need to talk." Rawls nodded toward the door.

"We're among friends. You got something to say, spit it out."

Rawls tossed his hat on a table. He knew he might as well talk to a stump when Marcus was drinking, but he had to try. "You boys, excuse my brother a minute? We got a little business." Rawls moved toward Marcus.

Rose sprang to her feet, turned a heel, and staggered. She almost fell, but straightened, and placed a hand on Marcus's shoulder. Her gaze locked on Rawls. It spoke of cold rivers and uphill trails. "You . . . ," she began, "you busted in on us once, cowboy . . . out at Plum Grove. Not this time. Marcus is tired. He needs his rest. You go on." She pointed at the door once she figured out where it was.

The brush popper called Blister stood. "It's OK, Rose, I'll handle it." He faced Rawls. "You heard your big brother. He's playing poker, and, right now, he's got a hundred dollars of my money. You got something on your chest, spill it. Otherwise, just sit down and be quiet."

As Blister tried to outstare Rawls, light from outside flooded the interior. The door thudded against the wall as Rawls wheeled to see Bess enter, closely followed by Lamb. She marched right up to the table.

Rawls put up his hands. "Now, just a minute, Bess, we were just going outside. We'll talk."

She brushed past him, her eyes fixing on Rose.

Rose opened her mouth, but Bess's right arm swung from low at her side and lashed forward. Her open hand struck Rose's cheek with the speed and bite of a snake. The slap sounded, sharp and brittle, snapped like a bolt of lightning. Rose twisted and fell.

Marcus's chair scraped backward, and Bess turned her fury on him. "How could you?" she screamed. Tears stormed down her face. She clenched her fist and drew back to hit him. But Lamb stepped in, grabbed her from behind.

"Even if you care nothing for me," Bess continued, "what about our friends, our neighbors? How could you?"

Marcus leaped to his feet, lunged forward. He hit Lamb flushly in the mouth. The preacher fell. Marcus glared at Bess. "Go home, woman! This is men's doings." He drew back his hand.

"Go home! Are you crazy?" She swung wildly with her left hand.

Marcus's arm lifted, and, as Bess staggered backward, Rawls jumped forward, swinging a left that caught Marcus in the gut and doubled him over. The follow-up right caught his brother's chin with a wicked, popping sound. Marcus fell, flattening Rose on the way down.

A glimpse of buckskin, then a terrible blow exploded like a howitzer in Rawls's head. He staggered backward, the floor inviting, the ceiling soaring away, as he realized Blister had pistol-whipped him. Rawls grabbed at the cruel face before him and caught soft leather in both hands. He pulled mightily and felt the floor on his back. He kicked up and vaulted Blister over his head. Above him, Marcus had managed to rise. He stood, swaying and bending over, his back to Rawls. Then a blur of motion swept past. *That damned kid!* Rawls comprehended through the fog.

Deuce had a heavy chair raised in his hands, and he

brought it down with force on Marcus's shoulders. The blow drove his face toward the floor. The boy then straddled Rose. His hands held two broken pieces of chair legs.

Rose kicked violently. She screamed, fighting to extract her face from the folds of her dress. Deuce tripped and fell.

Rawls hauled himself to one knee, saw Marcus twist and partially rise. His older brother wore a bewildered look, and his eyes were fixed maybe on Deuce, maybe beyond. His hand slashed for his gun with that blazing speed.

"God, no, don't!" Rawls yelled.

No one could match Marcus. Give him an edge and it was over. Rawls clutched desperately for his weapon. Marcus's pistol came up, swung in Deuce's direction, then past him. It moved toward Rawls's heart. He grabbed the butt of his .45, knowing he was too late.

From somewhere behind, Bess's scream clawed at him. White-hot pain boiled in his side. His belt jerked, and a loud gun blast echoed through his head. Fire and smoke poured from Marcus's weapon. *My own brother has shot me and is trying to do it again!* flashed through Rawls's fogged brain.

The echo of Marcus's six-gun seemed as loud as the shot. His own pistol swung, pointed at Marcus's chest. He dropped the hammer.

Marcus's eyes fluttered, opened wider, then the pupils rolled upward. A puzzled look appeared. Blood spread across his shirt. He stumbled backward, stiffened, then fell forward. Rose's scream joined Bess's while, on hands and knees, Deuce scrambled for the door.

A blur of lacey images spiraled before Rawls; his head throbbed. A foul liquid and terrible taste filled his throat. He choked back the bile and tears and wished for death. Marcus had shot him and died for it. He'd killed the better part of

215

himself, his own brother.

A shadow dropped across him as Blister lurched forward, holding his stomach with one hand, his pistol with another. The six-gun fired straight down as he slumped forward at the buckling of his knees. He crashed.

Rawls dragged himself toward Marcus. His mind reeled, fought for logic. The roar of guns in the low-ceiling room blasted over and over in his mind, driving in the truth. He'd not only shot Marcus, he'd done so while Marcus had been trying to save him. Marcus had not drawn on him, had not shot him. Good Jesus, God in heaven, what had he done? Pulled a trigger . . . orphaned a kid!

He reached Marcus, cradled his head in his arm, and hugged him close. There was a faint breath. He felt his brother's bloody hand on his face and heard him whisper: "Rawls . . . Rawls."

"You son-of-a-bitch," Rawls screamed back, "you-son-of-a-bitch, I thought you were trying to kill me!"

A light glimmered behind the film of death in Marcus's eyes. His lips twitched faintly. He nodded almost imperceptibly.

He knows. He understands, Rawls thought.

"My . . . hat . . . the sweatband . . . look. There for all . . . Be-Bess . . . Patina. No wooden nickels." His chin sagged, and his eyes went blank. There was no more. Rawls rocked and sobbed. He couldn't stop shaking.

Bass moved to the brothers. Rawls still held his weapon. It weighed heavily in his hand, but he wouldn't have fired if the man had held an axe. He was through shooting, forever. He'd killed Marcus.

Then Bess was at their side, bending over Marcus, sobbing, running her fingers through Rawls's hair.

"What happened?" he asked.

She looked him in the eye, shook her head.

Lamb stooped down behind Bess.

Rawls drew a breath. "The boy?" he said.

"He's outside," the parson replied, and then put his hands on Bess's shoulders, saying: "Let's go, Bess. You need some air."

"Take her back to the hotel, Lamb," Rawls suggested.

At the closing of the door, Bass sank down next to Rawls, checking his body for wounds.

"What happened?" Rawls asked again.

"Blister shot you," Bass replied.

"Who?"

"Blister Dickens. Marcus got him, but he caught one hisself." Bass pulled Rawls's shirt up, looked at the wound.

"No," Rawls mumbled, his mind swirling, trying to make sense of what had happened. "It was mine . . . mine was the one he caught."

"Looks like," Bass said, but didn't elaborate. "You're gonna be OK," he went on. "Bullet went through flesh from behind and came out through that belt in front. You ain't even bleeding much."

"Why'd that Blister shoot me? I thought it was Marcus. First I thought he was gonna gun the kid."

"He might have gunned the boy . . . might have gunned anybody, the way he'd been drinking, the way he was feeling." Bass moved to Rawls's good side, helped him stand. "Far as Blister was concerned, I didn't know him well. He met up with Marcus in Kansas. Somehow they put together a stake, a hell of a stake. Maybe Blister thought you had a claim on that stake. It don't take much, not for them Neuces brush poppers. They tote hair triggers, ride the owlhoot both sides of the river."

"Bass, let's go," said Jackson who was now standing at the

smoke streaked window. "There's a crowd growing up the street."

"Slaton, I got to go," Bass said. "The law will be here directly. I liked your brother. He drank a little much, too loose with his money, but he was straight with a friend, and knew how to laugh. Earlier today, out at the track . . . where we were running match races . . . a fellow told him you were looking for him." Bass stood up and walked to the door. "So long, Slaton, it's a bad day," he commented before heading outside.

Rawls pulled himself up and limped to the bar. He leaned there, locked eyes with the barman. "Help a man when he's down?"

"You got money?"

Rawls nodded.

"I can likely help. What's on your mind?"

"This hole." Rawls indicated his wound, and threw twenty dollars on the bar.

The *señorita* glided from the corner shadows. She was barefoot and carrying his hat.

Rawls recalled Marcus's words, looked around the room, and espied Marcus's Stetson on a hat rack on the wall. He turned back to the barman. "Can you clean this, maybe pour a little whiskey through her. Be good if you could find a clean pad and tie it on somehow."

The barman nodded at the girl. "Bring the coffee pot, Sylvia." He walked around the makeshift bar while Sylvia did as she was told. "Bend back there to the side," he suggested as he pulled the shirt aside. "That's it. *Aww*, you're all right. It'd been a half inch to the side, it would 'a' just been a crease. As it is, it mostly got tallow. Sylvia, the coffee."

"Coffee! You gonna use coffee?"

"Only thing around here that's been boiled today, and

cheaper than rotgut. It'll do. She'll wash the blood off and pour a little through that hole. Don't worry, we'll follow her up with a sprinkle of whiskey. A week you won't even be sore."

"If I'm alive," Rawls commented as Sylvia came back into the room.

"Either way." The barman handed the girl a clean apron from beneath the bar.

Sylvia tore the apron apart to use for a bandage, and began work on Rawls's wound. When she was done, she stepped back and smiled.

Rawls moved to the door. "What about him?" He pointed at Blister.

"I'll take care of it," he said, adding: "When the law gets here, what's your name again?"

"Rawls Slaton. And if I'm gone, when the law comes, you tell 'im them two shot each other. Tell 'em to check with the stage line up in Abilene. My brother there"—he swung his arm in the direction of the body—"Marcus Slaton . . . was wanted for stage robbery. I'll make arrangements with the undertaker?"

The barkeep nodded. "You got another twenty for me to watch him till then?"

Rawls tossed another twenty on the bar. "Tell you what, far as I'm concerned this Blister's gun and outfit is yours. Leave my brother's untouched. The same for his ponies . . . take care of 'em till I can send someone to pick them up, understand?"

Rawls picked up Marcus's hat on the way out.

Chapter Twenty-Seven

Rawls paused on the street outside the River *Cantina*. He dug inside the sweatband of Marcus's hat and felt a piece of paper. Carefully he pulled it out and read: **On the mission grounds—the old broken cannon.**

An hour later, having found Deuce and arranged for him to have a meal with Lamb, Rawls was in too much pain to ride, so he hired an old Mexican to take him to the Alamo. When they arrived at the fortress, the old man had to help steady Rawls as he climbed out of the wagon.

"A limb, *amigo*," Rawls told the old man. "I need a green, limber limb"—he held his hand chest high—"about so long. And at its end . . . like a hook or a thorn. You savvy?"

"Mesquite, perhaps?"

"*Si, si*, mesquite." Rawls nodded.

A few minutes later the man returned with the requested stick. At its end a small branch forked and supported a hardy thorn.

Rawls patted the man's back. "The cannon . . . where's the big gun?"

"By the well ees the old barrel." He indicated the location with a gnarled finger.

Rawls followed with his arm resting on the man's shoulder, the pain in his side excruciating. But on his first attempt, he snagged something soft, deep in the bore of the gun. He slowly withdrew the stick, hand over hand, till he was able to reach and grasp the canvas with his fingertips. A moment of exhilaration pushed at the dark mood and relieved the pain, but then disappeared, engulfed in sadness. Even money would not undo today's happenings. Still, he ignored the pain in his side and lifted the bag. Inside, coins shifted; their weight was heavy. He took one from the bag and held it skyward. Gold! Should he turn it in to the law? It was taken in a stage robbery. But Miguel had said they had taken from Rake Darrow only what he'd stolen from them in a crooked card game. Rawls knew Miguel wouldn't lie. Dirty gold, bloody gold, perhaps, but gold nonetheless. Gold that when distributed to ranchers along the Guadalupe would restore some respect to the Slaton name.

He handed a coin to the old Mexican. In the darkness he was unsure, but its weight felt like a double eagle. The old man lifted the coin up and down. He put it in his mouth.

Rawls laughed; the man had no teeth.

He held the coin toward Rawls.

"No, it's yours," Rawls explained. "Keep it. This night, here in the dark, never happened. It is our secret. Now help me tote this back to the hotel."

At the door to Bess's room, he bid *adiós* to the old man. He watched him shuffle away, fighting every fiber in himself that was aching to run. He had killed her husband. He stood, his head dropped. He stared at the grain of the pine flooring before he built up his courage. He raised his fist and knocked.

Lamb opened the door. Behind him sat Deuce. Bess sat, holding a Bible.

Rawls wanted to take off his hat, but the sack required both his hands. He struggled toward the wash stand. Bess jumped to her feet to help him across the room. He placed the money bag in the empty wash bowl. "This here's what your husband brought back to Texas. It's mostly for you and the neighbors."

Bess put her hand in the sack, pulled out a handful of coins, and let them fall into the bowl. She backed away, feeling her way along the bed to the chair, and sank into it. From outside, street noise, laughter, and Mexican music drifted through the open window. Bess covered her face. She spoke through her fingers. Her voice was distant, frayed with sorrow. "Rawls, that money was from the robbery. It's dirty money. It's got to go back. You know Jules told me what happened up there."

"Yes, but did the good parson also tell you it's money we were paid for that stock, and it belongs to folks all over that county back here? Don't you realize that money was taken from Marcus by a cheating cardsharp with a stacked deck, name of Rake Darrow? There wasn't nothing taken from that stage, but the money Darrow stoled."

"The sin of gambling pales beside that of armed robbery," Lamb reminded Rawls, while patting Bess's shoulder.

"Preacher, shut up. A man kills his brother, a parson don't weigh much." He'd never known a good man he so easily disliked. The parson's face was red and beefy-looking from Marcus's blow. For a moment Rawls thought the man was going to challenge him, so he added: "You know, some of that's probably gonna end up in your collection plate."

Rawls circled the room, leaning, holding his bandage. Deuce came up to him, wearing a worried look. Rawls clasped the redhead's shoulder and squeezed gently, thinking he had shown a bad example. He shook his head, and said: "I'd be obliged, Parson, if you'd let that slide. You've been a good friend to the Slatons. No call, me jumping on you."

"I'm man enough to put that aside for now, sir, for Bess's sake, if not religion."

Rawls stopped, thought better of arguing, and suggested: "It'd help if you'd take this coin and find an undertaker, maybe a barber or somebody to go get Marcus cleaned up. While you're at it, maybe send some grub up here. I'm hungry."

The preacher took the money and looked at Deuce. "You want to come with me, young man?"

Deuce nodded and followed Lamb out the door.

Rawls sat, gripping his side.

Bess reached, put her hand on Rawls's arm. "You poor dear," she said.

He let the hand rest a moment in silence before self-consciously pulling away. He wanted to wash, felt unworthy of being comforted.

"Rawls, about the money. You sure that's true?"

"It came straight from Miguel. He drank, but he didn't lie. For God's sake, Bess, we sold the cattle."

"Maybe, more to the point," Bess said nervously, "that man Darrow. I had the feeling you held back when you said he was killed . . . kept part of the story to yourself."

"I said a badman killed him. What I didn't say . . . I was the one." Rawls clasped his hands, placed them between his knees. "Bess, I done lots of poor things. Gambling, keeping questionable company, cussing, and using guns . . . those damned guns. But I don't make excuses, not when other folks' good is involved. What's been said about this money is gospel, as I know it. Men died on that drive, and since. Mostly, it couldn't be helped. Still, the idea had to do with making things better for everybody back home. It's what Marcus wanted, too. There was some good in him. I think the war affected us all."

"I know Marcus tried to change. And with the birth of Patina, I thought. . . ." Her voice trailed off.

He wanted to tell her it would be all right, about how he'd take care of her. "I won't ever try to fool you no more. Your husband pulled his regular shenanigans, you know . . . drank, put things off, gambled, and teased the gals, but he was trying to get that money to those it rightly belonged to."

"There in that awful place," Bess said, reaching out for his hand again, "I thought he shot you. Brother Lamb says he didn't. He said that other man shot you, and that Marcus killed him. Oh, Rawls, we both thought he was trying to kill you. If anyone's to blame, other than Marcus, it's me. I started the whole mess. I saw that woman and went crazy. Why couldn't I make him happy?" Finally she let go holding back the pain, and tears streamed down her face.

Rawls leaned forward, stroking her hand. "You did make Marcus happy. Why . . . why, he made me promise to bring you something special from Chicago. Described exactly what it had to be. Had the devil finding it."

"Rawls,—she looked up and met his gaze—"if I just could believe for a minute he really had that kind of thought . . . it wouldn't have had to be something bought. He could have whittled it from kindling. You know that, but thank you for trying to be kind. What would I ever do without you?"

"You never have to find out."

Back in the room, Lamb and Deuce counted $8,000 while Rawls ate. Beneath the gold they found three bundles of paper money. The parson changed positions on its proper ownership, saying he'd been praying about the matter. In light of the details brought to his attention by Rawls, the good ranch people of the upper Guadalupe, including the Slatons, were entitled to receiving their pay for the hard year's work it represented. They'd just keep its recent history to themselves. Perhaps some of it would serve the Lord, spread His word. Miracle of miracles, maybe, even a church steeple would rise higher than the Posey.

At mid-morning the next day, with Bess beside him on the seat, Rawls drove out of town in a new buckboard. Lamb rode horseback. Deuce rode the gray. Marcus, in a cypress box, rode tied snugly behind Bess, on the springboards.

When they neared home, the parson took the buckboard and Marcus on to town. Deuce doubled with Rawls, and Bess mounted the other horse. They rode to the Meadows place and spent the night. The funeral would be the following day. Marcus would be buried in a small, but growing, burial plot in sight of the Posey.

When Lamb had proposed burying him at the ranch, Bess had shaken her head. "He got lonesome at home," she had commented, and lowered her eyes.

Chapter Twenty-Eight

For two nights after the funeral, Bess and Rawls worked by lamplight, counting money, creating piles for each of the various ranchers based on Marcus's original contract. Rawls ended up with $1,300 above the amount he had received in the initial pay-off in Abilene. Bess kept a like amount. The ranchers ended up with an amount equaling $9 a head. That doubled Texas prices.

He had Lamb deliver the money to Snort, and he notified the ranchers to come to the Posey to receive their pay. Neither Rawls nor Bess attended the gathering. But Mr. Meadows had been there, and he told them that Snort had set a gallon of his best on the bar and, after some encouragement, received payment for all bar bills owed. Lamb took the opportunity to close the session with a request for each rancher to donate a tithe for a new church and closed with a prayer of thanksgiving.

Later that week, Bess had Rawls build a bunk in the loft for Deuce. She gave the boy a shovel and kept him busy enlarging the garden for next year's planting. She enjoyed having the boy around. He did the work with little grumbling, but even above cowboying came his first love, Patina.

In December the mesquites dropped their leaves. Bare, gnarled branches swayed and formed stick-picture images against dull skies. On the ground, the foliage dried and crisped. The leaves caught in other débris, hanging in old stubble and forming waves of little, raised wrinkles across the bare sod.

Bess's thoughts, like the little designs, wandered, went nowhere. To break the darkness of the present, she traveled backward, but found no light. Marcus had treated her badly, killed their love. He'd been cruel and a cheat in life, and in death he had dealt her the greatest blow of all, shame—shame in the belief that she had caused his death. If only she'd stayed out of it. She'd longed to be free of him, but not like this.

Now Rawls, the glimmer of brightness she'd so desperately clung to, would not talk. Like her, he felt responsible. They'd never work it out. It seemed that in Rawls's eyes, Marcus became a saint with his last breath.

She'd survived the long lonely months of the trail drive on make-believe stories with dream endings. Always Marcus disappeared from natural causes: snakebite one night, a bad horse the next. Each time, Rawls stormed to her rescue and damned Marcus for the wife beater he'd become and carried her off to happiness, gave her child a caring father.

Child—that child made it bearable, nourished her bruised spirit by giving reason to an otherwise purposeless existence. And the boy—loveable, bright—he proved more dear every day. Mischievous like Marcus and sensitive like Rawls, he had more questions than the world had answers.

Winter howled at the door, and the barn was no place for a man. Bess thought they should take some of the money and build another room onto the shack. Rawls could do it. He had a way with tools, but he'd probably say no, too damned noble to stay under the same roof with her. He'd not met her eyes since the funeral. He worked, gulped his food, rushed from the table to the barn, and the next day followed the same pattern.

On one occasion he did sit on the porch and smoke. It represented the saddest sight she'd seen. Another time, she'd offered him Marcus's pipes, but he declined; he now preferred rolled tobacco. Like her, only the boy and Patina offered him peace.

Bess gazed out the window and struggled to rid her mind of heavy thoughts by soaking in the view of this land she loved. In spite of a few showers, summer dryness still gripped the range. The creeks ceased to flow and new trails appeared and old ones deepened by cattle coming from all directions to water at the springs. The cottonwood, bare of its huge leaves, towered above the brush, and the ditch ran less rapidly. Today, the wind settled, but cattle moved down the paths and over by the cottonwood, raising dust. It powdered the house, made more work.

Bess hung four stockings for Christmas. Deuce had helped embroider their names on them. That night, Rawls watched and smoked his cigarettes behind that barrier she couldn't penetrate. He played with Patina. His only comment was— "Much obliged. Good night, ma'am."—when he departed for the barn.

She cried that night. Deuce climbed the ladder, and the corn shuck mattress rattled, then it was only she and the incessant wind that blew through the eaves. Its moans saddened her further.

Time passed slowly and the evenings were like the mornings and today unchanged from yesterday. But neither the wind nor the season formed the ice crystals that gathered in her heart. Like a river beneath the ice, her spirit ached for a thaw, resisted being impounded. She'd had enough. Her drought was Marcus's memory, her winter his brother's coolness.

Christmas Eve arrived, cold and cloudless. Rube roused Rawls's musings with enough energy and excited barking to put the Plum Grove mutts to shame.

A buggy, a wagon, and two horsemen turned the bend and stopped outside the house. The neighbors offered loud and joyous greetings. All sang "Silent Night" at the top of their voices. Cowbells hung clanging from the team's collars.

Rawls walked with Patina in his arms to greet them. Bess and Deuce followed closely. The wagon belonged to Wells, who'd made the drive to Abilene. He raised his hand. "You folks, grab your presents and coats and jump aboard. We all got family too far east to visit. Come along with us! We gonna celebrate in Plum Grove . . . there at the Posey. We want our friends with us."

Mrs. Wells sat beside her husband on the wagon seat. Her eyes twinkled, and she smiled. She looked at Bess, saying: "Don't worry, dear, Missus Meadows is coming. It'll be proper. The preacher is going to read the Christmas story."

"Jim, back there," Mr. Wells added, "brought his fiddle. Come on, Bess, Rawls, without you there wouldn't be no Christmas this year. Besides, Snort said he'd set up a round or two, and for us to be sure and drag your britches up there. That boy there looks like he's ready."

Rawls had not been to town since Marcus's funeral. Bess had gone to church a couple of times with the Meadowses, and she and Deuce had gone in once for supplies, but he had trouble with the idea of facing folks. It was hard to work "My brother robbed you" and "I killed him" into talk of weather and screwworms. However, this group's smiling faces erased his resistance. These people were his friends. It would provide an opportunity to get that bonnet out here, anyway.

In town, Lamb had Patina on one knee, a boy of similar age on the other, and Deuce beside him while he read from the Bible. They were seated on Snort's bar. Lilly sat on the stool by the piano, and Jim Holmstead waited impatiently with fiddle and bow at the ready.

The Meadowses joined them. Other ranch families that had sent cattle on the drive were in attendance. Embarrassed by the friendliness and backslapping, Rawls hung back and enviously watched Bess's expression as the parson read.

Lamb closed his Bible. "I see Mister Holmstead over there has his fiddle and young Miss Lilly is at the piano. Why don't we open presents? Then all as wants to can dance a while. I understand Mister Snort's been stringing that popcorn for a week."

The presents were mostly stick candy for the kids, tobacco for the men, and a couple of lace hankies for the ladies. One man handed his wife a partial bolt of fabric, commenting: "Think you wanted this."

Holmstead pulled his bow across the fiddle, and Lilly motioned Rawls toward the stairs. He trailed her up the steps and all eyes followed him. He turned to see the parson's stricken look. Snort calmed the waters.

"It's OK, folks, think he's got a present stored up there."

Several minutes passed before Rawls came down the stairs with Bess's bonnet in the box. He held it in front of his chest with two hands. Lilly had taken the trouble to wrap it in colored ribbons. He heard Deuce brag: "We brung it all the way from Chicago." Rawls could not see his feet, the stairs seemed endless. His heart pounded. Lilly pinched him through his shirt from behind. Finally the last step.

Then he stood before Bess. He had to lie about the present, and so kept asking himself: *Why am I doing this in front of a crowd?* He hadn't thought about this beforehand, so he finally just plunged in: "Bess, my brother wanted you to have something elegant. He told me, when I was getting on that train to go north, to see could I find you a bonnet. 'Rawls,' he said, 'she's partial to bonnets like fine ladies wear. She told me about seeing one in San Antonio. Not just any bonnet, get her one from Yoorup, a two Pie Saint, if you can find her.' " Rawls grinned, and turned to the merrymakers. "Well, they had one better than that. This here's a three Pie Saint."

Bess's chin quivered. For a moment a flood threatened, then, somehow, she pulled herself together and took the box.

Rawls patted her shoulder and fidgeted, and Mrs. Meadows ran over to her side. Together, the two women released the bows while Bess smiled meekly. The lid was off the box. She removed the present, held it high for all to see, then placed the hat pertly on her head, and tied the ribbon. Bess curtsied, stepped forward, and her lips brushed Rawls's cheek. "Thank you, Rawls," she whispered. She stepped back and faced the group, and grace and charm were all there. He wanted to hold her and tell her of his love. Instead, he stepped back.

"You have all been so nice," Bess announced. "I know my husband disappointed you . . . all of us . . . on occasion. But I don't know in the end, if it had not been for Rawls, if any of us would ever have gotten what belonged to us. Thank you for remaining our friends. Rawls, thank you for that terribly hard trip."

To Rawls's amazement, everyone in the place jumped to their feet and applauded. They praised Bess, then Rawls, and ended with a Merry Christmas to everyone.

Rawls headed for the bar.

Several weeks later, Bess watched Rawls ride toward the west range. He carried overnight supplies she'd prepared earlier. For the balance of the day, she busied herself about the house and attempted to gather her emotions. After supper, Deuce played with Patina near the fireplace, spinning a top. A barrier built by Rawls protected the baby from the fire.

"Deuce, do you like me?" Bess asked as she sat down.

"Yes'um, you're top drawer."

"That's a Rawls saying, isn't it?"

"Guess he says it some."

"If I asked you something real important to me, and you weren't sure what Rawls thought about it, would you just tell me the truth? You know, even if maybe he'd told me a little white lie?"

"You talking about that bonnet, ain't you?"

"That's right. Do you think my husband asked Rawls to buy me that?"

Deuce studied the low flame in the fireplace. He scratched his neck and frowned. "Boots has a weakness for lying, if it'll help others. I heard him tell folks that one all the way from Chicago. No, ma'am, that bonnet was his idea. I was across the street when he first eyed it. Even at that distance you could see him perk up like Rube on a rabbit. No, ma'am, something about that bonnet jogged his memory. You like it, huh?"

"I love it, Deuce. Thank you. Do you think we could keep this talk between ourselves?"

"Don't worry, me and him don't much talk important stuff. Makes him nervous, I think."

"He's missing a good adviser."

So, it was true. He remembered her story. She knew she'd never told Marcus that incident. It was just part of the difference between the two. *Rawls . . . Rawls, wake up you fool. Swallow that damn' nobility before we both drown.*

Chapter Twenty-Nine

Days after his return from the west range, Rawls and Deuce rode toward the barn. Rawls frowned at the horse and buggy hitched to the lot fence. "Looks like the Meadowses' rig," Rawls commented with a frown. "Probably that preacher . . . he's wearing the wheels off that thing. Before he came here, that old horse had a pretty good life."

"Boots, ain't you scared of not liking a preacher?"

"Who said anything about like?"

"I'd be scared was I you. He might put you on a list or something . . . maybe duck you under that water and not let you up." Deuce laughed at his own humor. "I can see you kicking now. You ain't a pretty sight, all soaked down."

Rawls looked at him, unsmiling. "What do you know about baptizing?"

"I've seen it. Seen near everything."

"I believe it. Knowing you, one thing you can bet, if we take another herd north next year, I ain't going to Chicago. A week up there ages a man five years. C'mon, hurry up."

"What for? They're just talking Bible."

At the barn, Rawls placed his saddle on the top rail of the lot fence. The boy released the horses into the corral. Bess and Lamb approached from the house.

"Our good luck. Look who's here," Bess said, nodding at Brother Lamb.

"Howdy, Parson." Rawls forced a smile. He noticed how big the kid grinned at the man.

"Brother Slaton, Deuce, my pleasure."

"Jules is going to stay for supper," Bess informed them. "It'll be early. I'll start it as soon as we return from the spring."

He watched them move away. *Fool has probably never seen a spring bubbling up*, he thought as he went into the barn. He marked a pattern for a new latigo on heavy cowhide, then took pleasure in forcing the sharp blade deeply into the leather.

He heard Bess laugh and looked toward the spring through the barn doors. She was bending over and Lamb was nodding, moving closer to her.

Rawls took his rope from the saddle and walked toward the lot. He passed Deuce near the gate. "Boy, tell Bess she needs to set only three plates. I'm going to the Grove."

"Wait, I'll go with you."

Rawls shook his head. "One of us needs to stay here."

Soot held a lope all the way into town, and, in short time, Rawls tied him in front of the Posey.

Snort greeted him. "Happy New Year, pardner! What's it been . . . two weeks?"

Rawls nodded, approached the bar. "Whiskey, and just leave the bottle."

Although he hadn't seen her when he walked in, Lilly came up to the bar and nodded at Snort. He filled her glass from Rawls's stock.

"Hi, handsome. How's the queen?"

"Who?" Rawls downed the first shot.

"Bess."

"She's fixing the Lord's Supper."

"What?"

"The Lord's Supper. Brother Lamb dropped by. I got thirsty." He glanced at her and saw that she was at it again— that damned, knowing smile.

"You poor thing," Lilly sympathized.

"Don't say that. Makes me feel like some kind of varmint. Heard Tur . . . Waldo stopped in here."

"Yeah, he did. He's getting everything together to haul to San Antonio. He's selling out and going to New Orleans. Said he'd be by 'fore he left."

"Son-of-a-gun! I miss him. Tell him hello." Rawls filled his glass, downed it, and poured another. He looked at Snort, and sensed a glow of friendship. He took another drink, reached over, and patted the front of Snort's shoulder. "Had a swell time Christmas." He drew his arm back, put it around Lilly's waist. "How's about us going over there to that table and see can we finish this bottle?"

Sometime shortly before daylight, Rawls belched, waking himself. He found he was on Lil's bed, and he wasn't alone. Outside a rooster challenged the world. Down the street another answered. Rawls clasped his head. "Serve them devils right if somebody gave 'em a pass to Snort's sour mash," he growled. "They'd not be rowdy so early."

He touched his chest and moved his hand down to his belt. He wore shirt, pants, and socks. He located a match, struck it, lifted the globe, and lit the bedside lamp.

Lil pulled the covers over her head.

Rawls swung his feet over the side of the bed and sat with his face in his hands. "What'd we do?"

"Nothing!" Lil answered. "Sober, you were gallant and unwilling. Later . . . you were willing and unable. Rawls, I'm gonna quit being with you. You're killing me . . . not to mention what's happening to my pride." She wiggled upward, pulling the quilts along to cover her breasts. She leaned against the headboard.

"I didn't misuse you?"

"No, dear, you didn't. Well, you did snore pretty bad, and, before that, the talking . . . you nearly wore my ears off."

"What'd I say?"

"Told what a bad ass you are. How you're going to hell for killing your brother, loving his wife, and hating a preacher."

"I didn't!"

"Well, maybe not exactly those words, but that's the picture."

"You sure we didn't do nothing?"

"No, Rawls . . . a thing like that I'd remember. It wouldn't hurt a lady to think you might, also. Only sinning we did was up here." She tapped her head.

Rawls laughed, grabbed his sore head, and whispered: "Where're my boots?"

Lil pointed beneath the bed.

He retrieved the boots, and pulled them on. "We square on the bottle?"

"We're square, cowboy. Tell the queen hello. Tell her for me, she's leaving a good man go to seed."

He reached, cushioning her chin in the palm of his hand. Her lips and those teasing eyes baited him, and he kissed her. For a second it was tender, friendly, and then his insides ignited, and he squeezed her in his arms and worked hungrily at her mouth. She responded, gave herself to him for an instant, but she jerked away.

"Go home, Rawls. Straighten yourself out. If you come back, I'll be here."

When he arrived at the ranch, he released Soot in the horse pasture. He raised his hand in greeting to Deuce, who waved from behind the barn. The boy rode the roan, carrying the shotgun. "Bess says duck or prairie chicken, she don't care which!" Deuce yelled as he took off at a run.

"Try Willow Sump," Rawls yelled back, "down the cañon! Mallards been there the last two months."

He freshened up, went to the house, and knocked on the door.

Bess answered—"Come in."—and he walked inside.

Her gaze ranged over him. Whatever she saw, she didn't like. She returned to the potatoes, fed their curls into the wooden bucket for the sow, seemed to find satisfaction in removing their eyes. "You missed supper . . . breakfast, too. Jules was disappointed you left."

"I don't think so." Rawls stood, slowly turning his Stetson between thumbs and fingers of both hands.

She turned with a potato on one hip, knife on the other. "Rawls, what is it?"

"We got to talk."

"Yes, we do."

"You first," he said, losing his confidence.

"No, what's on *your* mind? Where were you last night? Is it something in . . . in the family with you Slaton men?" She put her hand to her mouth. "I'm sorry. I've no right." She put away the potatoes, wiped her hands on the apron, and brought coffee and cups to the table. "Sit down, and quit fidgeting with that hat."

Rawls took a seat on the bench. He tossed his hat to the back of a chair, clasped his hands, and stuck them between his knees. *Well, here goes,* he thought. "I been sort of off my feed. Sort of like an old cow following her tail in a circle, looking for a soft spot to lay down. It's been going on ever since . . . since Marcus." He paused, relieved that at least he'd got that much out. He poured a cup of coffee. Bess remained quiet, opposite him. She pushed out her cup. He filled it. "Thing is," he continued, "they ain't no soft spot. You know what I'm saying?"

"No, but it's easy to see you've been uncomfortable . . . and still are."

"Uncomfortable! My God, woman!"

"Don't you swear in this house. We got two children here." Pink showed for a moment on her cheeks.

He pulled out the makings, nodding. He raised his eyes from the tobacco to look into hers. "Bess, I used to have bad feelings about you."

"Bad feelings?"

"Used to think unbrotherly thoughts."

"Rawls, I'm not, nor ever was your sister."

Patina crawled to the table, pulled herself up, and stood at his knee. She lifted her arms. "According to the law, you was."

"The law . . . *posh!*"

Rawls raised an eyebrow. He put Patina in his lap.

Bess's look changed. She appeared a little less out of sorts. "You said you *used* to think."

"Then that with Marcus happened," he tried to explain, "and since then all I can think about is how I took your man. How I'll always be dirty in your eyes and. . . ." He looked at Patina. "And her . . . what about her?" A shuddering, gasping sound erupted, surprising him. Suddenly Patina felt heavy, bouncing on his legs, and he feared dropping her. He wanted to talk fast, loudly, blabber his love to this woman, instead he battled to not cry.

His gaze remained fixed on Patina. "I killed my brother, her . . . her dad." There, it was, out. He'd said it. Bess's hand enclosed his. He met her gaze, and for just a moment he saw a brightness that immediately went into hiding.

"Rawls, Rawls, you'll never be dirty, never anything, but gallant in my eyes. Yes, once I loved your brother, and, no, we did not wish him dead. Still, you must accept what he'd become, what he did of his own free will. He brought this doom on us all. It was his doing. None of us should have ever been in San Antonio. Rawls . . . dammit! He hit me, he cheated on me, and, he caused the death of an innocent guard . . . and Miguel, you know that boy followed Marcus's lead. He caused both those men's deaths as sure as there's a God. As far as any thoughts you may have had for me, don't blame yourself. I egged them on. Trust me, I lapped them up and wanted to run away with you. But I guess you've answered my question."

"How's that?" Rawls said.

"You said you *used* to think about me that way. I take that to mean that now you don't still think about me as a woman . . . don't have those same feelings. I guess last night proves that. Tell me . . . tell me, damn you! Am I right?"

He'd never seen her like this. How could he make it better for her? "I want to take care of you," Rawls admitted, but then added: "Things just went against us. Things were put where we couldn't fix them. Nothing seems right no more."

Bess's face dropped to her hands while her shoulders shook and her low sobs tied knots in his stomach. But then she drew in a deep breath, straightened, and wiped her face on her sleeve. She said: "You through?"

He finally had the cigarette he'd been working on around Patina's thrashing arms finished. He lit it. "Yes, ma'am."

"Well, it's probably not important, but last night Jules asked me to marry him."

Rawls's mouth dropped. The cigarette shook, and Patina screamed. Startled, he looked at the girl. The sound was too loud for one so small. She reached for her mother. Rawls saw the smudge of hot ash on her little bare shoulder. He stood while handing her across the table.

The world gained weight, and he sat, and his head hurt. It

seemed nothing turned out right any more. Outside, Rube barked. Patina started yelling louder. Bess carried her to the water bucket and dipped cool water on the burn. He went to them, saw a small blister rising on the child's shoulder, but, at least, Patina was settling down, sniffling softly now.

"You said he asked," Rawls said, studying the back of Bess. "What'd you answer?" He was afraid of the answer.

"Told him I'd let him know. If you'll hitch my rig," Bess snapped, "I'm driving over there and tell him . . . yes."

"When?"

"Soon as I get this child happy."

"You don't want to wait?"

"I've been waiting, Rawls."

"She told me," Deuce declared. "It's set for in a couple months. You just gonna let her marry that preacher?" He dropped his armload of wood into the kindling box. He returned, standing out of the way while Rawls's axe took deep bites into a limb that branched from a main trunk of firewood.

"Don't see much way of stopping it. She's old enough to know her own mind."

"She don't. You don't, neither. She don't care about Jules."

"What you mean, I don't?"

"You ain't no rancher. Meadows is a rancher. Brother Jules is a preacher. You're a trail man, a scout, always looking up the road. I've watched you. We're alike, you and me . . . we're always looking for richer shoes to shine. Still, you're always saying how you want to stay around this spread. It's her draws you here."

Rawls chuckled. "Got it figured, have you?"

"You know what I'm saying. You're a fool, Boots, just a fool cowboy."

"What do you mean about her feelings for the parson. She's gonna marry him. What makes a kid like you think you got the answers. What makes you think you're so smart, anyway?"

Deuce thought for a moment before answering: "Sometimes a fellow knows more about what he never had than others about what they got."

That one set Rawls back, put him to studying. Was the kid talking family or what? "So . . . what's all that mean?"

"It means you killing your brother is a sad thing for you both, but it don't make her no never mind. It means that woman loves you. That's what it means."

"She loves me, so she's gonna marry the parson? You ain't very convincing, boy."

"I seen it. She thought I was asleep the other night, and I looked through that crack in the floor. There she was a hugging that old crooked walking stick of yours, up next to her. Had her eyes closed and her arms around it. She wasn't thinking of no preacher."

"Walking stick."

"Yes, walking stick. That one of yours, there over the fireplace. She told me how you leaned on it all the way from Tennessee. Women are crazy, you know. And you, I seen you toting that bonnet all the way from Chicago. That was your idea and nobody else's. Heck, you came all the way from Saint Louis a second time for it. Besides, I was watching from across the street the first time you seen it. Henry said you laid eyes on it and slobbered like a sick calf. We laughed at how love sick a cowboy you must 'a' been. If you were half smart, you'd do something. Tell you for sure . . . I would."

Rawls clamped his jaw. Maybe the kid was right. She same as said it when they had talked. He knew he hadn't misread that kiss a long way back, all them smiles before they headed

241

north. She same as said she wanted him for her man. She didn't act like she held a grudge. If only he could believe she wanted him as much as he wanted her. To hell with it. Sometimes he just wanted to take her and run off somewhere. Tell her that, if he had it to do over, he'd shoot Marcus a dozen times for what he had done to her.

What had he been doing lately? Just moping around, that's what. Life was too short, death and grief too long, to waste any of the good on what might have been. He had a mind to go grab that gal and tell her. He had a mind. . . . He sighed and wagged his head and handed the axe to the boy.

"Here, bub, see can you finish this. Gonna wash my face. Don't worry, whatever comes out of the chute around here, as long as I'm standing, you and me will find a place."

Chapter Thirty

The morning of the wedding, Deuce approached Rawls as he saddled the chestnut. "You owe me a nickel for that shine."

"Price gone up?" Rawls asked, handing him the coin. "Did a good job, though. May last forever."

"Regular price for a wedding polish," Deuce informed him, then added: "Mind if I ride in with you? If I go in now, business ought to be good. 'Most everybody spruces up for weddings."

Rawls nodded.

An hour later, traveling toward the Grove, neither spoke. The air sparkled with freshness, not too cool, but neither was it warm. It offered baby calves a time to frolic, colts the spirit to offer mock battle to others of their kind. The sun stayed longer in the sky now, and mares teased with seasonal stirrings, and studs sniffed the air and trumpeted their power. Rawls rode, head down, deep in thought.

Plum Grove appeared in the distance. Bess and the Meadowses would arrive in late afternoon. The ceremony would take place just after sundown. The parson's partially completed new church stood east of town on a slight rise. So far, the framed building consisted of a finished floor and roof, a front wall and steps, and a front door. Filling in the sides would come later. The benches had been added prior to last week's sermon. Rawls knew about the church. He'd heard plenty. It would house his tragedy.

In town, they left their horses at the livery, and Deuce opened for business in front of the barbershop. Rawls entered the Posey. Through the back door he could see the huge sandstone rock marking Marcus's grave. *You're lucky,* Rawls thought. He ordered whiskey.

Lilly kept up with him through the first three drinks, then switched to coffee. Snort followed his lead, and the liquor seemed to unhinge the bartender's tongue. His interest in everything from business, to weather, even dog fights perked up.

Rawls took it as long as he could before he blurted: "You ain't mentioned the coming event . . . neither one of you. Tell me what you think. You reckon Marcus would rather see her hitched to a damn' psalm singer than a cowboy?"

"Marcus was a pretty good cowboy," Lilly admitted, wiping a bead of perspiration from her upper lip. "The question is, would she be better off with a psalm singer with his brand stitched in new thread among the others on Rose's petticoat or with a stay-at-home cowboy?"

"You mean that? Rawls said. "That young scalawag's been up them stairs?"

"Regular," Lilly admitted while Snort nodded. "And the sounds coming from that bed make you think he's the one being converted."

Snort downed another shot, grinning.

Rawls wagged his head. "And to think the old hypocrite wouldn't even dance at Christmas. Means she's jumping from the pan to the same old fire, huh? So what's the answer?"

The intensity of Snort's stare forced Rawls to meet his eye. "You fill that glass up," Snort announced, "and listen to every word I put on you."

Rawls gladly did as directed.

"About a year and a half ago," began Snort, "you came staggering in here, bareheaded. You didn't have nothing, and

244

this whole damn' country had less. I give you the only hat in a hundred miles that wasn't in soak for a drink. The kids around here were hungry, the men had no tobacco, and the womenfolk were making coffee out of ground maize and scorched corn. Everybody was sitting around, wringing their hands and cussing the Yanks." Snort paused to take a double gulp. He smacked his lips and slammed the glass to the bar. "Everyone that is but that no-good brother of yours and you. You two stood up on your hind legs and showed us all the way. You two could see farther than the rest.

"I liked your brother, but he weren't no good for women or horses . . . a mean so-and-so when he drank. If I had a herd of hides to go north, I couldn't think of anyone better. I heard about the job he did. A long trail takes a real hard man. But if I couldn't get to my money before he got to a bottle, I'd've left you in charge.

"Them feelings folks told y'all about on Christmas were real. It ain't so much how a man lives as it is how he dies. From what I hear, Marcus was a little slow getting some things done, but he died the way he'd 'a' wanted. Boy, it's time you mourned the man and forgot the death. There's a good woman and baby and a boy out there that need all you got . . . all of it." Snort leaned forward and slapped Rawls on the back. "Now go on out there and ask your brother about that preacher thing. Go on, right out there where we're all gonna end up."

Rawls pushed back from the bar, moved slowly to his hat, picked it up, then reversed his steps, and walked out the back door. He wore the hat only a minute, removing it before the stone with **Marcus Slaton** scratched deeply into its face. He'd worn out a good knife doing that, and still needed to put Marcus's dates on it. He bowed his head and breathed the fresh cool air.

He'd thought a word or two might come to him, but there was none. The mound of dirt had settled to form little cracks around the firm outline of the hole. A few ants braved the chill. He looked to the southwest and the blue of the mountains arching the desert. Compared to the hills and that poor ground between, he reckoned himself just another of those ants crawling the earth, grooming Marcus's grave.

He felt the knot in his jaw as he turned and looked at Brother Lamb's partially finished church. *The boys could probably use a hand on that siding,* he thought.

"If anyone has reason this man and woman should not be joined in marriage, let him speak now or forever hold his piece," the judge declared as Rawls assessed him, thinking he didn't look too steady.

"Excuse me, Your Honor," Rawls answered from the back of the church.

"What . . . what? Who's that?" Judge Blumfield looked from the candles' soft light into the room's dark recesses. He appeared not to see Rawls standing near the door. He continued: "Surely no one speaks!"

"Judge, I speak. Back here, it's me," Rawls's voice echoed.

"What do you want?" said the judge.

This was as far as he'd figured the caper. What earthly reason could he give this man? But he plowed ahead. "Judge, I got to make a citizen's arrest. That woman there, Bess. She's got to come with me. You see that's my bonnet she's wearing. She's a thief. A big one . . . she stole my old ticker, then she stole that bonnet."

Bloomfield looked at the bonnet, and then said: "Missus Slaton, have you any idea what that man's talking about?"

Bess looked excitedly about. Her stomach did that little jerk, that little crow-hop that Rawls's presence caused. She whispered his name under her breath. She put her hands to her bonnet, turned, and then she saw him, halfway down the aisle.

The judge raised his voice: "Some of you boys take this man over to Snort's. I'll be there directly. Tell Snort the drinks are on me. Now, as I was saying. . . ."

Rawls heard the church door slam against the wall as it was again opened. High heels *clicked* behind him.

"Hold it, Judge," came the order from Lilly.

Rawls stopped. Then Lilly stood next to him. At the altar, Bess held her hand to her mouth. Her eyes showed surprise, shock. They opened wider, questioning; still, somehow, he knew they welcomed him. Only a few steps divided him from heaven. He'd just grab Bess, tell her how badly he wanted her.

The judge's eyes were on Lilly now. "Young lady, we're in the Lord's house. This is a gathering of Christian folks. Maybe we can discuss this later at the Posey, maybe you better. . . ."

"That man, there . . . the parson . . . don't marry him, arrest him," Lilly said, walking toward Bess. "He's stole more than that dear woman has. He's been fiddling with my here-after. Stole my salvation. . . ."

Brother Lamb's face darkened, turned purple. "Brother Rawls, you've gone too far. Whiskey or not, I. . . ."

Rawls interrupted, approaching Bess, the preacher, and Blumfield. "Judge, you need to find another pony. That hoss don't ride. Besides, I got more to say."

Now Lilly stood beside Bess. She clasped her hands, fingertips to fingertips, prayer-like, before her lips. "I'm sorry Judge. I'll be good." She turned to the congregation. "Folks, I apologize. He's just another man . . . just a man with a man's ways. God love 'em."

At Lamb's side, Rawls put his hand to the side of his mouth, turned his head, and whispered to the preacher: "Reverend, you just hold on. I don't want to defrock you in front of these good people, but some might wonder at your visits to Miss Rose Velure."

The whiskey burned in his belly, but he was sober as death on a battlefield. He looked at Bess and saw his life, his fear, and his future flickering in the candlelight glowing upon her face—that face now looking at him in disbelief. "Bess," he addressed her, "Brother Lamb's a good man, better than me, but I'm in love with you, woman. We gotta be together. God forgive us!"

He reached to take her in his arms. Bess stiffened, pulled back. Hope followed his heart to his boots. The word *"fool"* stabbed at his brain, and he struggled with a vision of standing before these people, barefoot up to his hat.

Bess stood silently for what seemed an eternity to Rawls before turning toward Lamb. Her gentle words were balm to the ache in Rawls's chest. "Jules, dear friend, forgive me. I've almost retraced old mistakes, done you the gravest injustice a woman can do. I love this man. I have since he came back from that dreadful war. Forgive me."

A look of confusion showed on the parson's face as Bess blotted Rawls's view. Her lips were on his, and soft kitten-like whimpers came from her as she moved into his arms. His senses drowned in the warm world she ruled. Her aroma cloaked him, and all he could think of was a room at the end of Snort's stairs, and her there, beside him.

Lilly's voice came from behind him: "Come on, Parson. Let's get us a bottle. You hold my hand while I do a little confessing. Maybe I'll let you cry on my shoulder." She led the baffled parson down the aisle and out the door.

Rawls put on his best hound-dog smile, turned to the

judge, and handed him a gold eagle. "Go ahead, Your Honor. Slaton is the name . . . Rawls Slaton."

Their kiss lasted longer than the ceremony, although nothing had been skipped. Rawls thought the judge seemed in a bit of a hurry. For his part, he took a minute to glory in the taste of his new wife. Then he turned with Bess and faced the crowd. He guided her slowly down the aisle, awash in smiling faces, watching them—weathered ranchers, men he'd ridden with, happy women, bouncing children. They were all grinning over the shining, new, wood benches that, like the pens of Abilene, separated one from the other. Their faces shown with approval, joy, and promised hope, said: we are with you, the past is behind, and only new trails are ahead. Patina jumped up and down on Mrs. Meadows's ample lap. Deuce winked, holding up a fistful of nickels.

RED WIND CROSSING

John D. Nesbitt

Clevis always says that when he sees a pretty girl walking down the street and looking over her shoulder, he pays attention, especially if she is walking fast. From the time he sees Helen hurrying down the street, Clevis knows she is in some sort of trouble. First he is curious. Then he wants to help. But helping Helen is no simple matter, as he soon finds out. She is trapped in a dark web of lies, deceit . . . and murder. And the more he tries to help her, the more the sticky strands of that web snare Clevis too. Clevis knows there has to be a way to free both of them. He just has to find it while they are still alive.

Wayne D. Overholser

WILD HORSE RIVER

The Wild Horse River is the dividing line in San Marcos County, with the ranchers on one side and Banjo Mesa on the other. But the small ranchers and the Banjo Mesa residents got together to elect Jim Bruce as county sheriff, an act of defiance and a slap in the face to Holt Klein, owner of the huge K Cross ranch. When the owner of Gray's Crossing, a small ranch over the river, is murdered, Klein insists all the evidence points directly to the Banjo Mesa people. But Jim Bruce isn't convinced that everything is as neat as it seems. Could Klein be trying to set one side against the other? Asking questions like that will make the sheriff even less popular with Klein, and Holt Klein is a dangerous man to cross.

Will Henry
THE SCOUT

Will Henry remains one of the most widely recognized and honored novelists ever to write about the American West. As demonstrated by the three novellas in this brilliant collection, throughout his career he was able to create exciting, authentic tales filled with humanity, adventure, and empathy. "Red Blizzard" is the tale of a Pawnee scout caught between the U.S. Army and the Sioux in the time of the wars with Crazy Horse. "Tales of the Texas Rangers" recounts the courageous battle waged by the Rangers against any danger, from Comanches to John Wesley Hardin. The title character in "The Hunkpapa Scout" is a trail guide for a wagon train set upon by rampaging Sioux. He will be the only hope to warn the nearby cavalry troop…if he survives!

LOREN ZANE GREY

AMBUSH FOR LASSITER

Framed for a murder they didn't commit, Lassiter and his best pal Borling are looking at twenty-five years of hard time in the most notorious prison of the West. In a daring move, they make a break for freedom—only to be double-crossed at the last minute. Lassiter ends up in solitary confinement, but Borling takes a bullet to the back. When at last Lassiter makes it out, there's only one thing on his mind: vengeance.